Bloody Massacre

A Thriller Anthology

Copyright © 2023 by Phoenix Voices Publishing

All rights reserved.

No portion of this book may be reproduced in any form without written permission from the publisher or author, except as permitted by U.S. copyright law.

CONTENTS

Dedication	1
Content / Trigger Warnings	2
Annihilation At Bayou Pointe	
Ashes to Ashes	
Bloody Masquerade	
Dark Cravings	
Her Dragon Knight	
Rabbit	
A Soul's Decay	
Where the Dead things Lie	

Dedication

To all the readers, writers and everyone in between that support us and help us achieve our dreams...

CONTENT / TRIGGER WARNINGS

This is a thriller/horror anthology and should only be read by those eighteen and older. If any of the following are triggers to your mental health, please be wary as you read:

Abduction, Ableism, Abuse, alcoholism —actually everything.

Bondage, brutality, blood

Cannibalism, car accident,

Death, dismemberment, disembowelment, drunk driving,

Emotional damage, emotional abuse, eyeball earrings, bad employees, eating disorders everything.

Fat phobias, Friends with benefits, family turned to lovers.

Gangbangilia, garage, general horror, genital mutilation, gore, gun usage,

Hateful language, homophobia, it's horror.

Idiots, incest,

Justice

Kidnapping

LGBTQ+ scenes might be present in this book.

THE BLOODY MASSACRE

Mental breakdowns, mental illness, literally everything.

Nonconsensual and consensual sexual acts

Ohhh, did we mention it's a horror, bloody massacre book? So, yeah, everything.

Pedophilia, poop swallowing, pornographic content,

Questionable behavior

Rape, Risqué behavior

Self-harm, suicide, sexual assault, Sexual misconduct, sex toys misuse, sex toys properly used,

Torture, human toilet

Underage violence

Violence

Wrecks, workplace violence,

Xenophobia

"Yes men".

Zoophoric scenes.

Again: This is a horror/triller book with the title: Bloody Massacre. It is to be understood this is not for anyone under the age of eighteen or with traumatic triggers. Read at your own discretion.

Enjoy. =)

Annihilation At Bayou Pointe

Brittany Wright

Phoenix Voices Anthologies

CONTENTS

Content/Trigger Warning:	#
Prologue	#
Chapter One	#
Chapter Two	#
Chapter Three	#
Chapter Four	#
Chapter Five	#
Chapter Six	#
Chapter Seven	#
Chapter Eight	#
Epilogue	#
Debbie Downer	#
Slave	#

About the Author

#

CONTENT/TRIGGER WARNING.

Basically, if you know this is a horror story, and you have triggers, close the book, and go read a fairytale. If you can handle most but some might be mental triggering, this is what you should look forward to, or otherwise: Anal, workplace violence, harassment, CNC, rape, forced oral sex, murder, abuse, revenge, sexual abuse, flight and flight mode, PTSD, snapping, tea kettle bursting.... Etc....

Terminology that might be useful for those not in the medical field:

DON- Director of Nurses (nursing)

ADON- Assistant director of nurses (Nursing)

RN- Registered Nurse

LPN - Licensed Practicing Nurse

CNA - Certified nurse assistant.

Union- a service provided for hourly workers who might get taken advantage of.

MULTIPLE AUTHORS

Union rep/Stewart- those who are the backbone of the hourly worker in the union.

PROLOGUE

Warning: <u>The shit is about to hit the fan.</u>

When you make tea with a kettle on a stove,
you add the cold water to the kettle,
Then put it on the stove to heat.
Once it's done, the kettle will hiss and steam.
Then, the kettle will make a 'ding' sound.
Ding, tea is done.
My temper was the same way. Nobody was there who could calm me down.
I tried so hard to make the right choice.
However, that wasn't in the cards for me.
The more I tried, the less I succeeded.
I kept to myself. I helped others.
That was my weakness.
My strength was my temper.
The temper was caged.
However, something would unleash the beast,
And I would wreak havoc on the ones who tormented me.
Harassed. Abused. Bullied.

With no regrets, I'd lick the blood off the knife and walk away from the nightmare I lived in for a very long time.

I thought back to how life has been for the past few years.

I moved away from paradise. I submitted to harassment and bullying.

I've seen it all. I've been through it all.

There was one point I fucking exploded.

Literally, I couldn't hold it back anymore. *Water went into the Kettle.*

Months and months of abuse and harassment. I was always nice.

I was always there for everyone. *Kettle was on the stove.*

I helped when asked.

I offered to help when I was done.

I was a true team player. Everyone has a breaking point.

The water was hot enough, steaming.

And I fucking reached mine. I went too far.

If I had to admit any of this to anyone, I'd lie and say I was joking.

This is the truth. *The kettle was rattling.* Just a bit longer.

They harassed me to where they needed me to kill them.

I couldn't let them hurt anyone else.

Stalking me throughout my shift.

Sabotaging my job, so I would need to quit.

Pissing me off to where I was ready to snap.

I was a grown ass woman, but I was bullied by other adults.

In the end, they might have succumbed to their death, but they deserved every single bit of their ironic demise.

Ding, tea is done!

CHAPTER ONE

I t all felt like a dream...

I meandered through the hall, taking in all the sights and sounds. I was completely alone; it was an eerie feeling. Constantly having too few staff members to adequately run the facility caused employees to feel emotionally and physically exhausted and undervalued. There was a stark contrast between the previously bustling staff and the eerie silence that now filled the room. The air was filled with a metallic smell, a reminder that everything was covered in a brownish paint. An excruciatingly sharp pain ran through my body, causing me to scream in pain. I screamed. *Shit. Did I do this? Was I finally pushed to my limits?* I'm hazy about the details of what happened. An intense pain spread outwards from the point of the stab wound in my skin. My beautiful blue scrub top was tarnished, covered in blood and sticky from whatever bodily fluids remained. My legs were bare. *Where are my bottoms?* I looked around the room for the blue bottoms. I don't remember taking them off.

The smell of death lingered in the air as I saw the pile of bodies behind the file cabinet. Rotted corpses were filling the room. I woke to the smell of death, a noxious odor that filled my senses. The smell of sweat and fear hung heavy in the air as I surveyed the scene of bodies scattered in many positions. Haley, the evil administrator, had blood trickling down her body from a multitude of cuts and marks. Her face and arms were mangled from vicious wounds, which ultimately ended in her demise.

The deep red fluids were all over the office. It smelled like a dumpster behind a Memphis barbeque joint after six months. I recognized the bodies. Sweet, sweet, Hunter. I placed my hand on his neck. He was still breathing, but he was definitely asleep. A strapon was left on the desk and it was covered in dried flaking cum. And to the left, I saw Dr. Death herself. When I saw Dina lying there, with the gun still in her hand, I felt a chill of horror, and I couldn't help but let out a wicked cackle. *What happened?*

The last thing I recall was the overwhelming feeling of anxiety as I stepped into the administration office. My job was on the line, and I fucking loathed Haley. Since the day I started at Bayou Pointe, everything was overwhelming. I moved to this state to make life easier for my kids and I, and to feel the comfort of home. They offered to pay for the move, and they secured a home that was perfect for my small family.

As a single mom, they sold me on the idea of the many conveniences these benefits could offer me. As soon as I stepped through the door, I felt the heavy gaze of everyone in the room, very aware of their whispers, a constant reminder I didn't belong–I was an outsider, a pariah. I was constantly barraged by their anger-filled glares and hostile words. Whenever something went awry, their accusing glares were directed towards me. I was the target of their frustration and anger.

They pinned the situation on me, and their words filled the air like a cloud of condemnation. Although the hall wasn't mine, I was there briefly when they attempted to attribute the incident to me. I had all the facts and evidence to help me. Going into the room together with the employer representative, we had an undeniable feeling that we were going to win the case.

THE BLOODY MASSACRE 15

When I left the floor, it was brought to my attention that I had neglected to remove the hazardous chemicals that were close to the bed—despite the assertions of the two nurse assistants who worked the shift following me that they had left no items on the tables. Nothing.

What did I do to contribute to this situation that has made it my fault? Whatever. For the last six months, I was the person they were aiming to target. All I could think of was how the meeting had gone and it had not gone in my favor in the slightest. Haley confessed to harboring a desire for revenge, despite having no good cause to do so. I gritted my teeth and forced the thoughts out of my head. In a moment of foolishness, I tried to stand with a knife protruding from my side, undoubtedly one of the least intelligent decisions I had ever made. I removed the knife from the wound while fervently hoping that I had done no damage to any of the vital organs.

Blood squirted from the flesh wound. I didn't know this much blood could exit a singular hole. The pain was unbearable. Despite the pain, I was on the mission. I had to carry on. After finding my bottoms, I forced the bottoms back on, wiping the knife's blade across the leg of my scrubs, a crimson line now tarnishing the immaculate pale blue material. My heart was racing. I didn't know how much time I had left. I gingerly placed the knife into Dina's icy hands, feeling the chill of death. I had a foggy recollection of Dina not being at the meeting, but I couldn't quite recall why or how she had arrived.

The only way to discover what was going on was to review the surveillance cameras. Something reminded me the cameras were in the Director of Nurse's office. I stumbled over in pain as I limped to their office, sat my ass in the chair, and pushed the rewind button. I'm glad the sound was recorded, too. While being careful to not put too much pressure on the wound on my side. I awaited the recording to finish rewinding.

I couldn't help revisiting the past. I knew how I got to this point. It's not like this was a one time ordeal. No. Not at all.

This wasn't the first meeting with Dr. Death and the Crypt Keepers, as I called them. They've been accusing me of anything and everything they could to gain the evidence that they needed to fire me. I put one of the rehab residents on the toilet and ran to the bathroom because the urge to pee spiraled through my stomach, damnit. I had taken a fucking water pill earlier and now I had to pee like it was nobody's business. The urge stifled my need to do anything other than race to the bathroom. My bladder felt like it was going to explode.

When I made it back to the floor, only five minutes later, the resident was screaming. Acting like she was traumatized. She insisted I had left her for thirty minutes and nobody had checked on her all morning. These residents were a pain in the ass. Got no peace around this facility. Dina, one of the nurses, admitted that was false, because she went into the room after me and saw me getting her ready for breakfast and putting her on the bedside commode. I had to write out a statement. The family was pissed, and she was removed from the facility. The reason? Accusations of lies and neglect. After that day, Haley had been after my job. My first freaking week at the facility and there were already red flags and trouble brewing. I was aware of the drama in the building. I was also aware of the staff shortage, but I wasn't prepared for the animosity I'd get from simply walking in the door.

After that, there was another incident where a nurse, Mona, told me to get vitals and make sure I was charting on the residents. I didn't mind. I always do what I'm asked. However, on this day in question, we were not only short staffed, but the State was in the building, following up on another complaint.

"The machines aren't working. I've tried two other tablets and they're not connecting to the server." I explained to Mona.

"Well, you need to tell Haley. She's just going to tell you to find another machine." Mona shot back at me. Mona was a backstabbing bitch. Of course, she rolled her eyes in her spoiled-nurse fashion.

THE BLOODY MASSACRE

"Well, if she wants it done, she can find me a working machine and I'll happily do it." I added sarcastically. I would still do it. However, I had a lot of residents to tend to and I was an hour away from the end of my shift. My residents were more important than their paperwork.

"Well, you can tell her that yourself," Mona stated, before stomping out of the room.

What I would give to make her blood rain down on the white tile. Marring its pristine sterilization with a defiling of the worst kind.

Whatever, I said to myself and continued to care for my residents. I finished all the resident care I was provisioned to do. There were only two I needed help with, and I was done.

Before seeing my last patient, the Director of Nursing approached me. "Haley wants to speak with you in her office." *Oh great. What did I do now?*

CHAPTER TWO

I looked for my hall partner to let her know I needed help with room 202 and I'd meet her after I spoke with Haley.

Not knowing I had to have a representative with me, I went in unarmed. Everyone at the nurse's station looked at me. Their eyes shooting fire. If looks could kill, they would have murdered me a long time ago. I told Mona I could get the machine to work, and I'd redo the vitals once I finished my last couple of people. I stomped on to the Administrator's office. It seemed the more I tried to stay invisible, the more they could find shit to yell at me about. The second I walked in, Haley came at me with the most disrespectful tone.

"Don't you ever instruct my nurses to tell me what to do! If something isn't working, you report it to me. You work for me. I do not work for you..." she rambled on for a minute. All I could see was blood as it dripped from my hands; the warm corrosive, coppery feeling sticky on my fingertips. A metallic tang rising in the air. I just wanted her to shut the fuck up. Kayla and Tally were in the office with her while the abuse was going on. Being a survivor of domestic violence, I loathed being yelled at and my fight-or-flight instincts kicked in. I wanted to run, get away.

THE BLOODY MASSACRE

Protect myself. Panic clawing at my stomach. Tears burned my eyes as I fought to hold them back. There was no way I would show her she was winning. I was at my breaking point. Anger flowed through my veins like lava. My words and sense of self were nonexistent. I shut down, but stayed alive enough to stand up, look her in the eyes and say what I needed to say. "If you keep up with that attitude, I'll show you where the goddamn door is!" Haley shouted as I walked around the corner. *Better yet, I would bury a knife all the way to the hilt.*

"Are you done yet?" I asked her, my voice wavering with fury. I was being disrespectful, sure. But I was done being talked to like a child. I was a grown ass woman. I wouldn't allow anyone to talk to me like that.

"Yeah, I'm done." She snapped. Her eyes glinted with disappointment, daggers of anger shooting right at me. I'm not sure what I ever did to her, besides trying to stay invisible. It never worked. My ADHD made me over share too much information and my need to belong kept me at the table where I didn't belong. I'm not sure I'd ever want to fit in or befriend any of these assholes here though.

"Good. I'm going to finish taking care of my residents," I said, turning to leave. *Enough is enough.*

"Keep being disrespectful and I'll make you hit the time clock and go home," Haley snarled as I was walking away. I wanted to slit her throat right then, watch as the blood dripped down, staining her perfectly pressed shirt. Listen to her gargling as her throat came apart; but instead, I went back to my duties. Before I could complete my shift, Kayla entered the room of one of my last residents.

"Karman, go clock out and go home," she demanded without explanation. I stared at her for a second. I wanted to skin her alive and watch her flail as she lost her most important organ. Then, use her skin to suffocate Haley. Just to watch her gag on her flawless skin and choke on her disgusting anti-human blood.

Paint her entire body with the rest of her wet and thick life source.

"There are still a few people I need to take care of. Once I'm done, I'll go home." I was running behind. I looked at her in confusion, but obeyed. *Twenty two minutes left. Just fuck off already.*

"I'll have Sunny do it. Just go home." Her voice was hard, leaving no room for argument. As cold as she was, the bitter glare from her eyes told me I had no foot to stand on. *Do it. Or wish I had.*

Kayla's hand was on her hip and she stoically stared at me as I finished putting the resident into her bed.I walked out of the door. I held back every bit of pride I had left. Everything inside me screamed for me to release the beast. I don't know how I didn't slam Kayla's into the concrete and force a dresser onto her face.

Instead, I held my head up high. My lip blistered as my molars pierced my cheek causing blood to seep through my teeth. I could taste the metalish bitterness as I walked away from her, before I really did something I'd regret. Biting my cheek and lip, or hell even biting my tongue saved Kayla's life at this point.

I went to the nurse's station and asked for the information for the Union representative. When I received all the information I needed, I logged out and went to my car. I threatened to go through the proper channels and file a grievance against the nurses and Haley if they continued with the harassment.

I drove home, rage simmered just below the surface, and made the first call. They claimed it was insubordination. I had a careless attitude problem, but my resident care was perfect. Because they terminated my position without a Union Representative with me, they didn't follow proper protocol, and didn't recognize my plea for needing a Union Rep with me, we effortlessly won the case. I was beyond my first ninety days and was no longer on probation. No write-up, no disciplinary

THE BLOODY MASSACRE

actions, no action was taken. However, the torment didn't end there.

After that day and winning against Haley and Kayla, I knew things would just get worse. My bullseye was proudly displayed on my back as I walked into work the following day. I wish I could say I was confident, but my body was displaying every other emotion. I was sick of fighting these fights. I was sick of defending my truth when they had more lies on top of lies.

After bringing in the Union and proving them wrong, I was and would be their target for a long time... I'm not sure it was ever off me. Anxiety combined with an overwhelming feeling of wanting to have perfect results completely overshadowed my commitment to having a good work ethic. I continued to push myself harder. I continued to help others as they needed. But, no good deed goes unpunished in this facility. Dr. Death and her henchmen required you to bow down to them, or face the wrath of not succumbing to their wishes.

The more I tried, the more I struggled to survive. For the first few days, everything was decent. I still had the nurses on my ass, and they still pushed me to do tasks that the others refused to do. I did everything without hesitation. I'd love to say I respected everyone until given a reason not to, but they gave me nothing to work with. When my name was brought up, I believe Haley was wondering, "How could I get Karman this time...?"

Everyone was as fake as a pair of silicone implants. I stayed true to myself and continued to carry on. I tried to be the best I knew I could be. Sometimes, even that's not good enough. I still pressed on. I kept my head up, I tried to stay in the shadows. I just waned to make it a year so I could get my nurse's license and move away from here. *No good intention goes unpunished...*

CHAPTER THREE

About three months later, we get a new Director of Nursing and the next issue occurred when the new director of nursing arrived. Her name was Davina and I had so much hope for her. Of course, what Haley wants, Haley gets. Not one, but two incidents happened that day. The first was when Haley took all the supply carts from the halls and told us if we wanted them, we had to go to her office to get them. *I didn't want the carts, so I didn't go get them.*

And the second thing, the nurses claimed I failed to provide care for a gentleman on my hall. I had a total of twenty-two residents that I was responsible for. It would take me at least two hours to finish one round on all the total-care rooms.

They claimed the man had a brown ring around his bottom, and I didn't change his soiled brief and allowed him to sit in filth. *Another lie.* I could prove it, because the evidence was still in the trash can and I time-stamped every one. I was accused of willful neglect due to not retrieving the cart from Haley's office. "I didn't want the cart, so I didn't go get it," I snapped at the nurse and new DON. I stayed true to my convictions. I said

THE BLOODY MASSACRE

what I needed to say. Janie, the Union Steward, was in the room with us, so I didn't think it mattered.

"This is a written warning. If it happens again, you will be suspended pending an investigation. If you need assistance, please don't hesitate to call one of us to help you. Not only are we your nurses," Davina wooed, "we are also here to help you." *Yep, another lie.*

I laughed. Maniacally. "You realize we have gone through seven directors of nurses (DONs) since I've been here. It's just a matter of time before you're next. When you don't bow down to Haley's wishes, you'll be next on the chopping block. You're a dime a dozen." I was trying to be helpful, she, clearly didn't see it that way

"Write your statement. Relay what happened and make sure you sign it." Davina said, ignoring my comments.

"They've been out to get me since I brought the Union in here the first time. It's only a matter of time before they chop up another bullshit ass story and try to get me out again. But you won't be here to see that. You'll be gone within the month." I taunted. I knew how evil Haley was. I knew how her mind worked. I'd seen it all play out in the last six months.

"Okay, if that's what happens, I'll deal with it when the time comes. I'm trying to help you out, Karman. I'm not out to get you."

I took a calming deep breath, wrote my statement, and signed the paper. I rolled the pen in my fingers. *I cannot let this be what breaks me.* The pen was a well needed distraction. I wished it was a knife, the wooden hilt secure in my hands. To feel the blood dripping beneath my fingers, the warmth seeping into my pores. I could stab each of them. "Are we done?" I asked, dying to bolt out of the room, annoyance swirling through my body. I didn't want them to win again. I wanted to paint the walls with their blood. Watch it drip down the walls, like a splotch of wet paint. I had a weird yet serious fascination with the chemistry of blood and how it splattered when it hit something. Yet, sadly, I wanted to cry. Never have I been accused of neglect before. I had a firm determination to do my job thoroughly and with commitment to the end. If I had to, I would stay late, but the needs of my job and residents always had to be taken care of first and foremost. Bullshit. When I visited the resident I was accused of neglecting, I pulled back the sheet on his bed and noticed that there were no bed sores or ring-shaped stains. His brief had been changed, and he barely wet the new one. That's when I noticed the soiled brief was still in the trash can. How the fuck?

I was being set up again. I ran into Haley's office. "Could you show me the resident you're accusing me of neglecting? Because this is fucking bullshit." I knew I should have watched my language, but I was reaching my breaking point once again. I didn't know how much more I could take.

Not looking up, Haley told Davina, "You saw it and you had a witness with you. You don't need to do anything further." I was dismissed. Further proof they were setting me up. I'm not sure why I stayed at this job as long as I did. Maybe it was convenience, maybe it was because I was hardheaded. Who k new.?

"This is fucking bullshit, and you all know it," I screamed, leaving the hallway and going back to finish my last rounds. I took out the trash and then clocked out.

The next few months went as predicted. They left me alone. Davina was fired, and we had a new DON. This time, it was Renee. Renee was nice at first. I didn't see her lasting beyond May, hell nobody did. She was a pushover.

Haley continued with her cart audits and was always checking mine first. My nurse, Dina, had me move a resident to another room, so I placed my coffee on the cart, and handled business. Before breakfast trays came out, Haley removed my cart from the hall and yelled at me in front of everyone. "Your drinks do not belong on the cart. Your belongings do not belong on the cart. If I tell you again, I'll take away your cart."

"Okay." I bit out.

THE BLOODY MASSACRE   25

Two weeks later, I worked my usual shift. I took two halls, East and West. I took care of my residents, loaded up the carts, and left. The next day, the new girl had West Hall, and I had East Hall. I went through and helped get all the residents up who were coming to the dining room, and had a few minutes before trays came out, so I took a smoke break. The West Hall was where we could smoke. One of the resident's lights was on, so I checked it. They needed ice water. The new girl was busy with resident care, so I filled her ice cup, sat both residents up and went out to smoke.

That's when all hell broke loose. I was in East Hall, passing out all my trays. I got to the last one, whom I had to feed.

"All morning shift CNAs come to the nurse's station immediately." Dina said over the loudspeaker.

We all went to the nurse's station to be told something that should have been common sense. "When dealing with the residents, don't leave out any chemicals. The elderly with dementia should never have this on their bedside table or on their tray table. It's a safety hazard." We all agreed and went about our business.

I completed all twenty of my residents and was finishing up tending to the last one when Dina came to the room as I was leaving. "I need you to write a statement about what happened in Ms. Fawner's room."

"Yes, ma'am." Here we go again.

I went to the nurse's station, completed my statement and Dina shot at me, "once you're finished with your report, clock out and go home. There's an ongoing investigation. Once it's completed, we'll call you."

So, I called Union as I was walking out the door.

"I'd like to file a grievance and I might need you back at Bayou Pointe for another issue. The harassment has not stopped," I told Iris. "It's best to put my two-weeks in and let this place burn to the ground in its own time."

"I'll call and get the details. Sign nothing." Fuck!

"I already filled out the statement."

"Oh, what did it say?" She asked.

"I said what happened. I arrived early. I helped the residents get up, then I went to smoke and call to make sure my kids made it to school. Then, I went to the dining room to get my trays. No chemicals were left near her bed." I answered.

"Okay good. Was there anyone in the room with you when this happened?"

"Other than the residents? No."

"Okay. Call me when they get back to you about the investigation and we'll go from there." She advised me.

Three days went by. No phone call. I called Iris to give an update about the lack of a response.

Forty-five minutes later, she called me to tell me they weren't firing me. The resident didn't die, and no harm was done, but they still had to act against me. Of course, they did.

CHAPTER FOUR

The loud click of the recording as it finished rewinding, snaps me out of the past memories of how they tormented me for so many months. The recording stopped rewinding. I knew what led me to sitting in this chair, what led me to this situation. Making up my mind, I made sure everything was in place.I could leave after handling everything and nobody would know I was here. Easy.

I pressed **play**. Watching myself as I walked into the room. We all sat down. Haley, Renee, Joey, Iris, Kayla, and myself. We all sat in the room, discussing what happened. I had the knife in the pocket of my scrubs, and I'd planned on recording the meeting to let my other coworkers hear exactly what took place. The Union and I were planning on a class action lawsuit against the facility and administration. The harassment was not only targeted at me any longer-, but the new nurses and DONs were a lso targeted.

"Karman, we called you in here today, because we had to do an investigation. The investigation was simple. We found you guilty of neglect and compromising the safety of a resident. You and I both know, if something had happened to Mrs. Fawner, you'd feel bad and wouldn't be able to live with yourself. Therefore, we have to suspend you without pay."

Shit. I needed the money.

"How am I guilty of something when I wasn't here and I never even worked that hall?" I asked, my tone curious as I seethed.

"We have many witnesses who placed you in her room before you took your vacation days." Haley said, a smug look on her face that I wanted to rip off.

"Again, that is not my hall and if I ever worked or was in that hall, it was to go to the smoke hole, and I would barely pass the rooms. If any of their lights were on, of course I'd answer to make sure they were okay, and it wasn't an emergency." I refuted.

"We're only giving you a written warning, and it's not the worst of all offenses. We're dropping the neglect point and we're going to just cite you for the safety hazard." Haley added, ignoring everything I said.

"I refuse to sign it," I said, handing it back to her.

"You can refuse to sign, but it's still going into your file," Haley said. She was the best liar. Actresses could learn a few things from her. "You've been slacking with your resident care lately. We need to address this issue before I report you to the State Board and you lose your license. I know that would be detrimental to your career and your livelihood." She was snarky. She was brave. My anger brewed, reaching its boiling point. I was ready to snap, but I waited.

"I don't see how my resident care has been slacking. When I have done everything, you have asked of me. I work short-staffed, long hours and I'm always cleaning up the messes the previous shifts leave me. Second, I follow the state and federal guidelines when providing resident care. If anything, I could report this facility to the State again, and this building could be shut down. Play the cards you want, but choose wisely." I

THE BLOODY MASSACRE

threatened. My anger was like a tea kettle, sitting on a burning stove about to whistle. The steam was building, but there were still a few minutes before I reached my breaking point.

"If that's how you want to play it, let's both make the call now. I'll report your negligence and you report the facility's faults. We'll see who gets put down first." She threatened back.

"Are you that brave?" I asked. Daring her to push my last button.

"In fact, on Thursday, you didn't go into Mr. Jaffer's room at all, and he was neglected. There were also two feeders that you forgot to change their sheets and give them bed baths." She pu shed.

"Is that all you have? Where are your witnesses for that?" I challenged myself.

"I'll pay someone to put their statement down. It's easy, Karman. You think you have me on the chopping block, but it's you who is being chopped."

My blood pressure rose. I went to grab the knife to throw at her throat, but Iris interrupted my thoughts before I even had a chance.

"Ms. Haley, you're admitting to using others to lie about Karman. We can't allow this to happen. As a representative, I now have proof that you are harassing Karman and I will allow her to file a grievance against you." Iris said, informing my demon administrator. I'm not sure if she was a demon, but she had to have demons in her bloodline somewhere. Stupid bitch.

"Okay, we'll let it go for now, but one more fuck-up, Karman, and you're out of here." Haley said, thinking she would intimidate me.

"No, Ms. Haley. You will leave Karman alone and let her do her job and go home. With no further harassment." The plebeians have another point on their board. The corrupt administration has none.

I laughed. "That will not happen." Once everything was done, the union representatives left the office. Kayla and Renee stayed for a minute. I handed Haley back the company phone with my resignation letter dated three days before. I was not going down for something I knew I didn't do.

"Haley, if she really drank the chemicals, and I didn't have the hall, how did she open the bottle?" I knew the resident couldn't open the bottle. It was a trick question.

"She opened the bottle because she was thirsty. You know you can't leave things around dementia residents. They don't think like you and I do."

"That's false. She can't open her own milk. She can't feed herself. And if I did somehow go in there and leave the chemicals beside her bed, in a hall that wasn't mine, why would I have the chemicals if all I was going to do was smoke? I always pour the chemical into the wipes and toss the bottle. It's less to keep up with, plus I had permission from the State to do it that way." I asked. I would prove my point.

"The chemical wasn't a big deal. It's just soap and water. It's the fact that you gave me something else to pin on you. And I won this time." Haley waved her hands as if to shoo me away. Dismissing me from her presence. Of course, this was after she admitted everything I confirmed. What I *should have done and what I did are two totally different things.* I looked at my watch. The next shift would arrive soon.

CHAPTER FIVE

*D*ing! Tea's done.

With one swift movement, I slapped her as hard as I could and with all the hatred I had withheld for the last six months. I was over it. "Kayla, Renee. Please come to the administrator's office!" She screeched as I laughed maniacally.

"You think they're going to stop me from giving you what you deserve?" I kept laughing. Watching me on screen was one thing, but the memories hitting me were another.

I pulled the knife out of my pocket and stabbed her in the knee she had recently had surgery on. "Ya see, Haley, you think everyone is afraid and walks on eggshells around you?" I pulled the knife out and stabbed her again in her arm. "I'm so sick of being your scapegoat! I refuse to let you pin all the facility's wrong doings on me." I pulled out the knife, she screamed. Grabbing the write-ups she documented, I ripped them into pieces, shoving them into her mouth.

I took the stapler and stapled her mouth shut. "Swallow it." I demanded.

Renee entered the room first. I threw the knife, and it hit her square in her diaphragm. I walked over to her, pulled it out, and slit her throat. Unfortunately, she didn't die a painful death, but either way, she was dead.

I went back to Haley, took my fingers, and pulled her mouth open, ripping the staples out and tearing her lips. The papers were gone. She swallowed. "Good girl," I said, in a mocking tone. "You know how to listen to others that are beneath you. I'm almost proud of you." I took the peri wash chemicals I was accused of leaving in front of the resident and poured it down her throat, forcing her to drink it. "Don't miss a drop. Your life's on the line." I laughed maliciously

She coughed and some of the blue liquid sputtered out of her mouth. "Uh oh, you're going to pay for that." I raised my hand back, with full force of my anger, my hand slapped her face, making the fat on her neck wrinkles and ripples like a tidal wave. "That's for the first time you dismissed my side of the story." I hit harder the second time. Grabbing her keyboard, I added money to my check and gave me a little overtime. I cleared every write-up and added notes to mine and my coworker's files. In addition, I added that we were exceptional employees and that we should all get a decent salary. *If it worked, it worked.* I went through the drawers of her desk and found a gun. "Why would you have a gun in your desk, Haley?" I mocked her.

"We had threats of family members wanting to retaliate for their family members. I've almost been robbed several times.." I cut her off before she could keep explaining. That was an entire federal offense. "Self defense doesn't work in the swamp, Haley..." I laughed as I checked the pistol to ensure there were enough bullets for my plan..

I turned back to Hayley, my heart beating loudly in my chest. I couldn't take it. Not now. Not ever.. I am fucking done. I gripped the wooden handle of the knife firmly, now or never. Pressing the blade against her skin, I felt it slice through each of the layers. Blood cascading onto the floor. Her skin fileting open with my skilled touch like a flower opening to blossom. The irony of it all was breathtaking. For the first time, Hayley was ac-

THE BLOODY MASSACRE 33

tually beautiful. A heart wrenching scream tore from her throat. I smiled, her voice never sounded so beautiful. Sliding the blade deeper. My thoughts whirled in agony. Every time I thought about a time when I could have landed in jail because of her, or lost my license because of her, I sliced a little deeper. The feeling of blood dripping through my fingers sending an exhilarated high through my body. She screamed in tortured agony, my ears ringing from the sound. The louder she screamed, the more I laughed.

"Almost done, Hayley, darling." My voice taunted, the bittersweet symphony of her screams and my maniacal laughter cascading through the air. I turned back to Haley, stabbed the knife deep into her arm, and literally cut off her skin. It was a bittersweet symphony. The remix.

I ripped Haley's shirt off and used it to grab the gun. I paged for Kayla again and waited for her to enter the room. She was the one who told me I had a poor attitude problem.

When she entered the room, Haley was still alive. I stabbed Kayla four times. Once in her stomach, the blade slid easily into both her legs and a fourth time right above her wrists. She would not bleed out, but I had to make it look like a struggle. The death crew would die. I threw Kayla over to the side and had her sit in a chair while I continued to torture Haley.

Placing Renee in the other vacant chair, I sat her up as if she were part of our audience.

Returning to Haley, I slapped her again, this time with a stapler. I added more pay to all the workers who had slaved over this facility. Giving us all a quintessential raise, I would bump our hourly pay to an actual exceptional wage. I also fixed the time for those who weren't at work, that were getting paid. Finishing and sending to payroll, I received a call from Corporate, well Haley did, but I answered. I explained the increase in pay and how we needed more staff. I also needed to replace the DON and ADON again, but they couldn't speak right now. They were fuming with Haley. Haha. I punched her again. The fear in her eyes was worth every bit of harassment I went through. Watching her eyes beg for me to stop, but not having the words to beg. "Karman, please. We can work this out."

"It's too late, Haley. You wronged me and others far too many times."

"What did Renee do to deserve that?" She asked, trying to get me to calm down. It was too late. I already gave in to the darkness. I was tired of being upset over a woman who could have made this facility much better. Instead, she was an asshole and made it an absolute nightmare.

"Renee got it easy. She had a simple life, and she died a simple death. I can't say I'll spare all of you the same fate." I spat. I was so full of rage it felt like my blood was fire in my veins. Anger can only simmer for so long before it bursts. I exploded.

Watching the screen, I think this is where I blacked out. Looking at my eyes, they were completely black. I laughed, recounting what had happened.

CHAPTER SIX

I paged Mona into the Administrator's office. She came prancing in as if she were ready to lick more ass. She was a swinger, and she and Dina often swapped husbands and women during their little fiascos. I waited until the door was shut and I shot her kneecap, causing her to hit the floor immediately. Without a flinch, I pulled my pants off and sat on her face. Even though I knew not wearing panties could cause UTIs, I still didn't like the restriction. "Eat me." I demanded, pushing my clit into her nose. My back against the wall, we were both facing the same direction. She bit my clit at first. I stabbed her straight into her stomach.

"Try that again and you'll have no clit left." She finally chose to be a good girl, and I rode her face like it was my most favorite ride. Once I reached my orgasm, I pulled her over to Haley. I pulled off Mona's scrubs, cut off the panties, and told her to lie on the desk. Since I've been body lifting the residents, I was very strong. With her laying there, I told Haley to eat Mona's cunt and show her how she's been a good girl. Haley refused at first. Her face was so bloody. I hit the back of her head. "If you want to live, you'll eat her." I whispered into her ear. She reluctantly went to her pussy and ate it as if she had no other choice in the world, which she didn't. "Don't stop until I say so." I said, walking over to Kayla. Kayla was beautiful, so was Renee. I shouldn't have been so hasty with Renee. This could have been a nice orgy. "Kayla, you've been such a rude bitch since the first day we met. You lure me in with false promises and then turn into the biggest cunt."

"Karman, whatever this is about, we can work it out." She begged, "I have kids at home, Karman." Tears ran down her face. She grabbed her scrubs, struggling to breathe. I took the knife and made a beautiful canvas out of her arms. It was a horrible attempt at making a flower, but she was a horrible person, so it didn't matter. Bored with making her a work of art, I snapped.

"So do I. But that never mattered before when you consistently tried to pin this bullshit on me time and time again." I cackled. I wanted to blow her brains out right there, but I had something more instore for them.

"Karman, I'm sure we can make this work to where you don't have to kill anyone else. This isn't you. You're a phenomenal person. Don't let this place corrupt you. Get out now while you can." Kayla pleaded. She tried, so I gave her that. She didn't try hard enough.

"Nah, I'm having too much fun." I laughed, "we're going to work it out alright. Get on your knees." I ordered.

"Bring me to another orgasm. However, you must beat Mona. Mona is very talented, but I don't trust Haley, and she's had a head start. If Mona gets off before I do, you die. If I do, she dies." I knew it would take me a long time to get off.

At that moment, Tina walked into the door. She recently had a baby, and the daddy was the maintenance supervisor. I shot her between her eyes. She landed. I'd check her for a pulse after I got my orgasm. "Wait, a second." I said to Kayla. I pulled Tina's body out of the doorway. And put her behind the desk. She could be discovered later. I returned to my throne. "You may continue," I told Kayla. She was fantastic. If I were able, I'd take

THE BLOODY MASSACRE

37

her home and keep her as my slave. Nobody would know where to look for her. Nobody would ever guess it was me. I rode her face.. I was getting so close to the second orgasm and Hunter, the maintenance supervisor-Tina's baby daddy- walked in the door. He saw Kayla eating me, and Mona being eaten by Haley. Renee was just there, bleeding out. "I think I came at a bad time," he said, trying to get away. "No, your timing is perfect." I told him. "Come in, shut the door. Are there police outside?" I asked.

"No. I thought I heard gunshots, but nobody else heard them. What's going on?" He stuttered.

"Lick my asshole, Kayla. " I demanded. "Hunter, come here, pull your pants down. It's party time."

They both obeyed, and I was about to make this my own little party. I heard Mona reaching an orgasm. It's okay. I wouldn't forget. Nobody was leaving here alive, anyway.

"Bring me that juicy cock, Hunter," I whispered to him. I took his cock into my mouth. "Deeper into my ass, Kayla. I need it nice and wet. Use your fingers." She obeyed. I made sure Hunter was nice and hard for me. I stood up, looked at what I had to work with. I threw everything off the desk, except Mona, and I told Kayla to get up there and lay on her back. I angled my ass over her face. "Don't stop what you are doing. I want ano ther orgasm."

"You're going to pay for this. This is a felony, Karman. There's no way you're going to get away with this. We have security cameras. There is video and audio recording." I was listening. I didn't know about the cameras before this. "And might I ask, where do you keep the footage of everything that happens in here?" I needed to know, so I could destroy it.

"It's all in Kayla's office." Mona answered. I guess she was the master ass kisser of all. She immediately gave me my evidence to get me off scott free. "Thank you, Mona. I might have a use for you after all." *But you're still going to die.*

"Hunter, fuck me or you die." I said to him. I've known Hunter a lot longer than I've been at Bayou Pointe. We met when he was dating my ex husband's sister. She was like a best friend to me back then. Serenity and I vowed to hate him for all of eternity. Part of me wanted to kill him, the other half wanted to see if his sex addiction was worth they hype. Today, all his efforts paid off. He stuck his enormous cock inside my pussy and thrusted into me as if his life depended on it. I didn't plan on killing him. I would keep him forever. His dick was amazing. I could see myself crying over him moving on, but I would never let him know that.

"Kayla, lick his asshole and his balls while he fucks me," I ordered. She was a good little slave. I honestly wanted to keep them both. The faster and harder he fucked me, the more I felt like everything was spinning. The orgasm was brewing, and I knew it would hit me soon.

I remembered Haley kept a hidden bag of gag gifts in her office. "Hold on, Hunter, walk over to that closet and look for a purple bag. I think there are some toys in there. If there's a strap on, strap it to Kayla's face." He went over there and sure enough, there was a beautiful strap on. "Is there some lube, too?" I asked. He nodded and pulled it over to us. He hooked up the strap-on to her face, having her mouth as the center point where she would have to lick whatever touched her face. Which would be Hunter's balls. I laughed. He added the lube to the dildo, and I slid it into my pussy. "Now fuck my ass, big boy." I purred. And he did. I rode the dildo, and he slammed into me with each thrust. I was building a bigger orgasm. Once he came inside me, I slid the dildo off her face, squeezed all his sweet nectar into her mouth, pushing all the boneless children and shit pebbles and muddy sludge to the back of her throat. *I shouldn't have drank coffee earlier*. I heard her gag and choke. "Chew it up!" Hunter and I both cackled like two sanctimonious maniacs on a mission. *Serves you right, stupid bitch*. "Now suck his dick and taste my ass on his cock," I taunted. "Do you like the taste of

THE BLOODY MASSACRE

39

my ass?" I laughed harder. I pushed her to the side. She started off doing an amazing job, but with her life fading out of her, I had no more use for her. She couldn't lick properly, and I think she choked on a brown log. I needed one more orgasm. Kayla was damn near dead already, so I took the gun and shot her. I looked at Hunter and nodded. He tossed her over to where Tina's corpse rested. *Three dead bodies. Go big or go home.* I thought about the rest of the employees. *Who else wronged me in this place?* "Wipe your dick off before you put it back inside me." I moaned.

Not giving anything an extra thought, Hunter took his nearly exhausted cock and wiped it on Kayla's pristine face, leaving a brown track mark where my bowels were pounded to oblivion.

I snuck a peek at Haley and Mona, who were sitting statues. I forgot about them for a minute. "Haley, eat her ass until she comes," I demanded. I needed to keep them busy until I knew my ultimate plan.

"Hunter, will you come home with me and fuck me like this every night?" I asked him as he was driving me to a pure euphoric high. Getting my revenge on all the torment they put me through was one thing. Getting to do it and receive orgasms was an absolute bonus, and I was cashing in on the whole prize. "Yeah, I'll do whatever you want, baby girl." He kept fucking m e.

"I killed Tina. So, you don't have to worry about her anymore, either." I laughed. "I'll take care of the baby, if you want me to." I offered.

"Okay. That sounds good. How are you going to get away with this?" He asked, not at all confident.

"Why are you so calm about this, Hunter? Are you not mad that I killed Tina?" I rushed before he could get another word in. "I know how I'm going to do it. Just trust me. Keep fucking me, I'm so close." He was a good boy. I had no clue what my plan was, but I needed this orgasm. I was working on another o ne.

"I'm not sure why I'm so relaxed about this. It feels so surreal. You're not usually this demonic, and I'll do whatever it takes to live." Hunter mocked me. I rolled my eyes. I still didn't plan for his survival.

"Mona, is your ass ready for me?" I asked, knowing I was about to fuck her while Hunter fucked me. Haley was eating her ass. She must have known it was her last meal.

CHAPTER SEVEN

Once she was ready, I grabbed the strap on off Kayla's face and walked over, bent Mona over the desk, and shoved the dildo into her ass. I took a letter opener and stabbed her clit, watching the blood pour out of her. I fucked Mona's ass. I stabbed her back with each thrust. I took the blood and rubbed it all over her. She was the first person to stab me in the back and I would not let her live. She didn't deserve that. I put the Karma in Karman. And I was out for vengeance.

The more I fucked her, the harder Hunter stared at me, "do you know how long I've waited to fuck you, Karman?" He asked.

I kept stabbing Mona's back with every urge to scream for more. I shook my head. "Tell me, Hunter. I have no patience for games right now."

"Since the first day you came over to your sister's house and pulled out your tit to breastfeed your daughter." I remembered the day. Serenity threw a party for my son and I nursed my daughter. That was over eight years ago. *When things were different and easier...*Butterflies tormented my stomach. I wasn't allowed to be sentimental right now.

"That turned you on?" I stuck the knife deeper into Mona's back and looked at him.

"Very much. I was jealous of a newborn, and I wanted to fuck you while sucking your tits and drinking your milk. I wanted you for myself." He smirked. Sneaking behind me, he slid his beautiful cock into my womanhood. I took the dildo in my hand and shoved it all the way inside Mona. The more I tortured the ones who tormented me, the more release I felt. I was finally getting my vengeance. I released a deep breath.

"Pull my hair! Slap my ass! Fuck me, Hunter, like you fucking mean it!" I screamed. I was so close to one of the biggest orgasms of my life.

He pulled my hair, bit my neck, and fucked me so hard. We both came so hard. I'm not sure what came over us. He kept coming repeatedly. "I don't think I can last any longer, Karman. You have literally drained me dry." He held onto me. "Let's go home. We can figure this out later." I laughed. *Could I keep him alive long enough?*

"Not yet," I hissed. I have so much more I need to do and it's not even four o'clock yet.

"What can I do to help you with this? If you're going down, I'm going down with you." Hunter fiddled with his shirt. He got dressed fast and sat down where the newly vacant chair was. While he was rebooting, I took Mona over to the pile of bodies. Haley was barely hanging on.

"Can you go get me a machete, a saw, an ax, chainsaw, any of the tools from the shed? Including rope, or whatever else you can get for me. If you see any of the other assholes, you can bring them in here, too. Nobody that's been a bully will survive this alive." He stood up, "Yes ma'am." I wasn't sure what I was going to do with Hunter. I honestly didn't think I could trust him, but if he would have betrayed me, I would have sought out for my revenge on him, too. He was much too calm and relaxed about me killing his boss and girlfriend. He stood over

THE BLOODY MASSACRE   43

two feet taller than me, and could easily out power me. *Why was he allowing me so much control?*

I pushed the thoughts out of my head and paced the office, arranging the bodies, cataloging my revenge for future reference. I looked into Haley's eyes. "How are you even still alive? I figured your gimp ass knee would have bled out now." I laughed in her face. "Who knew you had that much blood in you? You never seemed human to me."

"I guess the little bitch ass nurse assistant packs a punch, huh?" I spat in her face. I never gave her a chance to speak. The more I looked at how pathetic and dog ass ugly this woman was, the more I felt sorry for her. She was miserable and enjoyed making others miserable. A bully. The very definition of a bully, Haley's face, would be on the front pages. She had no remorse for anyone she yelled at, cursed at, or talked down to. If they didn't serve her and bow down to her needs, then they were shit to her. Now she was at my mercy.

"What am I going to do with you, Haley? Fucking Haley. I literally don't understand why you're such a bitch!" I sat on the desk and kicked her face.

"Karman," she struggled for air, "what is your ultimate goal here? You're going to go to prison and your children won't have a mother anymore. Your husband won't have a wife anymore. And all of this was for nothing."

"Are you trying to make me feel guilty? After the hell you put me through. Get a fucking life. Well, you can't do that anymore." I laughed, "I'm doing this because I want my kids in my life. I don't want my kids to run away from me like yours did. My husband? I divorced him five years ago, but Hunter... mmm, I'll keep him for a while. Once he's served his purpose, he'll be dead like the rest of you." I took a piece of paper and cut her body in various places. Papercuts were the absolute worst! I felt the paper cut into her skin. I watched the blood drip down her body. I laughed, "does that hurt? Does it hurt knowing you drove me to do all of this? Your abuse, harassment, and continuous disrespect drove me to this point. And what did I ever do to you?" We were going to get the answers I wanted. There was no faking her way out of this.

"I'm sorry, Karman. I shouldn't have treated you how I did." She pouted. I was waiting for her to apologize for six months, and it never came. She begged. Snot poured out of her nose. Her makeup was ruined. *What a masterpiece...*

"You're a day late and an hour short, Haley." I shrieked. "Why did you harass me? What did I ever do to you?"

"I just didn't like the way you came into the facility pointing out all of our flaws." She answered. I noticed her eyes were having issues staying open. She was fading away.

Hunter returned with my requested tools. "See who is left awake in here," I ordered.

"Besides you and me? Looks like Haley is the only one still conscious," he answered and kissed me. *That was odd.. Why did he kiss me?* I was glad he came back, I looked at the tools and tried to figure out how I wanted this to end.

CHAPTER EIGHT

The bodies were accumulating, and the smell of death infiltrated the air. The heat was on in the office. I turned off all of the fans. The next shift would be arriving soon, but I knew they would be two nurses short, and needing an entire new crew. I heard a voice inside my head whispering two options. I could frame Haley. The other, I frame Dina. Every hand is unique depending on how the cards are played.

Sunny left early, so she was spared. I knew where she lived, so I'd stop by another day.

I was almost out of time, and I could feel the pressure of the clock counting down. I felt an excruciating pain radiating up my spine from the hours of extra work I had done that day. I desired the feeling of the water cascading over my skin. I longed for a safe refuge, where I could escape from the world. The urge to grab my kids and flee was so strong that I could almost feel the cool air on my face. I double-checked everything to make sure I had done it correctly.

I made my last announcement over the loudspeaker.

Dina, please come to the administrator's office.

Dina stepped into the office, feeling a chill in the air, and saw the splatters of blood strewn across the walls. "What the hell..." she gasped, trying to walk backwards. I leapt out from behind the door, and the sound of the latch clicking reverberated around the room. She was startled by the sudden realization that I was in the room. I gripped the handle on the knife, jabbed into her arm. Blood cascaded all around her juicy muscles and my face. I removed the knife and put it in my side pocket. I grabbed the gun, shot her temple as she was in shock, trying to figure out what the hell happened. Removing the cloth from my hand and the gun, I placed the gun into her hand. With her digits, I positioned the gun perfectly and aimed, shooting Haley three times. My job was done. I didn't leave anyone alive. Sleepiness came over me, so I took the knife and stabbed my side. I felt the stab and realized I wasn't dreaming. It hurt like a motherfucker. I curled into Hunter, who was still asleep. I was drowsy. I took a catnap and then woke up confused about where I was. It had only been twenty minutes. We still haven't been discovered. Here I am now, in the ADON's office, watching the events play back to me.

I laughed, bringing myself back to the future. I hit stop and deleted the footage. I cleaned all the fingerprints and blood off me and changed into another set of scrubs, throwing my bloody scrubs into the pile of bodies. I had no use for my scrubs anymore. Either I could fake my death, or I could get away with murder. Either way, I would not be charged with this bloodbath. I walked back to the administrator's office, slapped Hunter until he woke up, and told him to go sit in my car. I closed the double doors separating the front offices from the residents. I poured bleach and alcohol all over Haley's body. I grabbed a small pile of papers from Haley's desk and set them on fire before I threw them at Haley. Then, added more flammable fluids to the pile of bodies. I set them ablaze, too.

THE BLOODY MASSACRE 47

I walked out of there with a hat on. In the car, I kissed Hunter, "If anything is ever said about what happened, I was with you at home and we were fucking." He kissed me again.

"Yes, ma'am." He seemed as refreshed as I was.

"How long have you wanted to kill Haley and the Death crew?" I asked him.

"Since the beginning of my employment there. They were blackmailing so many people." Hunter said, "What made you snap?"

"It wasn't just one thing, honestly. I just couldn't take it anymore, I guess. Did anyone see you come into Haley's office?" I asked. He shook his head.

"Did anyone see you go into Kayla's office?" He asked. I shook my head. "I cleared all the tapes. I burned my scrubs and everything I was wearing, including the gloves, with the bodies in the Administration office."

We got away with the Bayou Pointe Massacre.

It was very much a bloody massacre.

My daily torment would now be put to rest.

Six months later, I was no longer working at Bayou Pointe. Everything closed down because of the bloody massacre. The entire corporation surrounding the facility and administration was closed because of a huge investigation regarding the staff. They framed Dina as the one who snapped and killed everyone. Dina's husband mentioned her and Kayla having an argument, because she didn't want to be the new director of nursing. Mona's husband mentioned how she wanted Kayla to join them one weekend. "I guess she got cold feet. It's ironic that someone stabbed her in the back to death." The rest of the staff was stunned. Yes, they were harassing others, but there's no way Dina snapped like that. The detectives determined it was all sexual harassment and everyone was trying to tell Haley. Once she sought to fire them or reprimand them, that's when they snapped. Hunter and I laughed.

48   MULTIPLE AUTHORS

"I'm glad we got out of this alive, Karman." I never knew I'd find love in someone who chased me for months at a time. For years, he was always nice to me. Hunter would come over and help me put together shelves, cribs, and beds, and he and my sister-in-law actually broke one of my beds. He would wink at me and tell me it should have been with me. Some things can't change. She was a good woman. He had a sex addiction. I was just a good-hearted woman who wanted to be there and help everyone. I loved to be there for others. Maybe that was my weakness and my problem.

"Me too, Babe. Now fuck me again." We laughed.

I vowed to let no one take advantage of me again. PTSD wouldn't be the winner here. It would be me. No matter what, I wouldn't let another adult harass or treat me like a child. I knew better. I knew my worth. And now, I know my breaking point. T he end...

Beep, beep, beep. My alarm went off bringing me out of my melatonin induced slumber. My daughter was sleeping next to me. My hands were swollen from the day before and my feet literally felt like I had been walking on them for hours. My husband pulled me closer and kissed my neck. "What are your plans today?" I looked at him, confused. *Where is Hunter? Did I lock him in the basement?*

"I'm not sure. I have a lot of stuff to figure out today." I forced a laugh. Something wasn't right.

"Come here, babe. We need to make up for lost time. Want to take a shower?" He wrapped his hands around my waist. I flinched not wanting to hit the self-inflicted stab wound. Only when he touched my side, there was no stab wound. Nothing on my side hurt me.

Some things are truly too good to be true.

Me: When are you coming home?

Hunter: What do you mean? I'm at home with Tina and the baby. I'm off work today. It's Sunday.

THE BLOODY MASSACRE

Me: That's amazing.

I was stumped. *I guess it was all just a dream.*

On Monday, I decided to go to Bayou Pointe to confirm everything didn't happen. It felt so real. I dressed in my scrubs and walked into the corridor. I turned left, nothing was shut down. There was no blood on the walls. Mona and Dina were at their nursing carts and Kayla was in the ADON office.

"Why are you here? You're off work today?" Kayla asked me in the most condescending manner.

"I'm not sure. I knew we were short staffed, so I figured I'd come in and help." I laughed to myself. *It really was just a dream.*

I vowed at that moment to rededicate myself to never be subjected to another's unhappiness. I wouldn't be bullied. I wouldn't let them bring me to my breaking point. If they tried, I'd simply walk away and find something to ground and center. I'd find my happy place. I'd find my own solace.

The next week, I put in a notice for a different schedule. I refused to work the morning shift during the week and put up with the constant belittling. I wouldn't allow my mental health to be the casualty of another's horrible demeanor.

After the dream, every day following, I was in a better mood. The other shifts were a lot nicer and there was actual teamwork. The nurses, administrator, and ADON and DON never bothered me anymore. I guess that's what I needed to move on.

I forgave them and laid to rest everything with the closure I gained from killing all of them in my dreams. My sex life improved with my husband and I was a much better person for it.

I guess some dreams are just symbolization of what could happen, whereas other dreams bring the necessary means to a new beginning.

I still can't believe it was just a dream.

One, two, dreams can come true,

Three, four, the beast is at the door

Five, six, We're not done yet
Seven, Eight, It's not too late.
Nine, ten, we'll be back again...

EPILOGUE

Beep, beep, beep.

My alarm went off bringing me out of my melatonin induced slumber. My daughter was sleeping next to me. My hands were swollen from the day before and my feet literally felt like I had been walking on them for hours. My husband pulled me closer and kissed my neck. "What are your plans today?" I looked at him, confused.

"I'm not sure. I have a lot of stuff to figure out today." I laughed.

"Come here, babe. We need to make up for lost time. Want to take a shower?" He wrapped his hands around my waist. There was no stab wound. Nothing on my side hurt me.

I looked at the newspaper and laughed. Some things are truly too good to be true.

Me: When are you coming home?

Hunter: What do you mean? I'm at home with Tina and the baby. I'm off work today. It's Sunday.

Me: That's amazing.

I was stumped. *I guess it was all just a dream.*

I decided to go to Bayou Pointe to confirm everything didn't happen. *It felt so real.* I dressed in my scrubs and walked into the corridor. I turned left, nothing was shut down. There was no blood on the walls. Mona and Dina were at their nursing carts and Kayla was in the ADON office.

"Why are you here? You're off work today?" Kayla asked me in the most condescending manner.

"I'm not sure. I knew we were short staffed, so I figured I'd come in and help." I laughed to myself. *It really was just a dream.*

I vowed at that moment to rededicate myself to never be subjected to another's unhappiness. I wouldn't be bullied. I wouldn't let them bring me to my breaking point. If they tried, I'd simply walk away and find something to ground and center. I'd find my happy place. I'd find my own solace.

The next week, I put in a notice for a different schedule. I refused to work the morning shift during the week and put up with the constant belittling. I wouldn't allow my mental health to be the casualty of another's horrible demeanor.

Every day I walked into work after the dream, I was in a better mood. The other shifts were a lot nicer and there was actual teamwork. The nurses, administrator, and ADON and DON never bothered me anymore. I guess that's what I needed to move on.

I forgave them and laid to rest everything with the closure I gained from killing all of them in my dreams. My sex life improved with my husband, and I was a much better person for i t.

I guess some dreams are just symbolization of what could happen, whereas other dreams bring the necessary means to a new beginning.

I still can't believe it was just a dream.

DEBBIE DOWNER

A Poem

Debbie Downer

One, two, you're being
rude.
Three, four, Karma's
knocking on your door
Five, six, you're making
me pissed.
Seven, eight, you're not
doing great.
Nine, ten, you won't
harass me again.

I see through your mask,
when you're chipper
and glad,
Your life is miserable,
you're incredibly sad.

You act as if you're holy
and who the world re-
volves around. Not true.
But if faced with choos-
ing who lived or died,
could you choose you?
Life, as you know it is
about to change,
For your organs and
face, I want to rearrange.
Every step you take, and
promise you break,
There's a piece of skin
and bone for me to give
pain.
I'll break and destroy,
piece by piece, lie by lie.
I'll take back my control,
and laugh as you cry, cry, c
ry.
You may be the ad-
ministrator, but you're
nothing but a clown.
You're a Debbie Down-
er, and you're going.
Down, down, down.

SLAVE

A Poem

Slave

Tick. Tock. Tick Tock.
The clock spun on the
wall.
Drip. Drop. Drip. Drop.
The water went down
the faucet.
Of all the things they
asked for, I never stalled.
It's probably the thing I
ultimately regret.
It's crazy how it all went
down,
Life is funny when you
feel you're going to
drown.
When I moved back to

this small town, I didn't
know you were around.
When you walked
through the doors, I
wish I would have
pushed you away,
But you stayed, so now
you will forever be my
slave.

About the Author

Brittany Wright lives in Arkansas with her two kids, works in the healthcare field by day and writing as much as she can by night. Fun facts about her: she has never completed the Star Trek or Star Wars movies. She fears thunder. She has been writing since she could form words. My inspiration for writing is always to bring light to mental health issues. And leave the reader feeling like I hugged them. I do not shy away from emotions, nor do I hide anything or sugar coat the scenes.

"I tend to always include poetry and an extra laugh or hug with everything I write," she says. "Sometimes, I tend to be too gross or weird. Sometimes, my ADHD will kick in and we will have a blast trying to figure out what I'm meaning. Eventually, I'll go on to the next things. I promise I'm not trying to make anyone mad."

She has three published novels: Curse of the Raven, Tragic Peace and Red Market Exchange. I was also featured in the Spice and Steam anthology and Lovely Benefits anthology.

Stay in touch:

https://linkr.bio/author_Brittanywright

Ashes to Ashes

Tammy Godfrey

Phoenix Voices Anthologies

CONTENTS

Chapter One	#
Chapter Two	#
Chapter Three	#
Chapter Four	#
Chapter Five	#
About the Author	#

CHAPTER ONE

"Dee, please, no more whiskey; you don't want to get drunk again," She whispered to her husband. She didn't want to be noticed. Like most guys that age, Nicole's husband had an impressive body when he was younger, but didn't care about getting in shape after they had been married for ten years. So, Dee didn't work out. If he wasn't sixty pounds overweight, his five-foot-nine frame would look great. Instead, he was going bald and trying to hide it, yet he never hesitated to tell her if she gained over five pounds.

"Oh, shut up, woman," said the man who drank too much alcohol." Who am I to refuse the Dennings' invitation to the party?"

Dee and Nicole had been married for thirty years. Nicole knew how difficult Dee would be when drunk. At the end of the party, she didn't want to cause an ugly scene. Nicole was worried about what people thought. She knew certain people would believe that if her husband was drunk at another party, they would ban them from being invited to other parties. In other couples, Nicole has seen this. Dee told her that the women who drink too much are the only ones banned.

THE BLOODY MASSACRE

63

"I feel great, Nicole," slurred Dee, tottering from one foot to the other." I am fed up with these people."

Nicole was happy that her husband wanted to leave. He pulled her long blond hair as he put his arm around her. But he told her he would divorce her if she tried to cut it shorter. Their children were married and had children of their own. She had part-time jobs because she had to be home at the same time as Dee and make dinner. She helped Dee hide the fact that he was drunk. After saying their goodbyes, they headed for the front door. Even if he wasn't sober, the people at the party would think he was.

"You get into the passenger seat. I'm driving." Dee wasn't able to get the key in the car. Nicole didn't want to fight in front of their friends.

"No, come on, don't be silly. You cannot drive. Please give me the keys. I will take us home," she said calmly.

"I'm not drunk. I can drive my car to my home. Dee blurted out. Shut your mouth and get in the car." I will not be a questioning voice. If they were home, she would fight back, but not in front of their friends. They have a reputation to protect.

She didn't want a yelling fight in front of their friends, and she could see the other guests leaving.

After starting the car, Dee didn't stop and turned not on the usual street. Nicole could only pray the traffic was lighter in this direction. But, instead, the houses shot past quickly when Dee pressed his foot down. She held her hands in her lap, and the knuckles on her hand turned white. She hated it when Dee was drunk. It wasn't possible to argue or reason with him. He is a pain in the ass when he is drunk.

Nicole screamed. The dump truck was suddenly in front of them. He hit the brakes hard. Too late! The compact car smashed into the back of the truck, and Dee and Nicole were thrown forward.

Everyone who has known Dee, for better or worse, has known he was paranoid. His suspicious nature won't go beyond a new phone every six months. It extended to his car and who worked on it. He had probably heard through some websites that mandatory passenger-side airbags were just a scam by the government to track your whereabouts. So no one will tell him where and when to drive his car.

The steering wheel stopped Dee, leaving an impression on his forehead. However, the windshield did not prevent Nicole from going through the windshield.

The full impact of the crash hit Nicole headfirst. Unfortunately, there was no airbag because Dee had removed it because he was told that the government had tracked where he was going. He wasn't having anyone follow him. Dee had replaced the radio in the car and take the airbag out, thinking they were stupid to have airbags in a vehicle.

Dee remained unconscious for just a few seconds. He shook his head to help clear his foggy mind. He felt his face; there was a cut above his eye, his left hand felt broken, and the fingers were stiff and painful.

Nicole lay partway through the window. He quickly pulled her back into the car; her head was flapping on the back of the seat, facing the window. He tilted her face toward him and nearly vomited. Nicole's head had almost been severed from her neck. The hard edge of the glass had sliced through her windpipe right down to her spine. Her face looked like the glass was sticking out all over her face, and her eyes were wide, like she was scared to death. She must have died instantly.

He looked up and saw the truck driver stumble from his truck and stagger, then sit down on the sidewalk's curb.

He quickly crawled over to his wife and dragged her into the driver's seat; pain shot through his broken fingers as he took her weight. But it has to be done, he thought. If the police found out he had been driving while drunk, he could go to prison for a long time. But Nicole has already died. What does she have to worry about? He saw it as the last thing she would do for him. He felt sick from the accident and somewhat guilty about what

THE BLOODY MASSACRE 65

Dee had just done, but self-protection overruled all notions of decency?

The colorful lights he knew were coming had arrived. "Are you all right? What happened?" the police officer asked after seeing Dee outside the driver's side with the door open as he sat on the ground.

"My wife Nicole fainted while driving," lied Dee. "There was nothing I could do." But then Dee heard more police cars and ambulances coming. Maybe someone can fix my hand and arm now.

"Have you and your wife been drinking?" the police officer asked, moving closer to check on Nicole.

"We were at a party," said Dee, the reality of the situation striking home for the first time.

"She's dead," the police officer said.

The reality of Nicole being gone finally hit him. Or was it the alcohol? He wasn't sure, but a mist formed in front of Dee's eyes, and he fell unconscious for the second time that night.

CHAPTER TWO

I t was the pain that woke him up. Shape-directed pain. Dee's eyes opened to a nurse staring at monitors, and a police officer staring at him. His name on the nameplate said 'Miller.' He seemed eager to talk. So did the other two officers by the door. "Can we call you Dee?" officer Miller asked.

"Sure," Dee said, convincing himself it was a routine visit to offer condolences on his dead wife.

"Dee, did you know your alcohol blood level was .025?" - Officer Miller kept talking like he didn't want an answer. "You would have felt dazed, confused, and disoriented, would have balance and muscle control deteriorated, and would need help walking."

"We were told by many people from the party that you got in the driver's side. After you had a fight about who was driving because your wife wanted to drive," another officer, Smith, stated, "Then you hit a trash can and turned the corner."

Dee had to make this up on the sly. Then, finally, he had to talk his way out of it. "Yes, I got in the driver's side when I hit the trash can. Nicole started yelling at me to pull over, and I did.

THE BLOODY MASSACRE

She started the car and began driving, then she passed out. Then the truck came up, and I tried to turn the car away."

"Was your wife drinking at the party?" Officer Miller asked.

"Yes, I saw her with a glass at the party," Dee replied. Dee wasn't sure if she was drinking. She always had to be the perfect person at parties. But he liked that because it made him look g ood.

"Your wife didn't have any alcohol in her blood, and the doctors can't find a reason why she passed out, as you said," Officer Smith said.

"I don't know what to tell you," Dee mumbled.

"The injuries show she didn't have any marks from the steering wheel, but you do." Officer Miller pointed out.

"I was trying to get control of the wheel. Maybe that's how I got mine," Dee offered in desperation.

"Why did you take the airbags out of the car?" Officer Smith asked.

"I'm a proud republican, and one of the radio stations said that liberals had put chips in the cars to track us, so I pulled them out," Dee said.

"Only thirty-seven percent of people who used an airbag died. So the airbag could have saved your wife's life," Smith said. "Don't listen to everything the radios tell you. Most of the time, the information is faulty."

"Do you know your wife and you both had a seventy-five thousand insurance policy?" Miller asked. "Dee watched the other guy and took notes."

I didn't know it was that high. It was Nicole's idea to get it. I just signed the papers to make her get off my back about it.

"We will check on that with the company," Smith assured him.

"Go ahead. I thought spending money on an insurance policy was stupid. Still, Nicole wanted one because of her new job," Dee stated he didn't want it but gave in to his wife.

"How long has Nicole been working at her job?" Smith asked.

"A year. My job cut back my overtime, and Nicole asked if she could find a position to make up the difference." Dee said.

Each of the police officers gave Dee that look that they didn't believe a word he said. Then, they closed their notebooks, put their pens in their pockets, and left, sharing whispered options on their way out. Dee was just glad they went.

In a matter of moments, he forgot their names, the scowls on their faces, but not the dollar amount of the life insurance policy for Nicole J. Jonson. Instead, he thought of the places he could travel without a nagging wife telling him what to do and what not to do. She was such a killjoy.

That's when he heard the voice.

It wasn't loud. Just a whisper, like someone standing next to his bed, next to his ear. There was no one in the room, no cops, no nurses. The only sounds were the beeps of his heart monitor and the whispers in his ear that sounded familiar, even unmistakable.

Nicole.

"If you drink any alcohol, I will make you pay," said the voice.

Drugs. Obviously. It had to be the pain meds coursing through his veins. He wasn't the type to hear heartbeats under the floor, brought on by guilt. He didn't have the heart for it.

"Dee, if you drink any alcohol, I will make you pay," the voice stated again.

Suddenly, Dee felt an overwhelming need for companionship. So he pressed the alert button for the nurse... repeatedly.

"What do you need?" came a sure voice of a middle-aged nurse named Peg.

"I have an arm that is killing me. Can you give me more medication so I can sleep?" Dee asked.

"Let me ask the doctor?" Peg walked out of the room.

The doctor came in. "How are you feeling?"

"My arm is killing me. Can I have something for it?"

"I was planning on releasing you today from the hospital, so we will give you something that won't cause a problem so you

THE BLOODY MASSACRE

can get home. I will provide you with a prescription so you can get the meds. Take one every four hours, and don't take more than that."

Throughout their marriage, Nicole made every attempt to watch her favorite soap operas, usually very late at night when Dee was sleeping off a six-pack of whatever beer was on sale. When the children were at home, they knew when mom was sneaking into the living room at two in the morning. They could hear the TV from their rooms, even when it was turned do wn.

Nicole's son was named after his dad. Dee insisted. On the other hand, her daughter Carly was named after her favorite soap characters. Her kids loved her very much, and they both just returned home after receiving the heartbreaking phone call from the police.

They came to help their dad, so of course, the first thing to do was to get rid of the beer. Carly was sure her father would insist on mixing his terrible-tasting medication with a tall, cold one. She didn't want to lose another parent.

Carly made sure all the alcohol was removed from the house. When Dee told them what happened, he would have to do it sober. When he finished his story, Carly did not believe him. Dee knew she didn't and quickly changed the subject to the funeral. She took over the funeral details and didn't care what he wanted.

Dee wanted a simple funeral, but his daughter wanted to follow her mother's wishes. A casket was in a cemetery where her family member was buried. When he discovered the cost of a casket, Dee demanded a cremation. Carly was reluctant to agree, but it was probably best given the condition of her mother's body. Dee was to keep her ashes in an urn. I would be so glad when the kids left.

He would take the money from his wife's life insurance in a few weeks. And go on holiday to France, where they had spent their honeymoon. Before leaving, Dee would sprinkle her ashes off the cliff on their favorite spot; a rather touching gesture, anyway, it would get rid of them. However, he did not relish the idea of having the ashes in the house, as feelings of guilt he managed to keep at bay began to creep up on him like bony claws in his throat.

It's only natural for family members to show up in support during grief. Dee's brother, Jim, brought a sympathetic ear, a bucket of chicken, and a six-pack. "It's awful," said Dee's. "She was a fine woman, Dee; it must be a terrible loss for you."

"Yes, it is," replied Dee. "If only I had been driving, it wouldn't have happened. I keep thinking, over and over, that I should have died." His lies flowed like water.

"Don't be silly, Dee. It was an accident. It wasn't your fault that Nicole fainted. Your alcohol level was point two five. So, it only makes sense to have her drive home that night. It was a good thing Nicole was driving. You can't blame yourself for th at."

"No, but I still can't help but feel guilty, Jim." Dee had repeated these lies so often that he was almost starting to believe them.

"Well, life goes on, brother," said Jim, helping himself to another piece of chicken and beer.

"The cops didn't help," Dee began. "The police questioned me for hours about why I took the airbag out of my car. Why was my wife driving that night? Then, when people from the party saw me getting behind the wheel. After they turned the corner, I explained my wife demanded that she drive because she didn't want me to drive while I was drinking. So, I pulled over and let his wife drive."

Dee had always been a selfish man, always putting himself first, and though he would admit it to no one, he was glad it was Nicole and not him who had died. He knew it was wrong to think this, but he felt the same.

"It should have been me! It should have been me!" he repeatedly told his friends and family, not meaning a single word.

THE BLOODY MASSACRE

This continued at the funeral as if black would make the lies less noticeable.

The funeral had finished, and everyone vanished like spirits into the night. Dee set off for home in his car, whistling a jolly tune. Nicole remains in the car's back seat. They might as well have been cigarette ash in an ashtray. Dee had forgotten them already.

"Well, she's dead now," thought Dee, "no point in crying over spilled milk. I've still got a life to lead."

The car entered the drive to his house, and he was just about to close the car door when he remembered the ashes. With a sigh, he knew he would have to be the good and grieving husband for the neighbors until the money came in. He took her inside, looking for a place, and settled for the windowsill, temporarily. He continued searching, not wanting the urn in his bedroom or the house. Maybe the basement, but people would think he didn't care. Dee placed it on the coffee table. It looked out of place, and he liked to eat in the front room. That would not work. He put it on the mantlepiece. He didn't like it there, but it would only be there for a while.

He ditched the dull black and put on jeans and the Hawaiian shirt his wife hated, and went shopping and got a case of beer, frozen dinners, and some junk food. After returning, he turned on the TV and looked for the play-off game that started in ten minutes. Dee heated the dinner, grabbed two bowls, and filled one with Chex Mix and the other with Pizza rolls. He opened the beer and was about to take a drink when he heard a voice say, "Drink it, and I will hurt you," the voice said.

His blood froze. His beer dropped. Dee peered to his left, right, then up, and finally, cautiously behind him, in a fruitless effect to find what could not be seen. Nothing. No one. He picked up his beer from off the floor and brought it to his lips as it shook in his hands. Then, in the act of defiance, he took a drink
.

He felt the first sharp, intense pain on the top right of his chest. But it did not stop there. A razor-sharp, slashing pain continued across his chest, down to the left side of his beer belly. Then the blood came. He cried out in agony as he stood up and tore off his Hawaiian shirt.

"What the hell!"

"Every time you take a drink, you will be hurt just as I was, you bastard," the voice said.

"I rule this house, Nicole, not you," Dee said, and took another drink.

"I was hoping you would say that," the voice replied. "I will hurt you as you hurt me. Asshole!" the voice began. "You told my children, my family, everyone that I did it when you're the one who killed me!"

He felt another stab in his neck and blood trickling down.

Dee felt a deep cut on his arm, which wouldn't stop bleeding. So Dee, being too dumb for his own good, took another drink, slashed across the face, and had a sharp pain in his chest. "Dee, you killed me!"

Then there was a knock on the door, and Jim walked in. "Who beat you up?" he asked, running over to his brother. "We need to get you to the hospital."

CHAPTER FOUR

Dee started researching how to get rid of a ghost. If Nicole thought he would stand for her watching him, she had another thing coming. Why couldn't she die as everyone does? Why does she have to be difficult? He thought her job in my life was to make it difficult, and she was good at it.

He would have never considered this kind of research seriously before the voice spoke to him. Still, Dee started reading that ghosts stay in the house or where their urn is. In ghost lore, it's a home or other building often believed to be inhabited by disembodied spirits. The deceased may have been former residents or were otherwise connected with the property. Others say they are connected to their body or wherever it is located. Ghosts want something from us. Sigmund Freud said that *projection of mental entities into the external world*.

"What the hell does that mean? Sounds like a bunch of bullshit to me," Came Dee's rebuttal. He must get rid of Nicole and her ashes and sell the house. "I'm done with her, but how do I get rid of her ashes and not have the kids mad at me?"

Dee remembered stepping through his front door after work, and the smell of cooking that usually greeted him had gone, along with Nicole; he missed that. Since Nicole had died, the house seemed larger, almost empty. Yet, if he missed anything about her, it was her presence in the kitchen.

Although Dee had loved her in a selfish, overbearing way, he genuinely missed her, but thought that life without her was better than no life. This, he decided, justified his appalling actions at the crash scene.

Carly called a week after Dee's second time in the hospital and asked him not to take the ashes to France. Instead, she wanted some ashes for necklaces for her and her daughters. Of course, Dee being Dee, thought it was such a dumb ass thing to do, but one of Carly's daughters came up with the idea, and now all they talk about is having grandma with them always. So, Dee asked Carly if she wanted the urn and to have mom with her.

"Only if you can handle not having mom with you," Carly told him

"I think your mom would be happy watching the grandkids grow up," Dee admitted.

Carly jumped at the chance to have her mom's ashes with her. Dee didn't want to keep them, so why would he say no to his daughter and grandkids? Carly is doing him a favor by taking them.

The money from the insurance company came into Dee's account three weeks later, and the first thing he did was put the house up for sale. His kids thought it was too soon, but he told them it was hard to live here without their mother, and he thought a smaller house would be better for his needs. It was almost too easy to get the kids to understand. They all thought it would be a few months, but a couple loved the house and wanted the closing to be less than a month. I couldn't leave the house quickly, so he accepted their opening offer.

Nothing says a new start like a new house, and the house Dee found met three simple criteria: no mantle above the fireplace, no stairs, and a smaller yard. He offered a cash deal for less than

THE BLOODY MASSACRE 77

the asking price, and they accepted. He patted himself on the back for putting the insurance money to good use.

He smirked at the urn. "I'm moving out, and you are going with Carly. So, I will be done with you. Do you know I'm happy it was me who lived, not you? You complained about everything I did, and now I can do as I please. I can get a dog now without worrying about your animal allergy."

"As long as you don't drink, we will get along, or you can tell the kids, and I'll leave you forever," the voice said.

"When your urn is with Carly, I'm moving into a new house. So, my dear wife, you will be with Carly or in this house, but I'll be without you in my life," Dee happily replied.

CHAPTER FIVE

Two weeks later, when he moved, he had a moving company. Dee didn't want Nicole's stuff in this house. He didn't wish to have Nicole in his place. He knew his kids would eventually take the urn, but they were back home, and their kids were in school. He didn't like the cost, but it was worth paying for a storage locker to get her and her crap out of his home. He knew how it would look to those who were still watching him. He didn't want to appear uncaring, so he told everybody he was getting away to France to clear his head. They were fools, cops, and everyone who believed he was going to France, not Las Vegas. Until then, he kept up appearances. No booze, not a drop. In public, he would wear a frown and an ugly black suit. While there was no alcohol, there was no voice.

After all, there was a lot of sun in Vegas. He needed a new pair of sunglasses. The shop on the corner where he used to live sold them, and Dee liked the people there, so he picked up his wallet and set off to buy some.

"Hello, Mr. Huckabee. How are you feeling? You look much better now." Mrs. Brent, the shopkeeper, smiled as Dee entered the store.

THE BLOODY MASSACRE

"Oh, I'm holding up, Mrs. Brent, thank you, but I still feel sad. I think it should have been me that died and not Nicole. I loved her so much. She deserved to live, not I." But, unfortunately, this lie had become second nature to Dee.

"Don't be so silly, Mr. Huckabee. This had nothing to do with you. It was a terrible twist of fate that your wife fainted while driving. You can't blame yourself at all."

He smiled and shook his head.

Dee bought the sunglasses, said farewell, and set off for home. He had a vacation to look forward to.

The front room was pretty cool. There was one big window with a built-in shelf under it. Dee bought a new couch, and his recliner from the old house was sitting right in front of the television. The television, one of many, was fresh, seventy inches, and covered most of the wall. The other wall had a giant mirror with a leaf design that was light on the mirror. The couch was right in front of it. The coffee table was between the recliner and the sofa.

It was getting dark, and he felt like retiring early tonight. Dee had packed his bags and had them by his front door for the next day. He had gone to the store and got some scotch. He felt that moving to a new house got him out of the police's eyes. Finally, Dee felt safe enough to pour a drink.

"Don't drink that," the voice began. "You will pay."

Did he hear the voice, or didn't he? Dee wasn't sure. He didn't care. He would first help himself to a large scotch; even though this slow poison had been the main reason for his wife's death, he still wanted the drink and would not let his wife win. Since he was in a new house and his wife's ashes were in storage, he felt safe. "Don't believe everything you read," the voice said.

He settled into an armchair and downed the contents of the glass with one swallow.

The room seemed unnaturally quiet. Dee could hear his breathing. He held his breath, yet the breathing continued. Dee's first thoughts were of a burglar in or around the house. He fumbles for poker from the fireplace and walks towards the window. The breathing had come from that direction next to the window. He could hear it clearly now.

It was outside the window, close to the ground. It was a snuffling, husky wheeze, not human at all. Dee pulled back the curtain and then laughed out loud. It was a rat, a tiny, spikey rat.

He looked closer, and to his disgust, the little animal was devouring a mouse. He pulled the curtains shut. Not a pleasant sight, he thought. He laughed at himself again. Burglars.

He helped himself to another scotch, then retired to his bedroom.

The bed seemed larger. Of course, it was only natural. But the bed was also colder. This, too, should have been expected, but it took Dee some time to get used to it. He wore sweats and a t-shirt, a familiar look since becoming a bachelor. The actual term, of course, was widower, but bachelor sounded more optimistic. Normally, he wouldn't dream of wearing his shoes in bed, but now, fuck it, he can do as he pleases. So he decided to kick his shoes off, one landing on the bed, one on the floor.

He would lean back and relax on his pillow and hers when he heard the noise. You might listen to it from the kitchen, like a knife tapping on a plate, but this came from the living room.

He opened his door to the darkroom, reaching to the left, taping, then hitting the wall desperately, trying to find the light switch. The air felt dense as he finally saw the light. There was a strange haze throughout the room, as if someone had opened the window and invited in a dense fog. It wasn't possible. He was alone.

Again, he heard the metallic tapping noise. It was coming from the direction of the fireplace. Then toward the coffee table. At first, he thought his eyes were playing tricks. He couldn't be seeing what he was seeing. It was Nicole's urn...It was walking across the coffee table as if some invisible hand was moving it back and forth.

THE BLOODY MASSACRE

81

The movement of the urn became more and more violent. Finally, it leaped high and smashed hard against the floor, scattering Nicole's ashes. Dee was transfixed. He thought he must be overdoing the scotch, but what happened next was too horrific for alcohol-induced hallucinations.

A cold, shivering sensation crept up his spine as the first cut went down his back. He felt the warm blood moistening his shirt, and then the cold hit it. Then another cut, followed by searing pain, as it slashed across the front of his chest.

A heavy smell filled the air. It was Nicole's perfume, and it was everywhere. "I told you not to drink alcohol!" Then he was cut again. This time blood went everywhere.

"You never listen to me. Even when it would have saved my life," the voice said as Dee was cut again. "I gave you a choice."

"You will not tell me what I can and cannot do!" Dee yelled defiantly. The relentless attack continued as blood rolled down his arm. The front room floor was beginning to be covered in blood as it dripped from Dee.

"Yes, I can. You killed me, and now I can make you do whatever I want. If you do not, you will suffer the consequences," the voice said. "Suffer, Dee, suffer. The only way you can get rid of me is by telling the truth!"

"I'm sorry you died," Dee blubbered, tears mixing with the blood.

He was cut off by the voice. "Liar! You're happy I'm not alive. You can't hide what you feel."

"I will not tell the kids!" Dee yelled.

"Then stop drinking, you dumb ass," the voice said. Dee felt another burning sensation, and she had cut him again, coming dangerously close to his crotch.

"No! You can't tell me what to do!" His eyes burned from blood, sweat, and tears, so he couldn't believe what he saw next.

The ashes started to form into a body. "Are you going to tell the kids, or I will," the voice said.

"You can't talk to the kids," Dee smirked as he smelled Nicole's perfume all over the room. The ashes formed into a body, standing nose to nose with her husband.

"I will never stop drinking, and you can never make me tell the kids," Dee said in a quivering cry.

The form moved to the mirror and started writing in blood.

I lied

I was driving

I killed Nicole

"See, I can tell the kids," the form said. "Are you going to listen to me?"

"No!"

The ash from horror leaped upon him, enveloping him, its grotesque face from the car crash of Nicole pressed close to him. He opened his mouth to scream, and as he did so, this thing rammed its hands into his face. The thick, heavy ash filled his eyes, ears, nose, and mouth. He felt the ash being forced down his windpipe into his lungs, stomach, and whole body. The obscene, grey dust pushed its way into every opening. He could not see, he could not scream, he could not breathe! He was suffocating!

The ash had permeated every part of his being, smothering him.

As the last seconds of life deserted him, he could hear a voice. It seemed to come from within him. It was Nicole's voice,

"Now I can have peace, and the kids will know what you did." Nicole's voice sounded happy.

About the Author

Tammy Godfrey has called Southeast Idaho home for the vast majority of her life. She survived sixteen years in the military and is proud of almost every minute of it. After leaving the camouflage uniform behind, Tammy decided she needed to do something productive when she wasn't lost in the exciting world of tax preparation. She was hitting the books at Idaho State University, seeking a degree in something practical like business. During her time in the world of academia, she discovered a love for writing. After spending long days and nights overcoming her fear of the blank page, her first book was published in 2013. She is currently working hard on her next novel. Tammy loves everything geek, including her adorable husband, reading, and going to comic con. Tammy believes that Murphy's Law has played a large part in her life. If anything, weird can happen, it will. One thing that can be said about Tammy Godfrey, she's not boring.

Bloody Masquerade

Brittany Wright and Dakota Cole

Phoenix Voices Anthologies

CONTENTS

Prologue	#
Chapter One	#
Chapter Two	#
Chapter Three	#
Chapter Four	#
Chapter Five	#
Chapter Six	#
Chapter Seven	#
Chapter Eight	#
Chapter Nine	#
Chapter Ten	#
About the Author	#

PROLOGUE

*M*y heart and soul.

    My Bride. My unborn children.
Taking away the man within me
The story is never forgotten and never told.
My children never had a chance, Taken.
Never to be happy, the darkness provides,
I must end the entire bloodline,
If I want to make it out alive.

* * *

Payton

Self-hatred grows in me like a vehemently fervent and metastasizing disease. I loathed her family as much as I hated myself. I couldn't take accountability for this. Her father took so much from me. There's so much I can't explain yet. My heart and soul repudiated anything I wanted to do to get closure and move on. However, that night is on repeat, and I see the screams of my heart being taken away from me. Within a matter of minutes,

THE BLOODY MASSACRE

my entire world shattered in front of me, ripped out of my hands, and taken forever. The moment I lost my heart is the moment I became one with the darkness.

The poetry helped me live with myself. I concealed myself in the darkness for way too long. Jennifer and I agreed, we fucking agreed, she would stay in school, and I could look after her and the kids until she graduated. I had a copious amount of money. I was three years away from being finished with law school.

The steak knife. The blood. The cries and screams. The pleading. He took my life, so I took his.

Poor Penny. So innocent. Was she, though?

I stood by and watched her mother lock her up. I showed up to every court hearing and every appointment thereafter that was allowed. She never spoke of that night. Only how she wanted to go to her grandmother's house because they needed a lot of help.

Her grandmother never knew what happened. She passed away two years later.

I beheld them as they struggled to move on. Her mother was the vilest being I've ever witnessed. I'm not sure what pushed her to throw away her last living relative, but the day she chose work over her daughter, I pushed her over the cliff. One down, one to go.

Penny remained locked up because of the sins of her father. I'm not even sure she knew the extent of how much he was responsible for.

Out of all the things she could get right, she witnessed the Grim Reaper take away her father's life.

And since the day he took my bride's life, I vowed to ruin everything that came near his family. His wife, his progeny—anything that brought a smile to their face—would suffer.

I would stay true to my promise and seek revenge on Jennifer's life.

As soon as I got my hands on Penny, I'd let my anger free. I had plans for this little girl. Her innocence might have been able to be proven by me, but she was safer in the asylum than free for anyone to take advantage of.

More than she could imagine. I would rip her to shreds and ensure she'd submit to my every word. Her innocence, mine. Her beauty, mine.

Penny would be mine.

Miraculously, she ambled down the street close to my club. I used everything in my power to get her in the doors. I never expected it to be this uncomplicated. And as easy as it was.

I watched her walk through the doors to my new club. Everything was in place. A masquerade ball experience enhanced with the features of a rave. A DJ able to make every song into something perfect for those participating and dancing.

When she chose her dress, I knew there was a better option for her. I made myself invisible and gave the attendant helping her the instructions. It would be perfect.

* * *

Penny

I was so excited to meet with my mom after over three months of not seeing her. I was stuck in this asylum and held hostage within my mind. Every day, I was given antipsychotics, anti-anxiety, antidepressants, and three shots called an anxiety cocktail shot. My blood type was probably Xanax and Ativan. Luckily, when it was time for me to get my leave, I only had to take the capsules. *Small blessings.*

Once mom picked me up, we drove two hours to her house. She said little . I felt like an outsider in her world. Maybe she only came by out of courtesy. She was my legal guardian and with me being over eighteen, they had to rule me unable to sustain a healthy life for myself and others. Now, mom gets all of my inheritance from my father and sister. I didn't know until recently she added a life insurance policy on my sister and me.

THE BLOODY MASSACRE

91

My father had one on all of us and it paid out upon their deaths. *Talk about being the lucky one, and on the right side of the dirt at the right time...*

While having dinner with my mom, she received a phone call saying her job needed her. I did not listen to the conversation but understood what was doing on. She gave me my bag of pills and enough money to take the bus home. *She didn't trust me.*

"You have to go back, Penelope." She barked. She knew I hated when people called me Penelope. Everyone else called me Penny. My fucking name is Penny.

"Mama, I'll just sit here and watch TV while I wait for you to come home. I don't mind at all..." I pleaded, but she didn't listen. She didn't care. Her eyes aged more from our last video session. It was obvious mother wasn't happy.

"Penelope, you have to go back. If I let you stay here and something happens, it could be very bad!" My mom yelled at me. What could go wrong? I hurt no one.

"What are you so afraid of mama?" I asked. Trying to get her to look at me, "you know I haven't ever hurt anyone..."

"It's not you I'm worried about or afraid of..." she looked at me, "I'm not worried about you hurting me..."

"Then what is it?"

"I'm afraid of me and what I might do..." she said. Carelessly, she handed me the bus tickets and written instructions. I had my bag of meds and we drove to the bus station. Where she dropped me off, to figure this out on my own. Four bus stops back to the Asylum. I wasn't ready. Before she left, "I'm sorry I wasn't the best mom for you."

"You did what you had to do," I said, "I love you mama." I gave her a hug and she drove away not saying anything.

Here I was... alone again. Free to decide for once.

What's the worst that could happen?

Chapter One

Penny

Welcome to the Masquerade Ball!

Please pick up your mask and then move to the dressing room.

We understand that you chose your gown, but tonight, we'll make sure you look dazzling!

I read the sign and chased the signs. I snatched a white mask and walked into the second dressing room. A towering woman, also wearing a mask, smiled and pulled me over to her.

"You wear a size 10, yes?" She flirted.

"Fourteen, but I'll take the flattery any day!" I felt my cheeks heating.

"Perfect, darling. I have the best dress for you." She smiled again, walking through the dresses. I saw her peek around. "Question, dear, do you get hot easily?" I nodded.

"I'm a big girl. I stay hot and sweaty!" I laughed, trying to mask my feelings of insecurity about my physical appearance.

THE BLOODY MASSACRE 93

"Oh hush, you're definitely a beautiful woman. More to love, I'll say." She walked around the rack of dresses. "Close your eyes, darling."

I obeyed.

"Open now." I opened my eyes and saw the most stunning dress before me. Red gown with black lace. No sleeves. The back of the dress was invisible, literally a lace band, and made of a silk-like fabric.

"That is the most beautiful dress I have ever seen in my life." Butterflies fluttered in my belly. This dress was too good for me. "I'll have to choose a different mask. Mine is white, and that is the most rogue red I've ever seen."

"I am aware. I already bought another one for you." Meticulously designed lace on the mask would sit over my face, hiding my cheekbones and nose. The brow went up as if it were demon horns. "Oh, my goodness," I said, admiring the beautiful mask in my hand, "you truly outdid yourself."

"I hope so. This will be alluring on your face, and the dress will be fabulous on your body."

My face warmed. Compliments never made me comfortable. "How long have you been going to these gatherings?" I wasn't good at small talk either. But I wanted to try. This was my opportunity to emerge from my isolation, experiment with something uncommon for me, and show I wasn't all that they said I was. I wasn't a monster. At least, I didn't remember being a monster.

"Six months," she chuckled. "Undress and put on your stunning dress."

I nodded and obeyed.

Once my gown hit the floor, the coolness of the room hit my nipples, instantly, a mountain peak. "Step in." The dress landed at my feet. With one hand, she held my leg, and with the other, she pulled the dress over each foot. The satin or silk felt buttery and affectionately stroked my skin. Once it pulled over my hips and covered my breasts, she smoothed the dress out. I glanced into the full-body mirror. The dress seriously looked as if it were painted onto me.

"I knew this was the perfect dress for you," she smiled. "My name is Sadie."

"My name is Penny." I smiled. "Nice to meet you." I shook her hand.

"Let's adjust your makeup a bit and you'll be ready for the subsequent room."

"What's in the next room?" Curiosity knocked and I had to know what awaited me on the other side.

"You'll have to see for yourself." Sadie challenged my curiosity and raised me a smile.

My makeup was finished. Before I knew it, it was time to enter the next room. I wasn't prepared for whatever was in there.

I can do this. I lied to myself.

I'm not sure why I was so uneasy about leaving the asylum. It was something I could call mine. It was my room. Well, sort of, it's an inpatient room, but I was allowed two days LOA, which is a leave of absence, where I'm able to visit family and such. My mother brought me home for the holidays but had to work. So, she sent me back to the hospital. I never understood why I had to stay at the mental institution. I was placed here after I was thirteen. Since then, the drugs were poured into me every morning, afternoon, and evening. And right before I fall asleep, a magical three shots. They lock up the room, and I'm left alone, stuck in my head with no understanding of what's going on. Thankfully, they removed the restraints, and I was no longer strapped to the bed.

I had no social contact with anyone.

I was fed through a hole.

I was showered, yes; they showered me three times a week.

The asylum and hell are likely the same places. My parents are probably in control, too. Either way, I couldn't force a memory I didn't have. I remember little else.

THE BLOODY MASSACRE

I walked into the next room, and the colors were absolutely radiant. I loved how abstract one wall was from the other. To the left, was a crimson red, next to it was a neon green, then yellow, and orange, and to my immediate right was purple. I walked through and the sign reads:

Pick the color for the way you would like your night to end.

I was wearing red, so I went with red. I walked through the curtains, and everything shifted to a different world, it seemed. Red and black swirled the walls. Everyone was wearing either red or black and had a mask on. *They must be used to this place.* I noticed a food and drink area, so I approached it with the best intentions.

"Hello, would you like the red or the black pill to go on your trip tonight?" The guy said. He was tall, had a chiseled jawline, and long blonde hair.

"Which one does what?" I was puzzled.

"The red pill will undo anything wrong done to you, but you will feel amazing. Whereas the black one shows you how you got here but corrects anything in your past."

"Could I take both?" I challenged myself. I didn't understand the riddle of either pill.

"No."

"Do I have to choose one?"

"Yes."

"I'll go with black since I chose red earlier."

I took the black pill, poured some punch, and ate a few macaroons. "I felt nothing."

"You will."

"Are you always this cut to the point with everyone?"

"Yes."

I was sick of the one and two worded responses, so I walked away from him and sauntered around the room. Everyone had someone to talk to, except me. I found a nice table and sat down. I was glad to not be at the institution, but I still felt alone.

CHAPTER TWO

Payton

The girl was hurt as much as I was. I forced myself to listen to how she became institutionalized. Every second that went by, the more I learned, the more I needed to know.

The attachment. The need. The wanting. I felt bad for her. *This wasn't part of the plan.*

Yes, I wanted her to pay for what happened to Jennifer.

For my pain. But she has done nothing wrong? She existed.

She lost everything too. Her mom hated her existence.

The memory of previous events took over my mind.

Well, her mom swam with the fish now. Oh, the pure revenge extracted from her. I took her to the cliff, forced her to stand outside of the car. I had my shades and hat on, so she couldn't see who I was. Her screams danced around me. Her pleas were unheard. Nobody went on this side of town unless it was shady business, or they were lost. I knew where we were. I knew why.

Why isn't Penny with her? Penny was supposed to be in the car with her, so when I took her and forced her to watch her mother jump to her death, she would be scared enough to go anywhere with me. I didn't know if I was meant to be her savior or her anti-hero,

THE BLOODY MASSACRE 97

either way. I was hers to yield. I couldn't have known the amount of power this girl would hold on me.

"Where is Penny at?" I screamed at her mother.

"She walked back to the train station. Don't worry, she'll be in the Asylum until she dies. I'll never let her out again." The woman was clueless. I'd have her tonight if it were up to me.

"Why would you do that to your daughter?" I shook her. I had to know why she would throw her daughter away.

"Because she was his daughter. She wasn't mine. Jennifer was our daughter. I adopted Penny. She was a result of his adultery. When he killed our child, I wanted everything gone."

"But you raised her as your own. She's innocent in all of this." I gave her a mile to come back to decent humanity. She threw it away instantly.

"She's the child of a whore and a man who couldn't keep his dick in his pants," she spat. An evil, vile, broken woman, who only wanted someone to love her. I could be wrong. She didn't take care of herself anymore.

"Do you know who I am?" I asked her. She wanted to tell all of her woes and betrayals to a stranger, but I needed her to know who took her life.

"Yes, Nathaniel, everyone knows who you are. The best lawyer in town, but a snake if you ask me. Jennifer got lucky if you asked me," she spat. I seethed. The mention of her name made my blood boil. I felt my eyes get wider.

"I'm glad you know who I am, because you already know what's going to happen tonight," I whispered as I took her ID and keys off her body and threw it back into the car.

"Make sure you get Penny too. Her blood is tainted. Martin might have destroyed me by having an affair, but bringing their love child home for me to raise? That was the lowest. You should have taken Penny years ago. The worthless whore..." She rambled on and on. Yet, I realized my hatred was possibly misdirected. It fueled my direction and motivation.

"How is that her fault?" I asked her, before throwing her over the cliff.

I didn't wait for her answer. I really didn't want it. Either way, Penny wouldn't know the truth of what happened to her mom or why she was shunned away in an asylum.

*Oh Penny...*she's such a goddess, a broken, innocent goddess. *I wonder if she's still a virgin.*

Institutionalized at thirteen, which was over seven years ago. She's freshly twenty-one years old. It's a matter of time before someone stole her innocence.

My guilt got a mind of its own. The more she talked about Jennifer, her father and me and the night everything changed; the more I wanted to know about her since *that* night. I didn't realize she remembered all the details, yet never shared it with the police. *Did she remember me? Would that change anything?* My physical appearance hadn't changed. I'm still the same person, I think. Then again, she said she barely remembered my name. Although, she called me 'Nay.' *Payton Nathanial.* Very few people knew my middle name, and even fewer called me 'Nay'.

Penny's dress was stunning. It hugged her curves in the best way. She grew up a lot! Almost looked like Jennifer, but she aged a lot faster. In desperate need of the sun, she was a creamy pale white. Luckily, I was a lawyer and had a big house she could live i n. *Could I save her?*

Chapter Three

Penny

With every step I took, I felt as if I were on a spinning roller coaster, while in a funny mirror room. Nothing was steady. The room was topsy-turvy. I felt a little disoriented. I needed to sit down. I found a vacant table and claimed a chair. Everything was still spinning. I rested my head on my hands and shut my eyes. I needed my body to balance itself without the medications they poured into me for so long. I recognized it was like when I go through withdrawals. They change my medication every so often.

"Are you okay, ma'am?" A man asked me. I wasn't ready for conversations yet. I needed more time.

"I am." I shook my head no. I wanted to say, *Just a few minutes, please. I think I'm reacting the medications.'* Instead, I was short and rude, but I wanted to meditate–ground and center. I wanted to find my inner Zen. Or whatever it is they try to tell us during group therapy.

"My name is Payton. You seem very pale, from what I can see. Want to talk about it?" The new man was persistent.

"I'm Penny. I'm not sure what's going on. I took the black pill and now I'm just lightheaded and confused."

"I took the red one, so it was a bit of a fun trip as well. How did you get here?" He asked.

"I took the wrong bus and saw the masquerade event. I was already wearing an evening gown, so it felt right to come here. Now, I'm not sure if I made the right choice."

"I see. Where were you supposed to go?" His smile was brighter by the second.

"Back to the mental institution." I looked down and added, "The asylum."

"Oh, do you work there?" He still smiled. He was likely talking mad crap about me in his head.

"No." The room steadied as time went on. Perhaps it was a mixture between the pills and the masks. I definitely felt off.

"Do you volunteer there?" He didn't give up. He pressed.

"Nope," I snapped.

"So, you...." He paused.

"I live there. I'm a patient there." I did the one finger in a circle 'crazy' sign, "I'm a lunatic that belongs in the looney bin."

"I see. And how do you feel now?" *Typical man. Tell him you are crazy, and he will ask you how you feel.*

"I feel like I can't fathom why I was in there or why my mom doesn't love me enough to keep me in her life. I surmise that I have been maneuvered into this cube and I don't understand why because it should have been a circle." His eyes were a bluish, golden hazel... His hair was jet black and his mask was equally dark. "Does that make sense?"

"It does. Do you mind if I sit with you?" He never stopped smiling or looking at me.

"I don't mind at all. Have a seat." I motioned him to take the seat he was leaning on.

He grabbed a chair and placed it opposite me, then he sat down. "So why were you sent to a loony bin, anyway? You're so beautiful. Nothing as beautiful as you could be that crazy."

THE BLOODY MASSACRE

He paused for a minute when I looked down. "I'm sorry. Let me try that again. What was so bad that you had to be locked away, Penny?" Payton asked me, with his head tilted to the side.

"Well, that is the thing I don't remember what I did to be locked up at all. I just know it is bad enough for my mother to not want anything to do with me," I said back to him without breaking eye contact the whole time.

The room around us was darker. The others who were in the room were scarce and were fading away. It was only Payton and I in the room.

Did I know him? Impossible. I knew no one.

I don't have a clue what it is about Payton, but peering into his bluish eyes has me hypnotized. He feels like a soulmate. I can't understand it. It's like I've known him all my life, even though I met him tonight.

This smirk that he gave me tells me he feels as if he doesn't understand what's going on or why we even have this connection.

"So, tell me Penny, what do you remember?" Payton asked.

"Well, I remember I was just getting home from helping my grandmother with her store. It was during the summertime. I had worked two full shifts that day and I was exhausted. I hated being at home and my grandparents didn't care about me helping them out. I remember going to the front door with my keys in hand and opening it to walk into the house, only to hear something fall to the floor. I wanted to see what was happening, so I moved closer to the door that was down the hall. The door was open enough for me to look in and see my dad laying on the floor with a man standing over him and my sister stationary to the wall. I noticed that she wasn't moving. She had a blood stain where it appeared she was stabbed. I think Dad stabbed her with a steak knife. Surprisingly, when I looked closer to dad, I could tell he was holding on to his side. Blood rushed out of him. I ran to phone 911, to get my mom, anything...but it was too late."

I missed my grandmother. I take a moment to catch my breath as I look down at my hands and for some odd reason I get a flash of blood on my hands, but when I go to rub the blood off, it's no longer there.

What? I guess they were right. I must be crazy if I'm sitting here having delusions.

I looked back up at Payton and found him looking at my hands too.

Was he able to see the blood too?

What a fucking psycho, right?

What person likes the fact that they can see blood on someone else's hands? What does it say about me that I don't mind blood being on my hands? He said nothing. He just smiled and stared at me. "Keep going. Why do you feel like you're crazy?" He pushed.

"As suggested, I could be a psycho. From the moment I walked into the room to find my father, a man, and my sister, I completely blacked out. Then, I was confined in a padded room, strapped to the bed. I stirred from my sleep and my mother was the only one in the doorway to greet me. She told me this was where I was going to be living from this time forward. She was rooted to the spot, her face betraying her fear with no explanation. She kept her distance, as if she heard the silent plea in my eyes, asking her to stay." I had to take a break from the memory. It was too much. I never opened up about what happened with my dad and Jennifer.

"I have no memory of having done anything wrong. I have no memory of what transpired with my father, sister, and that man after I ventured into that room. Everything is shrouded in darkness as if my mind has decided that my life would be improved by never remembering what happened. Every time I try to remember, a searing headache overwhelms me, and I'm filled with a feeling of sickness." My voice was now a whisper. I closed my eyes and let my head fall backwards on the back of

THE BLOODY MASSACRE

the chair. I was ready for my medications again. This trip was to o much.

Payton leaned closer, so close I felt him almost on my face. I felt his breath on my lips. "Would you like to dance with me? Someone in a beautiful dress like the one you're wearing deserves to be dancing with a handsome man. Not sitting at a table all night, talking to him," he smirks as he offers me a hand to stand up from the table and follow him onto the dance floor. I nodded and shrugged my shoulders.

CHAPTER FOUR

Penny

"What's the worst that could happen?"

We danced to the music. It was a techno version of a rock song I've never heard before, and it was absolutely hypnotic. Each beat brought a distinct feeling and the more I danced with Payton, the more I wanted to get closer to him.

I grazed my hips on his and moved with the beat. "You're a brilliant dancer, Penny." Pulling me closer, the song went slower. He kissed me. I kissed him back, but wondered, *why is he kissing me?*

He tasted like a strawberry dipped in copper. A bloody strawberry. I broke away from the kiss. I noticed he's looking at me, scared. As if he knew of my biggest fears, he set this up to get me good. My feet planted where I stood, I couldn't turn away, move and I couldn't breathe. This was how I died.

Metallic paint dripped over the walls. Beneath my boots and all around me was a pool of thick, anticoagulated blood. I was dancing in a pool of blood. *This was actually fun.* Everything was *red*.

THE BLOODY MASSACRE

"What's wrong?" I stopped and looked at him. His face changed. No longer the most handsome man with a mask I've ever seen, but now he is a scary clown. Instead of paint on his face, he's covered in blood.

"You look like a clown to me, Penny." He licked my face, and I felt something wake up inside me. I felt alive. My bones were moving. My head was clear. And for the first time in my life, I had butterflies fluttering within my stomach.

"Your face is painted with blood." I yelled back to him. He wasn't understanding. *My biggest fear was clowns.*

"So is yours, Payton." I laughed. It had to be the drink and pill we took earlier. *This was all an illusion.*

"Tell me what else you remember before killing your dad and sister..." He asked to pull me onto the dance floor again. This time, the DJ played a slower song, and we danced a lot closer and slower.

"I never said I killed my dad and sister. I don't remember what happened that night. I helped my grandmother after school. I was exhausted. I came home and someone was standing over them. The next thing I know I woke up in a hospital and they asked me what happened. They said someone or something fell on top of me, and I had a concussion and long-term brain damage..." I paused for a minute. I still didn't know exactly what happened.

"So how did you end up in the mental institution?" He pressed further.

"I told them I saw the grim reaper." The truth.

"So, they thought you lost your mind. That makes sense," Payton laughed, "why did you tell them that?" I didn't laugh.

"I really saw the grim reaper," I confessed. "The look in his eyes was enough to tell me my father messed up. I felt the rage. I felt his heartbreak." I couldn't talk anymore.

Everything that was red turned black. Everything that was black turned red.

MULTIPLE AUTHORS

"What was your sister's boyfriend's name?" He asked. I leaned into him letting him hold me as I broke from whatever chains held me in the past.

"I always called him a snuggle bear. I was only thirteen. I think his nickname was "Nay", but I can't remember." I didn't want to talk about it anymore. The more I felt like I needed to tell him, the more I wanted to withdraw and hold back information for leverage. *For what, you lunatic?*

"Penny, I'm not here to hurt you. I'm here because I really enjoy your company and your eyes are so mesmerizing. I really enjoy spending time with you. You can trust me, okay?" He pleaded with me. I didn't know what his motive was, but I wanted to trust someone outside of the white walls I was limited to.

"I will not hurt you either. What happens next?" I brushed off the rest of the conversation.

"Well, it seems you have had an epiphany, so now it's time for us to go to the next room to see what could happen there," he explained.

We followed those leaving the room and took a blanket and washed off our faces and arms. The bloody paint came off easily. They did a fantastic job with this.

The next room was a solid black room with little neon lights sporadically around.

"Do you wish to change your dress?" A voice asked me as I was reaching the entrance. I didn't want to, but my dress was covered in paint. *At least I think it's paint.*

"Yes, please." I followed the voice to an empty room. I stripped down to my bra and panties.

"What color are you feeling now?" A very odd question to be asked. I wasn't sure what color I felt like. I just picked the next two that came to mind. The color of my first doll's hair and her car she drove and my dream destination.

"I think green." I smiled. This wasn't Sadie, but they could pass for twins.

THE BLOODY MASSACRE

"Perfect, and for your mask?"

"Purple." Green and purple reminded me of Mardi Gras, and I've always wanted to go.

The lady brought out a green strapless dress that barely reached my knees. She helped me into the dress, and I removed my bra. *It doesn't matter if I get this back. I'll never be let free again.* I put a pair of black boots on and walked into the next room. I looked around for Payton but didn't see him at first. So, I found a table and took a seat. *He must be still getting dressed or cleaned up.*

A server approached the table I was sitting at and asked, "Green or purple?" He had two cookies and shot glasses. "Can I take a green cookie and a purple drink?" I'm not sure what either did, but I figured I'd balance my choices out.

"The green will show your true intentions. The purple will reveal everyone else's." The server's eyebrows raised slightly. He enjoyed his job but wasn't fully aware of what was going on. He definitely didn't like playing twenty questions. *Neither did I.*

"So, either way, I could be fully exposed?" I guess it was worth the risk. All I've ever wanted was to be loved and understand why my mother hated me so much. I did not kill my dad. I did not kill my sister.

"Precisely." He rushed the words out and pushed the platter.

"Sounds good." I grabbed the green cookie and ate it, then shot the purple drink. It tasted like a Jolly Rancher mixed with a Starburst. Absolutely delicious. Green apple was my favorite flavor. The green cookie was a sugar cookie dipped in food coloring. I laughed to myself. I noticed everyone was walking around and introducing themselves. The music hadn't started yet. It was refreshing to hear again.

I hated that Payton wanted to talk about Jennifer and my father. It definitely wasn't the best part of tonight. In fact, I never wanted to think about that night. It wasn't my fault, yet I have paid for every second of it.

Remarkably, I felt amazing soon after indulging in the Mardi Gras duo. I saw auras, which I did not see before. Roughly, I want to say it was about twenty minutes later. I gave up waiting on Payton and moved around. *I guess he truly intended on never seeing me again.* I was sad, because he was my first human interaction without medications, and I enjoyed him. *Maybe he didn't get his epiphany yet? Maybe. Just maybe he's looking for me too.*

Chapter Five

Payton

The DJ started the music up again. I needed to change the subject for a few minutes. It was time to let the chopper free.

It's the perfect time to dance, spin and make a scene, so I asked her if she'd like to dance.

Every man woman and between looked and admired Penny. I had to kill them all. That's the only way she will survive. I'm not sure how or when my hatred turned to protection, but I had to keep her safe. I had to protect her.

But why?

What has she ever done for me?

I mean, aside from keeping me out of prison and away from the death penalty, saving my life and ultimately giving me the best night of my life that night, she did nothing for me.

So, she's done everything for me, but I'm an evil piece of shit who doesn't deserve her love, her touch, her smiles, her laughter...

Her innocence.

Her beauty.

No, I don't deserve this beautifully created angel before me.

But fuck what they say, because I will have her anyway. She is mine from here on out. And I will slice, dice, and disembowel anyone who tries to stop me.

Bring it on, motherfuckers.

CHAPTER SIX

Penny

I noticed different masks on others. Some were brighter, others were dull and dark. I felt a body sneak up on me. The warmth immediately soothed the chill I was feeling in my legs. Arms wrapped around me and a whisper in my ear, "Guess who?" I turned around fast. I went to take off my mask, but his hand stopped me. "You can't take off the mask. At all. In any of the rooms." I bit my bottom lip.

"Why?" The person I was talking to sounded like Payton, had his eyes, and resembled someone that could be Payton. In reality, I didn't even know what Payton looked like. I knew his mask and clown makeup were covered with blood. His lips. It was definitely him.

"Because it's part of the experience." He laughed. His precious, maniacal laugh.

"What colors did you choose?" I asked him.

"Red and orange." He laughed. "And you?"

"You can't tell?" I said, stretching my arms to form a Y. I spun around, making the dress flare.

"Everything is orange and red to me in this room. Including you."

"I chose purple and Green, though."

"It's your mask. It has a color filter." That made sense, I guess.

The room went dark. I saw various bodies that were brighter earlier go dull.

"Let's dance."

"What's going on, Payton? I'm not sure what's happening?"

He pulled me onto the dance floor. We danced. The more I looked into his eyes, I felt free. Maybe he was my redemption.

"Pick black and black next time, my dearie."

"Is it our last door?" I asked. I'm not even sure how long we were dancing for.

"It is for tonight. I want you to come home with me. I want to save you from yourself."

"How can you do that? I'm a ward of the state."

We danced. He ignored my question. I noticed lights were dimming all around us.

I went to wrap my arms around him and noticed his tux had a lot of sharp blades on it. I sliced my wrist open like a new blossoming flower. I felt the blood pour onto my skin.

"Damnit!" I said, grabbing my arm.

"What's wrong, Penny?"

"I think I cut myself on your jacket?" I was confused, but I knew there was no way that's what happened.

"Shit."

"It's time to go to the next room. Ask them to bandage you up." I nodded, even though I could barely see his face.

Before he left me, I removed the mask and looked behind, and the light turned on. There were over a hundred bodies on the ground, blood was everywhere, and my arm didn't have a scratch on it.

I looked back to see where Payton went, and he was gone.

CHAPTER SEVEN

Payton

The best idea I've ever had was asking Penny to dance with me. My mask didn't have the vision distortion lens. Instead, I saw everything clearly.

I loved feeling her hold onto me as if her life depended on it.

I loved smelling her hair and feeling her frail frame pulling me closer to her.

The pills she was taking? Random doses of Ecstasy.

I was a lawyer by day and a risk taker by night. I eliminated my challenges by removing them from the game.

Was Penny a challenge now? I really wanted to trust her, but she was related to Jennifer, which meant their father's blood ran through her veins. The pain rushed into me. I need more of this girl. I didn't know why I sought her demise. I'm not sure why I wanted her blood on my hands. Ultimately, one choice she made kept me alive. *Did I owe her a life debt?*

Would she trust me long enough to let me take control?

Could she be the one?

Every bitter choice has a consequence.

However, every choice has led me to her in every direction.

114 MULTIPLE AUTHORS

* * *

The ability to take out entire rooms and not flinch must be a talent few people possess. Then again, mass shooters are on the ride in the world again. I annihilated the entire first two levels and cleared out the entire room within thirty seconds. Nobody would live to talk about the last room. I took care of the bodies and sent them all to the research center. They all signed an agreement that we weren't responsible. And it clearly details that it's the Bloody Masquerade experience. What were they thinking it would be? Cupcakes and wine? Whatever.

Walking into this club is like walking into a new game of Russian Roulette every time you enter. I knew one day; I'd get her into my club. I just wished—no I prayed and begged to God or whomever to let me have one more minute with Jennifer so I could save her. And every time I do, Penny showed up.

I had to change everything up because the drugs weren't getting me the answers I wanted. She was pretty honest with me so far. I guess it was time to be honest and not be cryptic anymore.

It's time to tell her the Grim Reaper was real, very real, in fact, I know who he is...

CHAPTER EIGHT

Penny

"What color dress, Penny?" A familiar voice asked.

"Black dress. Black Mask, please," I whispered. I tried to remember what her name was.

"Okay. Take this and wash it off with these," the voice said, spreading soap on me as I climbed out of the dress. I took the drink and medicine she gave me. "What is this for?" I asked, not wanting to go on another psychedelic trip.

"This is for the inevitable hangover you're going to have tomorrow morning."

We both laughed as she handed me a black tank top and miniskirt. Sadie added a jacket to the outfit, and I felt like I was part of a new biker gang, at least the ones I read about.

"Don't touch anyone's jackets. Make sure you keep your wits about you. This is the last part of the experience."

"Are those people dead?" I asked her. Her eyes were wider than a doe caught in headlights.

"You weren't supposed to remove your mask, nor were you supposed to see that."

"Is this real or a dream?" I was confused.

"This is part of the experience," she said, skipping away from the answers I wanted. "Go have fun. This is your last room."

"I feel like I'm being punished, but I did nothing."

"Then the experience is working. Go on, Penny. Have fun."

* * *

I took two steps into the new room. Everything was rainbowish. I knew Payton would find me. Something told me he knew more about what was going on than he was letting on. I couldn't let go of the feeling there were dead bodies and a pool of coppery blood in the last room. Is that how it was painted on me? It was leaking from the roof. I didn't remember going up or down stairs.

I found a similarly placed table and moved the extra chairs away from it. I only needed two. One for me. One for Payton. Anything more was a waste, and I really just wanted to know what was going on.

"What is your poison of choice, Penny?" The server asked.

"How do you know my name?" I asked. It was okay that the lady getting me dressed knew, but now the server, too. Something was off. I felt it.

"You're wearing a name tag on your jacket." He said, pointing to his jacket. His tag said Eric.

"Nice to meet you, Eric." I forced a smile, "Do you have a rum runner? I heard they are the best."

"We do. And what to eat?" He was good at the server thing. If I gained my freedom, I wonder what career choice would be best for me?

"I'd really love a medium rare steak with a loaded baked potato and a huge salad." I drooled.

I felt his presence before he sat down. Reflecting, I never knew why Payton came into my life. I'm sure if I would have known, I would have flown galaxies away from him in the opposite direction. However, there was such a magnetic pull to him.

THE BLOODY MASSACRE 117

"A woman with a healthy appetite. I love it." We laughed.

"I'll have what she's having, but I want my steak rare." He licked his lips and winked at me.

"So, are you going to tell me why I saw a hundred bodies when I left the last room?" Straight to the point. I wanted only the truth. Small talk wasn't allowed at this table.

"Are you going to tell me the truth about what happened and how you entered the asylum?" His head turned slightly, and he grabbed my right arm. He used one finger to play invisible dot to dot with the goosebumps.

"My dad killed my sister. Her boyfriend went into a rage. They were announcing she was pregnant with twins and getting married. She was seventeen years old. Four years older than I was. My sister's boyfriend killed my dad. He gave me the spear and pushed the bookshelf onto me, nearly killing me," I confessed. I told no one else the truth about what happened. "The boyfriend was never seen again. To this day, I know he was the grim reaper, because he was dressed in all black." Chills overcame me. I shuddered at the memory.

"Why did you take the blame for the murder?" Payton's entire demeanor changed.

"Honestly, I was more pissed that my dad killed Jennifer than her boyfriend killing my father." I felt tears building. A sensation foreign to me since being locked away.

"Did your dad ever hurt you or your sister?" He pulled me closer. With one hand, he held my face, and the other he used his pointer finger and wiped the tears from my face. Then, he licked my tears off of his finger. *Odd...*

"I want to be honest with you. But I don't remember. Everything is a blur." I was honest and wanted to go back to the medications. Reality was too much to bear.

"Very well then. That's what really happened?" He pressed. Intently, he looked into both my eyes. I thought we were having a staring contest.

I nodded.

"I killed them. Every single soul that tried to approach you and take you away from me. I killed them. When we spin, my jacket turns into propellers, and it slices and dices everyone." He smiled.

"And the pool of blood? Were we really dancing in blood?" I liked this fast-paced conversation. I wanted the truth about everything. This club hadn't been here for long, yet everyone wanted to come for one day. No way.

"That's just for a sensual experience. Why did you take off the mask?" His head turned and he smiled.

"Why did you kill people for wanting to approach me?" I retorted. I would not end my interrogation with a question. Not fair.

"Not everything is what it seems. Be on guard, too." His smile faded, and he was more serious at this moment than any other moment.

"Why are you protecting me, Payton?" I really wanted to know.

Quietly, he kissed my forehead. And at the most unfortunate moment the food arrived. Payton handed the server a tip and he scurried away.

"How do you know me?" I asked quickly. I had to know more. I didn't like the silent treatment or him not answering my questions. The questions weren't hard.

"I'll tell you later." The food arrived, and we immediately ate. The steak was cooked perfectly. I didn't need a knife. Hell, I could have eaten it with a plastic spoon. No steak sauce needed, and the potato had the perfect amount of cheese. We ate in silence. The rest of the room moved around us, but that's part of the experience, I guess. The food outside of the institution, asylum, crazy person prison, whatever you want to call it, is different. There's flavor. It's not deduced into slop. The senses are alive outside of those walls. I didn't realize how hungry I could actually be. Between the medications and overwhelmingly not feeling alive, I only ate what I had to eat. There were weeks

THE BLOODY MASSACRE

119

where I wouldn't eat, and I'd lose so much weight. They put a PEG tube on me and if I don't eat, I get formula. I tried pulling it out. That's when they strap me down, put the guard belt on and I couldn't move or do anything for weeks. The more I fought them, the more they restrained and drugged me.

The more I ate, the more I wondered where I met him.

I didn't meet him from school because I went to an all-girl's school. I knew no boys aside from Jenn's boyfriend and there's no way he'd be interested in me, nor could he have pulled any of this off. None of dad's friends had boys, and most moved away, because of the news channels and journalism all wanting answers. *Who could he be?*

Don't mess with Payton's date or you will die. I didn't see that rule anywhere. I laughed, thinking about the possibility that many people died for merely approaching me.

"Why are you laughing, Penny?" He asked.

"What happens next?" I asked, before putting the last bite in my mouth.

"Would you like another drink, Penny?"

"Sure. Water, please."

The server brought another water without even asking us. I suppose they have some type of telepathy in this building.

"I just hit a button on my phone and let them know we wanted water." He smiled.

I nodded. *And they read minds too.*

"Would you like to dance again?" I wanted to, but I had so many questions.

"Will people die if they try to come near me again?" Challenging him for another question and answer.

"Yes." He took a bite of his steak and pointed his fork at me.

"Will they die if they look at me?" I took the bait and asked another.

"Yes."

"Are you the owner of this club?" I figured I'd ask the obvious ones.

"Yes."

"Is this really a club?" I whispered. I looked around the room. The colors were so vibrant, but at the same time, I couldn't explain where the walls were. Were they walls? It could have been a curtain. And the floor on this level was carpet. So, it felt like floating on a cloud.

"No." Payton shook his head.

"Where are we?" I really wanted to know because it was feeling like a dream. Everything was too good to be true. *Especially him.*

"Are you having fun?" He smiled.

"I am, Payton." Aside from feeling like I would float away, I really was having fun.

"Would you come here again?" He moved closer, pulling my hand to his lips. He kissed the palm of my hand. I giggled.

"I'm not sure how I got here. And if I ever got out of the asylum again, I'm sure they'd have a strict patrol around me." I've escaped before and the punishment for doing that was almost unbearable. If I had access to anything to end my life, I would have done it a long time ago. I took a deep breath. "Are you screwing with me? Or Am I dreaming?" I rushed to get my next question out.

"Not anymore and no."

"So, you are real?" I touched his face. I pulled my hands away from his and with one finger, I rubbed along his lips. He took my hand in his and kissed the palm of my hand, moving to my wrist and toward my shoulder. "Why were you screwing with me at first?"

"Do I feel real?" He whispered, breathing into my ears, pulling my hair out of the way.

"I'm not sure what's real or fake anymore?" He kissed my ears and kissed down my neck to my throat. Everything felt so right with him. But something was *wrong.*

"I'm very real, Penny."

THE BLOODY MASSACRE

121

"So, if you're real, but this isn't a club, but you own this establishment, and I am the sole motive for all the people being slaughtered today, what is really going on?"

"I'm recruiting you, Penny," he said smiling. "I was originally going to kill you and do whatever I wanted with your body. But I think Jennifer and Martin's deaths took care of my revenge plot and now I want to do everything with you. I even took care of Karen as well."

"Karen? As in my mom Karen?" Something was taking over me. There's no way my mom died. Did she? I literally just saw her a few hours ago. *I think it was a few hours ago.*

"Yes, your mom never intended to fully take care of you. You were a blight on her life. A burden. You were the result of an affair. Your parents hid the details, but I'm being honest with you. I'd still like to recruit you. I'll answer any questions you have." He was now holding my hands. Everything was going too fast. Overstimulation. I needed to breathe. *How do I breathe?*

"In order for me to fully explain everything to you, I need to go through everything, and I need to ask you questions. Consider this part of your interview for the recruitment."

Recruitment? What the fuck?

"For what?" I was officially confused. Absolutely nothing made sense. I was definitely on drugs. Very strong potent drugs. Hallucinogens. I was losing my fucking mind. I thought I was insane before. This confirmed it.

I was batshit, three sheets to the wind, out of this world, madder than the hatter, completely insane. Period.

"Okay. Close your eyes. I'm going to take this washcloth and wash your face. While I'm doing this, I'm going to explain a few things to you, and I need to ask a few questions. Please be honest with me. Somehow you managed to wiggle into my heart and change my plans. So, please don't anger me."

"Okay."

"From here on out, please say 'yes sir'."

"Okay, Payton."

"I see you want to be a brat. That's okay. I've been a tamer before."

"First question, are you still a virgin? I've been dying to know."

"I am. We met today. So why would you be dying to know that?"

"I've known you a lot longer than today. You could call me your dark guardian angel, Penny."

"What do you mean? I don't remember knowing you. I think I'd remember someone as handsome as you are." My eyes were still closed. I wanted to open them, but the warm washcloth siting on my face felt heavenly and was doing wonders for my migraine.

"What if I told you, you were right about what you remembered in your past?"

"I would have felt less crazy, I think." I didn't understand where this was going.

"What if I told you that your memory is a lot more accurate than you think it is?"

"Okay. So, Jennifer's boyfriend did kill my dad and he killed my sister? And then he left me there to die?"

"Perhaps not the last bit. I didn't leave you there to die," he hissed at the accusation.

"What the fuck?" I pulled the washcloth off my head. "Have you been stalking me?"

His mask was removed from his face. I saw who he truly was. He still looked as beautiful as I could remember. Jennifer would have been lucky with this one.

"I haven't been stalking you. But I did do everything I could to make sure you didn't go to prison for the murders. You were innocent and you're not insane." He took a deep breath, grabbed my hands. I snatched it back. I think he growled. "I forgot to mention, Penny, I'm the Grim Reaper. I want you to be my second in command and help me produce the next heir."

"You're the Grim Reaper?"

CHAPTER NINE

Penny

Lord Lucifer, what in the unholy hell is going on? Payton is the Grim Reaper. The Grim Reaper wants me to be part of his life, in a relationship, and have his kids. This can't be happening right; I mean I must be losing my mind like they have been saying I have been right? Confusion raped my mind; the lack of understanding assaulted my reality. I didn't know...I just didn't know what to say or do.

I knew everything in my life was a lie. Maybe I wasn't confused but betrayed.

I did not know why my doctors would say I was psychotic and lie. Why would my mother continue to keep the facade of loving me? For as long as I remember, she never said those words. *Maybe she didn't love me.*

The past few years I have been numb. And when reality sets in and I'm taken off the medications I was forced on, I feel like I am crazy with the way they are looking at me all the fucking time.

Am I crazy? I don't know.

Then, there's Payton. He makes me feel like nothing is wrong with me. He validates my thoughts have merit and meaning. There is an absolute bigger problem than whether or not I'm crazy. Someone knows I'm not crazy and I'm looking dead into his murderous eyes. They're keeping me in the looneybin to silence me. But, why!?

I know I'm not crazy. I lost my best friend and sister when they were murdered. Then, I lost my everyday life. No, I wasn't crazy...

I look over at Payton. "Are you saying that I don't have to be in this loony bin with these people that are saying that I don't know the difference between reality and imagination? All I will have to do is be myself. If that is what you are offering me then how can I say no to that? How can I look the other way while they get away with the way they are treating me?"

Payton looks me right in the eyes. "Yes, Penny, that is what I am saying that for now on as long as you stand by my side you will always have everything you need. You will never want for anything again if I have anything to say about it."

I am seeing the color red. The more I think about it, the redder I see. "I want their heads Payton, I want them on a platter, I want to look them in the eyes and rip their nails off with tweezers, cut them open and show them their insides. I want to be a Grim Reaper too. What I am saying is that if you give me this then I will agree to becoming your second and having your children. I will agree to anything that you ask of me as long as you give me what I asked for in return."

After I say this Payton has a smile on his face it is so big it reaches his eyes. "Then that is what you will have Penny starting today all of your wants will be answered." He bit his lip. "I do have one request, though."

"What's your request?" I asked without hesitation. There wasn't much he could throw at me right now that would surprise me.

THE BLOODY MASSACRE

"Do you remember in fourth or fifth grade, there was a kid who used to bully you all the time, do you remember his name?" He asked.

"I do. His name was Eric." I remembered him vividly. He would pull my hair and ask me to do his homework for him. He'd steal my lunches and make me beg for it back.

"I want you to kill him, then I will make love to you. Once we make love, I am yours and you are mine."

"Yes sir," I whispered. I looked at him like he was crazy. It's not like I meant that I wanted to hurt people. The longer I stayed around Payton though the more I feel like what happened in the past was something I never deserved. The reality of the entire situation is Payton, and my father should have been the ones suffering. Not me.

Maybe I may become the thing that they always said I am, a crazy psycho. At least now I will have something to blame it on. The more I think about it the more I love having blood on my hands.

"Open your mouth," Payton said out of nowhere. I obeyed and opened my mouth. "Close your eyes."

I did as he said. He placed something in my mouth. "Eat it."

"A marshmallow?" I asked after I chewed it.

"Very good." He gave me another and I ate it, too. The sweetness was perfect. "I remember marshmallows being your favorite treat when you were younger. I'm glad somethings never change. Are you ready for all of this?"

"I have no idea what we are doing. I am new at this," I said, trying not to show my ignorance. "So, how do we do this?"

"I'll guide you the entire way. Have you ever killed anyone before?"

"I haven't. That's your specialty," I laughed.

"Very funny. First, I want to undress you and see what all you are hiding."

"Yes sir," I said. He pulled me to stand and took off my shirt, then the skirt. I was wearing only my boots and panties. I really wished I had my bra on right now. The room wasn't warm.

"My gods, you are a beautiful sight to see," he said holding my hand forcing me to spin around.

CHAPTER TEN

Payton

Can I really trust her?

Within her blood is the very core of what broke me in the first place. I wanted to believe she would not betray me. How could I trust someone who is so innocent? That should be an easy question to answer, but she wouldn't even know if she was hurting me. She's been sheltered within an asylum, drugged to the max, and led to believe she's insane. Penny is not insane. There's not an insane element within this woman.

She agreed to be mine.

She agreed to kill Eric. I will miss having him around. He's been a good righthand man, but I need her to prove her loyalty. Not only will this give me leverage over her, and help me keep her on her toes, but it will be a great way to start our new lives together. Blood in, blood out. It'll even the playing field.

"Lay down on the table. I need to taste you," I whispered. My needs and wants were distorted with everything else going on. Perhaps if I focused only on her, I'd be able to plan this out perfectly. Penny being her wasn't within my calculations. I figured she would have hit the door running, but she succumbed to all of her issues and persevered.

I watched her lay down on the table. So feeble and fragile. She wasn't tall, definitely about five foot three. She weighed about 175 pounds and was thick in the right places. She had little confidence or self-love for herself. Her self-esteem has definitely suffered over the past years. "Open your legs," I growled. I needed to see what I was about to open up. I needed to feel her.

She opened her legs, and I dove in. Jesus with the twelve disciples have nothing on me. If this was my last supper, I was making sure it was an absolute feast. I kissed her legs, moving to her thighs. Her womanhood was screaming for me. Her love button taunting me, begging me to suckle the honey. I needed every drop she would offer. Once I kissed her forbidden lips, I used one hand to open her up, and the other to pull her closer. The instant my mouth contacted her clit, she pushed away from me. I didn't want to tie her up, but I needed to finish what I started.

"Don't fight me, Penny. But, before I keep going, do you want this?"

"Yes sir," she snapped, "I'm not fighting you. It just caught me by surprise. Please don't stop," she begged. I obliged.

Happily, I dove back into my forbidden platter. I focused on her clit at first, making sure her satisfaction was building. I wanted her to explode.

"This feels so amazing." She pushed back to me, wrapping her legs around my neck. If she squeezed, she could surely break my neck.

"I'm glad you love that, Penny." I pulled her down to me. "I want you to taste how delicious you are." I kissed her, forcing my tongue into her mouth. Without hesitation, she licked and sucked on my tongue. With any more force, she could have pulled my tongue out of my mouth as a souvenir.

I didn't want to take any chances. I sent a quick text to Eric letting him know we needed a refill. I know he was lurking

THE BLOODY MASSACRE

around somewhere watching me make Penny mine. *Little did he know...*

Eric ran over with a pitcher of water and looked at Penny displayed on the table.

"Would you like a taste?" I asked him.

"I would," he said stepping over to her. "Do you mind if I have a taste?" He looked at me, but I wasn't sure if he was asking me or her.

"Who are you asking?"

"She's your pet, I'm asking you," he answered. *Wrong answer.*

I placed a steak knife into her hands. I figured he could taste her before she killed him.

"Penny, do you mind if Eric tastes you?"

"I don't mind." I think she read my mind and knew where I wanted this to go.

"While he's tasting me, can I taste you?" She moved her head over to see me.

Eric and I both undressed. I headed over to Penny so she could get her needs met.

I moved over to Penny's head, so she was under me. She looked up at me and smiled. She took my cock into her hand, pulled me closer and took my cock into her mouth while upside down. Even though this was her first time, she wasn't a novice at this. Perhaps she had practice before? I didn't want to ask. The second her tongue touched the underside of my cock; I moaned out with pleasure. I put my hand into her hair only to help guide her through the motions, pushing to the back of her throat. Once I was where I could wait no longer, I held onto her head and thrusted into her mouth. I fucked her face as if it were the last time, I'd be able to do this. One thing is for sure, her mouth was made for me. I couldn't wait to teach her everything else there was to learn.

While I was getting the best fellatio a man could dream of, Eric dove into her lady bits and went down. I noticed he was using fingers and she wasn't moving as much. Once I came into her mouth, she swallowed every bit. I kissed her. Fair is fair, right?

"I'm ready for you, Payton. I want you to take me now. I can't wait any longer." Moaning, she was begging me now.

"Eric must not be satisfying you properly?" I joked.

"Absolutely not. But I have an idea if you'll indulge my crazy psychotic mind." She was smiling ear to ear. Eric continued on with his tongue torture. He apparently did not get the memo.

"Your wish is my command." I bowed my head and submitted to her. The first and last time this would ever happen for a woman. I usually had them submitting.

"I want you to make love to me, while Eric watches." Her eyes fluttered at me. *A cuckold in the making, I'm impressed.*

I helped Penny move from the table to the floor. I'm so glad I installed carpets on this level. "Are you sure you're ready for this?"

"I am."

"This is going to hurt for a few seconds. Just tell me if it's too much," I said, "close your eyes and relax."

"Yes sir," she said.

I positioned myself to enter and take the best gift a girl could give a man, and with one thrust, I entered and let her adjust to the intrusion taking over her body. "I'm ready. Give me more." She grimaced through the pain.

"Are you sure you're ready for this?" I was already thrusting into her, building momentum, and watching her body rise with every breath she released and held.

"I think I'm ready for you and Eric at the same time," she said. I was confused, but maybe this was part of her grand plan.

Eric moved himself over her mouth so she could taste him and prep him for entrance. She laughed.

"I'm not tasting you. I want to be on top of you, while Payton takes me from behind."

THE BLOODY MASSACRE   131

"So, he's going to have your ass, while I am your second?" Eric asked confused.

"Sure." She didn't give a full answer. I knew she was up to something. *My deviant little sex pot.*

Eric laid down beside her, ready for his turn at the action. "Do we have handcuffs?" She asked.

I knew we did, but I'd have to go get them. "Not right now," I answered.

"Okay." She climbed onto Eric, grabbed the knife, and the second I was inside of her again, she took the knife and severed his dick from the base. He no longer had a penis. It was in her hand. Eric didn't realize what was going on at first, but when he saw his dick in her hand and blood going everywhere, he tried to throw us off of him. How did he not feel that?

"What the hell you crazy bitch?" He yelled. While I was doing everything I could to keep him from knocking her off of him, she threw his cock at his mouth. Hole. In. One. With the first shot at that.

"Eric, did you know that you used to be a mean bully?" He shook his head.

She readjusted so I could enter her with no issues. The knife still in her grip.

"You used to torment the hell out of me. I almost forgot about it, but my little angel here reminded me." With another swift movement, she grabbed his ball sack, twisted, and cut his ball sack completely off. Blood was going everywhere. I could fall in love with Penny if I had a heart left to give her. Amongst all of this death, she made me feel alive again.

"Fuck you, Eric. I hope you choke on a cock," she laughed, "Oh wait, you are, aren't you?"

She laughed so hard she pushed me out of her. I turned her over, so she was laying on top of Eric, but facing me. "You're so beautiful my deviant vixen." I pounded into her with everything I had left in me.

"Did I pass your test, sir?"

"You still have a bit to work on, but I think you're off to a great start."

"Okay. So, what's the next test?"

"Well, let's see how you react to jealousy at my other job?"

"Your job as a lawyer?"

"Nope."

"What else do you do?"

"Oh baby, I'll show you," I laughed. "Will you accept me as your boyfriend?"

"Absolutely."

"Well, it's safe to say that your boyfriend is a murderous lawyer and works at a strip club." He moved me through the room, and we admired the bloody masterpiece that surrounded us.

"So, you're a stripper?"

To be continued....

About the Author

Dakota Cole is an emerging author. This will be her first published piece, but will not be her last!

She lives at home with her mom and younger brother. Her father passed away in November 2022. She has a furry baby, Dixie. She was born and raised in Kentucky.

She loves to watch LMN and has never been married.

If she could live anywhere it would be Florida or California.

Dark Cravings

Arianna Barton

Phoenix Voices Anthologies

CONTENTS

Foreword	#
Prologue	#
Chapter One	#
Chapter Two	#
Chapter Three	#
Chapter Four	#
Chapter Five	#
Chapter Six	#
About the Author	#

FOREWORD

This story is part of the Deception World. It can be read as a standalone as it contains it's own characters an plot-line.

TRIGGER WARNING

As this is a horror story, there are a lot of triggers. This is a list of the main ones, however there might be others. So please, proceed with caution and be ready for a frightful time!

- Torture
- Stalking
- Forced self-mutilation
- Murder
- Mind control
- Arousal from violence
- Flesh consuming
- Patricide
- Clothing made into skin
- Spousal cheating

Prologue

Prologue

T he sound of the clock ticking drowned out the silence. I stared at the front door, willing it too miraculously open. He was getting bolder, staying out later and not even bothering to message me where he was. He used to lie, but he stopped caring to put up any pretenses anymore. I glanced at my smartphone, the small object taunting me. I could so easily call him, to see where he was and try to catch him out, but that would force me to face a reality I wasn't ready for. It would make me have to accept that I truly was alone and make me let go of the fabricated idea that I still had him in my corner. It was pathetic of me, but I didn't care. When you were in your fif'ties you were allowed to be less brave. In my mind at least. Although, I knew numerous others would disagree.

The clock chimed. I sighed, seeing the hands pointing at 1 am. I had all the lights off, except for one lamp. It cast a faint orange glow that battled with the shadows, providing me just enough light to see with. I looked around our living room, trying to see what was so wrong with it he had to find solace with someone else. It was quaint, with outdated furniture and a small coffee table over a shag rug. Nothing fancy, but it was warm and did the job. Just like I thought our relationship did the job.

I slumped in my seat as I accepted, he likely wasn't coming home anytime soon. I needed to get some sleep as I had a big day at work tomorrow. I stood up and winced at the pain spidering through my back. I didn't bother turning off the lamp, just walked to the exit and into the hallway leading to our room. I had already brushed my teeth and gotten dressed, so I climbed onto my bed that felt endlessly big being in it alone. I shut my eyes and tried to get comfortable.

I exhaled and tried to calm my mind. The silence almost seemed to buzz, and my stomach twisted as the uncanny feeling of being watched filled me. I pulled the blankets higher, hoping it would somehow ward off the feeling. The feeling grew worse, and anxiety caught me in its net. I focused on my breathing and tried to relax my stiffening body. The moment seemed to drag, and right as I was about to lose my mind, the feeling went away. I let out a deep breath, only to scream as something slammed into my window. I shook under my covers and stared at my closed curtains with wide eyes.

"It was probably just a bird. Just shut your eyes," I whispered, forcing myself back down to the pillow.

It took a while, but finally the knot loosened, and I was finally able to rest. I fell through the gauzy glaze of sleep and the world melted away.

As I looked around, my dress flew out, the long white night-gown transforming me into some sort of ghost. The world looked like it did underwater, with the light streams coming in and making everything look ethereal. It took a few moments to recognize I was in my house, and more accurately, in my bed-room. I looked over and saw myself in bed, my husband missing. I floated over and smiled sadly. This wasn't how I envisioned

THE BLOODY MASSACRE   141

my life going. I expected him to uphold his vows just as I had upheld mine. Instead, he shattered my faith in him and left me with nothing but disappointment.

My sleeping form rolled onto her back; her mouth firmly closed. I watched her silently, not making a move. Was this normal? Did people normally see themselves in dreams? I supposed anything was possible when it came to the imagination.

Sleeping me began to groan, and I watched silently as her face screwed up. She moaned loudly, before her body jerked and she let out an ear-piercing shriek that chilled me to the bone. I wanted to help her, myself, but I was rooted in spot. I watched as she started to gurgle, her eyes flying open and her back arching and lurching off the bed. She looked possessed, with her wide eyes and the distorted shape of her body. Horror filled me as her hands went to her throat and her nails began to claw at the tender skin there, leaving red ribbons of blood and rips in her flesh. Bile snaked up my throat as I watched black legs push at the holes, ripping them open further. A moving black river slowly piled out and ripped my throat further, leaving mangled flesh and blood in its wake. I wanted to throw up as the river scuttled out, covering my sleeping figure's body. I saw specks of white intermixed and tried to curb the growing dread. The same blackness surged out of my ears and nose, another stream falling out of my mouth and covering my torso. I watched helplessly as my hands went to my mouth and pulled the corners with all my strength. A sickening, ripping sound filled the air and I stared horrified as tears formed in my face. More and more blackness came piling out, and my body continued to scream as tears and blackness fell down my cheeks.

It was only when my body was covered in the writhing creatures, I saw what they were, but by this time it was too late, my body was lifeless; claimed by the spiders and their unborn young.

I woke up with a start, my hand going to my chest. I reached out and touched my face and throat to ensure they were all intact. Finding no mutilated skin, I sunk back into the pillow, some of the terror melting away.

"It was just a nightmare, nothing to worry about," I said softly, hoping my mind would latch onto my words of reassurance.

"Just try to go back to sleep, you'll need it for work tomorrow," I whispered, trying to calm myself down by speaking aloud.

I forced my eyes shut despite the terror swimming through my body like a shark hunting its prey. It took a while, but I was almost able to pierce through that gauze again when something brushed against my ankle.

"What in the world?" I muttered, leaning over to turn on my light.

I lifted the blanket up, and deliberately ignored the shaking in my hand. My entire body froze, and nausea filled when I saw the culprit.

There, in between my legs was a black, hairy spider, the exact kind from my dream. I watched, paralysed in fear as it scuttled out of sight. Once I was able to, I pulled my legs away and ran out the room, deciding that waiting up for my husband to come home from whatever lady's house he was at sounded like a good idea after all.

CHAPTER ONE

I moaned as the insipid woman's delicious fear filled me. I tilted my head back and dug my nails into Raphael's head as his tongue laved on my exposed pussy. I could feel my orgasm crest along with the woman's fear and barely managed to hold back my scream as it washed over me. I felt myself squirt all over my lover, and my eyes rolled back into my head as the overwhelming sensations filled me. There was nothing more erotic than making people so scared they could barely function. It always got me going, and luckily for me, my men were always willing to accommodate me.

He kept laving me as I came down from my high. He let his tongue brush along my clit one last time, sending sparks through me, before he pulled away. He sat up and smirked at me, pride shining in his bright red eyes. Raph's face was slick with my come, and I thought he'd never looked more handsome.

"How was that my love?" he asked, his voice huskier than usual.

I moaned in reply, not wanting to use my words. He just chuckled and moved next to me, pausing only to open his legs and lift me in between.

"Tomorrow we will get inside that house, and you can have your fill of her fear before we torture her and drain her dry. I'd love to fuck you with her organs and limbs strewn around," Raph said, making another surge of horniness fill me.

"Don't talk dirty to me right now. We need to focus," I lightly reprimanded.

He groaned and placed his head against mine. We were in the bushes, and I had used my Deimos magic to encase us in shadows. We could watch her scream in terror all we liked, but she would never see us.

"Nice touch with slamming on her window," I complimented, looking up at him.

"She reacted nicely, didn't she?" he said, and I smiled knowingly.

"I just wish Leander was here to see this too, you know how he likes it when they scream," I said, pouting.

"He will be here with us tomorrow, Levana, be patient, my love. You know he prefers the more direct approach."

I smirked. "I still can't believe these idiots haven't realised he is Jack the Ripper; utter idiots."

"Humans are idiots, it's why they're so easy to wind up and turn into delicious juice boxes."

I smirked at Raph's reply and looked out at the house. A thin sliver of moon was visible above the roof, and the light from inside seeped out from behind the curtains. It didn't stop me from being able to see her; my eyesight was acute enough to see her pacing nervously. A slow, dark smile crossed my lips and I let my eyes flutter shut. I imagined black spiders appearing randomly throughout her house, just sitting there innocuously to taunt her, and was rewarded by the dulcet sounds of her terror-filled screams. I moaned as the fear washed over me, and

THE BLOODY MASSACRE

let it soothe my soul. I couldn't wait to rip her body apart and bathe in her blood. It was going to be a treat.

"Ready to go, baby?" Raphael asked, his red eyes radiating nothing but love for me.

"Let's go get Leander and get some sleep. We have a busy day tomorrow."

* * *

I smirked as I watched the glorious scene before me. Leander had a prostitute bent over with her ass in the air and her hands braced against the wall as he ploughed inside her exposed pussy. Her panties were around her ankles and her moans were anything but fake. Raphael sat without feet dangling over the edge of the roof behind him, watching the show. It was always hot watching Lee work, especially when he let the monster out. Raph was affected by the sight as well as he placed his hand between my thighs and rubbed me gently, making me moan as his dexterous fingers worked their magic. My orgasm built up, and I found my release the same time as the woman below. Raph pumped me harder, forcing me to crash into another before tearing his hands away and licking off the results of his hard work.

I leaned in to kiss him before looking back down. Leander's hand pulled out of her and had her facing him now. I leaned forward, eager for the show. I watched as he leaned down and whispered something in her ear. At first, she was smiling but it was soon replaced with wide eyes and a trembling pulse. She pushed him off her and he let her, his usual smirk resting on his lips as he watched her pull up her panties and stumble out the alleyway. Leander counted a few minutes before chasing after her, leaving a cloud of grime behind. Raph and I smirked at each other before leaping up and jumped from one building to the next, our own bloodlust rising. I saw her sprinting rather clumsily for a girl about to die and noticed her casting multiple glances behind her. Her heart raced enticingly in her chest, and I moaned at the sweetness of her fear. Leander was ensuring he was always in her line of sight but never too close as he followed her, ramping up her fear and making her blood pump deliciously through her veins.

We stood above her as she turned into an alley. I could taste her fear spike as she saw it was a one-way street. I looked and Raph and winked before disappearing and materialising in the dark behind her. I waited until she was looking frantically around before revealing myself to her.

"What are you doing in my territory, bitch?" I sassed, crossing my arms over my chest.

She whirled on me; her eyes wide. I watched as she ran back to me and let her grasp my hands. "Please, you must help me. I had a client and things were fine, but he turned and now he's trying to kill me! Please, you must come with me. It's not safe here," she begged, her eyes wet with unshed tears.

It was cute how she was trying to save the person who was going to be her undoing. Playing the part, I scoffed and raised an eyebrow at her.

"Are you serious? You're just trying to take my spot!" I spat, eyeing her like one would dirt under their shoe. "Get out of here now. You'll chase away my clients."

Never before had I been so happy about the way I dressed. My long black hair was slick straight and fell in a sheet down my back. My makeup was a bit excessive, but I loved to experiment with colour and intensity. I had opted for my dark red leather mini dress and heeled boots today, as I loved getting men's attention before I tore out their throat, plus the guys loved watching it too.

"You don't understand! We have to get out of here now. Before he——"

"Too late, little girl. The monster is already here."

I shivered at the sound of my beloved's voice and managed to stop my smirk from forming until her head swung back to the maw of the alley.

THE BLOODY MASSACRE   147

"No no no. Leave us alone!" she begged, already backing up and pulling me with her.

I smirked as my back hit the wall and I forced my face into a look of fear. She looked up desperately, hoping somehow, we could scale the wall. Taking her cue, I looked at her seriously and shook her shoulders.

"Climb on my shoulders and I'll lift you up. We can get out of this together, just pull me up with you," I instructed.

She looked back and exhaled shakily when she saw my precious just standing there, bathed in shadows with only his dark soulless eyes staring back at her. He was so fucking hot when he looked like that, and it took everything in me not to go to him.

She looked at me and nodded so hard I thought her head would fall off. "Okay, yeah, let's do it!"

I squatted down and let her climb onto my shoulders. Her motions were clumsy and her heels sharp, but my skin was much tougher than any human's. I helped lift her up and I waited for her to have her hands on the top, her fingers literally tasting freedom before I faked losing my balance and sending her falling onto the ground hard enough to leave a massive bruise on her arm, if not snap the bone like a twig.

She screamed in pain, and I ran to her, my eyes wide with fake fear. "I'm so sorry! God I'm sorry." I rambled and made a show of looking up to see Leander staring at us with a lecherous smirk and eyes filled with nothing but lust for the hunt.

I hurriedly helped her to sit, and we both backed away into the wall. I scrambled around for some kind of weapon and chuckled under my breath when my hand closed around two pieces of wood. I gave one to her as fast as a human would and wrapped my arms around her shoulders. I forced myself to tremble with her and focused on the staccato of her heart. It was hard not to moan as her fear washed over her, sweeter than any wine I had ever tasted. I wanted to draw this out as long as possible, to savour her before we ripped out her heart.

"Please. Please leave us alone. I didn't do anything to you! I gave you what you paid for!" she screamed, bordering on hysterics as she begged him, her stake held out like it could actually hurt him.

Leander just smiled cruelly as he slowly walked closer. He was as smooth as a predator, his focus lasered on his prey. He never once glanced at me, just made a show of licking his lips and looking her up and down. Her emotions flooded off her, and I breathed them in. The shadows around us parted for him like water and he stood there in the muted light with a wicked gleam in his eye. Leander was in his element; his prey boxed in and barely functional with no way of escape.

The scent of ammonia joined the grime, and I turned my head to hide my smirk. The little bitch had actually pissed herself. Clearly the excitement was just too much for her.

Leander took an exaggerated sniff and flashed a smile at her. "Oh, you gave me half of what I paid for. Why do you think I gave you extra? It wasn't a tip; it was to give you a bit of happiness before I stopped you from feeling anything else."

The dark tone of his voice made her squeak, and I felt her press against me for protection. I felt like snorting. Like I'd protect her, in fact, I'd probably draw it out more than Leander did. He was more likely to rip her from limb to limb and throw her mangled corpse around whereas I liked to play with my food, to milk every drop of desperation. I played mind games, giving them multiple illusions of escape and false promises that they'd survive before I finally gave them a reprieve, just not in the way I promised.

He chuckled deeply, the sound promising nothing but agony. I watched as he launched forward, using a sliver of supernatural power to cross the distance. The girl screamed as he grabbed her, and I responded by grabbing her hands and putting on my best terrified face.

"Let her go!" I screamed, wrapping my arms around her forearms and pulling her towards me.

THE BLOODY MASSACRE   149

Leander smirked and winked at me over her body before sobering. "Why would I do that? She is mine to play with," he replied, his tone holding a dark edge.

The girl met my eyes, and I absorbed the complete desperation in her bright green eyes. She was a pretty girl, and I could see the regret for her life choices flash in their reflection. I maintained eye contact, showing her how terrified I was and how desperate I was to save her. I saw it gave her a flicker of comfort, a little reassurance to know I wasn't giving up on her.

That's when I dropped the mask.

My terror changed to excitement, and I let the manic smile I usually hid rise to the surface. I stared her in the eyes, watching eagerly as her small reassurance melted away in the face of my shift.

"No! Please, you have to save me! Please!" she begged, and I just chuckled lowly.

"Who said I was going to save you in the first place?" I replied, amusement lacing my voice.

I looked above her at Leander and nodded. We both pulled harder, putting so much strain on her body that she felt like her spine was going to break. Her screams were such an aphrodisiac that I let my moan slip out, my eyes rolling back in lust. I considered letting her tear apart, to just let her guts and blood splat out of her and stain the dirty floor. To sever her spine so she was completely vulnerable, entirely at our mercy.

Poor girl: we had none.

Instead, right when I heard a slight tear in her body I let go. She gasped, and Leander wasted no time in spinning her around like she was a shot in a shot put game and slamming her body into the wall. I heard a faint crunch, likely her ribs, but that was nothing. He pulled her back and threw her into the wall again, this time letting her go so she crumpled into a miserable heap.

I smiled down at her, and she hesitantly looked up at me. Her eyes were wet with unshed tears, and she had a permanent wince on her face.

Oh yes, I was going to enjoy this.

CHAPTER TWO

I stared up at the two monsters, scarcely able to breathe. I couldn't believe I bought her innocent act, that I'd actually believed she would help me. No one would help you in this world; we were all at someone's mercy. It just so happened that tonight I was at theirs.

My ribs screamed in pain and tears streamed down my cheeks. Despite my attempts to act indifferent in my mind, I was terrified. I knew they were going to kill me, and it wasn't the threat of death that terrified me. It was the fact I knew without a shadow of doubt they were going to drag it out. They were going to make me suffer before they finally put me out of my misery and there was nothing, I could do about it.

The woman and man stalked over to me, their eyes shining with everything except humanity. Another stream of piss pooled in my underwear as the certainty of death washed over me. It was clear he was just playing with me before, corralling me like I was cattle to this very alleyway. They likely had this planned from the beginning, and I had signed my death warrant as soon as I accepted his offer of service.

The man hovered over me and flashed me his teeth. He was gorgeous, and that blinded me to the monster inside him. I let out a pathetic whimper, causing them to chuckle cruelly. The more upset I got the more of a thrill they'd get.

"Come now darling, lying there isn't going to help you. Why not get up and try to fight? Who knows, we might let you leave if you impress us enough," the man said, his smooth cultured tone making me sick to my stomach.

I looked up at them with as much heat as I could manage. I knew they were just toying with me. They were the cats, and I was the mouse. There was no way they'd let me leave, and if they did, they'd just bring me right back. I was starting death in the face and knew they'd be the last faces I saw.

"Even if you let me leave, you'd just do that same thing and corral me somewhere else," I said, my voice shaking as tears fell unashamedly down my cheeks.

The woman raised an eyebrow at me and smiled. "So, she does have a little fight in her, after all. Impressive."

I shivered at her cutthroat stare. She gracefully walked closer, a small smirk on her face. She forced me to meet her eyes. I watched as they took on a red glow, and the entire world faded around me. She was the centre of my world.

"Now, you are going to get up and run. You are going to keep looking back and the fear will keep eating you alive. You know we will murder you, happily so, but you will keep fighting as it is so much more enjoyable for us when they fight." Her voice had an ethereal quality, and I couldn't stop myself from agreeing.

Any thought of disobeying her vanished from my mind. A wave of dread and terror washed over me, and I scrambled against the wall. All I could think about was the fact they were going to kill me and I had to get out of here.

The man looked at me and his eyes took on a red glow. My brain was inundated with visuals of what he planned to do with me. I saw my own head being ripped off my neck, sending gore and blood flying everywhere in a red mist. I saw him grabbing

THE BLOODY MASSACRE

my head and violating my skull while his girlfriend watched, her mind and body riddled with lust. This was going to be my fate if I didn't get out of here.

I did the only thing I could do. I ran.

I stumbled past them and clumsily sprinted out of the alley. I looked both ways before running in a random direction. The streets were slick with a fine mist of water, making me lose my balance as I sprinted away from the psychos. I kept looking back, praying to anyone who'd listen that they wouldn't be behind me.

My heart almost exploded and frigid dread dripped through me when I saw their dark shapes. I kept pumping my arms and legs, willing them to go faster.

Despite the fright, I was going to do anything I could to survive. I would fight tooth and nail for my life; would keep going until my muscles turned to mush. I would not let them end me, not without my final moments being used to fight them off.

I saw another man on the side of the road, his figure half concealed in shadows. I wasn't going to be fooled twice. I ran past him, my breathing coming out in ragged pants as if the air was dragged over broken glass before being exhaled.

I ran for God knows how long, my adrenaline fuelling me as I pounded down the street. My ribs ached, but thankfully my urgency dulled the pain. I could feel them behind me, though they weren't getting too close. My traitorous mind told me they were just toying with me, but I kept running, not paying any mind to my growing suspicions.

I rounded a corner and spotted the park up ahead. I was surrounded by an ornate gate, but I figured I could scale it and find somewhere to hide. I wished I had a cell phone, but all my money went to rent and food.

"Come on, you can do this, just a little further," I whispered, hoping my words would stave off my growing exhaustion.

I could have kissed the gate when I reached it, and actually did when I saw it was open enough for me to slip between. The man had no chance of getting through, but the woman definitely did. I shimmied my body past the gate and ran into the darkness. I was lucky the streetlights chased some of it away, but at least they wouldn't be able to see me as well in the dark. It was creepy, but my mind was stretched so thin I could barely acknowledge that thought before the terror chased it away.

The park was open, but I saw a thicket of trees ahead. I glanced over my shoulder and saw what I thought were their shapes a few paces ahead. Steeling my resolve, I hurried forward, not able to think. My long blonde hair streamed out behind me, the platinum colour no doubt a beacon in the darkness. I ran as fast as I could over the grass and leapt into the trees, my thudding heart drowning out any other sounds.

My breathing was tortured, and I backed away. I collided with something hard, and dread coiled in my stomach. I looked behind me and screamed as Leander stood above me. Before I could think, his eyes turned blood red and his fangs descended. He snarled and leaned down, his arms holding me like a vice. I couldn't even think as they punctured me sharply, as the sheer agony pushed away all coherent thought. I sagged against him as the surreal sound of him slurping my blood and the weird pulling feeling of blood leaving my veins made my legs give out.

I tried to fight but my motions were weak, my heart skipped pitifully as the blankness blurred my vision at the edges.

Before it finally took me, he whispered, "Don't worry Callista, this is just the beginning," before I finally slipped away.

CHAPTER THREE

I grinned down at the dying girl. There was beauty in death, something that not everyone could see. She was one of the lucky ones though, as she wasn't going to stay that way. Raphael had caught up to Leander and I and was standing at the edge of the shadows looking at us curiously. I knew he was wondering what changed my mind but there wasn't anything really. A part of me called me to do it, told me she'd be more useful under my thrall. I strode towards her and knelt down, before biting into my wrist roughly and moaning at the pain. I shoved her over onto her back and forced it into her mouth. She moaned pathetically, but I pushed tighter and forced the blood into her mouth. When I knew she'd had enough, I pulled it back and smirked. Soon there'd be another member of the undead joining us, and this time, she'd be on my side.

I stood up and looked at my men. They were so handsome, especially Leander right now with the blood dripping down his chiselled chin and his shirt coated in the substance. He always was a messy easter. He even somehow managed to get some in his stylish light blond hair. I gave him a flirty smile and sashayed over to him. He smirked at me and pulled me close, his arms tightly wrapped around my waist. I fluttered my eyelashes at him and craned my neck. I was a tall woman, made taller with my heels so I didn't have to go far. I licked the trail of drying blood from the bottom of his neck, taking care to nip at his carotid artery, before going up till I reached his lips. We moaned into the kiss, letting the taste of her blood wash over us. She tasted so good on him; it made me want more. I lost myself in his kiss before pulling back. It was all so hot. The blood, him, Raph watching and the dead girl at our feet. The only thing missing was gore splattered around the clearing.

"Come on boys, we better head home before sunrise."

Raphael walked over and wrapped his arm around my waist. "What about the dead girl?"

I shrugged. "She'll sense me and find me as I'm her sire."

"You don't just want to take her home with us now?"

I gave Raphael a look. "No. If I wanted to do that, I would. besides, I want to see what kinds of carnage she'll cause on her way."

"And if she alerts the International Protection Agency?"

Leander and I shared a look and in unison said, "so much the better."

Raphael shook his head at us, a fond smile on his face. His black hair was a little shaggy and fell into his gorgeous red eyes. Man, he was sexy with his chiselled jaw. As soon as we got back, I was going to take them both to bed and fuck them till morning.

"Come on, let's get out of here." I said, earning nods from both.

"Last one there gets edged," I said in a teasing voice, before darting off.

I heard their shouts of indignation and just laughed, ready for whatever came.

* * *

I sighed at the traffic. God, cars were slow. How the cattle dealt with such pitiful transport was beyond me. To amuse myself, I turned on the radio and wrinkled my nose at the terrible

THE BLOODY MASSACRE

sound. Man, the owner of my stolen vehicle had shit taste. I suppose that was typical for cattle, since their minds were so small.

We had checked on the youngling this morning, and she was gone. A quick look through the news reports confirmed someone had gone on a murder spree, draining everyone of blood as they did so. I couldn't help but feel proud for my part in causing this and was already thinking of the chaos we could create with her in our midst. I might even let the boys fuck her on occasion if she was interested, but only on my terms.

The window was down, letting the cooling air in. It was seven o'clock at night, so the sun was beginning to settle in for the night. The only reason I was able to be out, vamps had a cream we could layer on ourselves to block us from the sun. Amazing what happens with a little mind control.

I turned at the next corner and lightly beeped my horn, signaling to put the plan into action. A thrill fizzed through me, and my bloodlust surged. I looked out my side and saw Raphael wearing a black hoodie following the woman with arachnophobia down the street. She was shaking, her eyes darting this way and that like she expected to see another spider. I smirked, her fear already wafting of her. It was a low dose, but I knew before she died it would rise to a wonderful crescendo just like it did a couple of nights ago.

The woman was looking for this way and that, yet somehow managed to not notice she was being followed. I bet she could sense something around her, something predatorial, but not exactly what it was.

I swerved and pulled over; my expression morphed into one of fright. The woman jumped as I appeared next to her, my wide eyes setting her off.

"Get in. There's a man following you. Pretend like we know each other," I whispered.

Her eyes widened and it took her a second to process. She nodded furiously and stumbled around, her entire body shaking. She opened the door and climbed in, shutting the door behind her. Her terror was visceral and was absolutely addicting.

I put my foot on the gas and peeled back into the street, giving her a chance to collect her thoughts.

After a few moments of aimless driving, she hesitantly turned to me. It was amazing how humans wouldn't question a stranger appearing to help them when there was a bigger threat. They just took the open hand and didn't even look for the concealed knife.

"Th-thank you. I didn't even notice him. I've been sleeping really badly and I... just thank you." she stuttered, her voice breaking as she spoke.

I gave her my best sympathetic look and reached out to take her hand. She squeezed it tightly, using it as a lifeline.

"You're absolutely welcome. Us women need to stick together in this world. I'm thinking we drive around for a while so we lose him then I can take you home."

"That sounds nice, thank you." She paused before looking at me with a small smile. "My name is Sarah."

I smiled back, still letting her hold onto my arm. "I'm Levana. I know, weird name. My parents wanted to be special," I pulled a face, and got her to crack a smile.

"I think it's beautiful. Thank you again, I don't even want to think about what might've happened if you didn't rescue me when you did."

Oh, I had a fair idea.

I kept my expression sympathetic and squeezed her hand to reassure her. "No need to think about that now, okay. Just so I know, will there be anyone at home with you tonight? I don't want you alone with that man out there."

The effect was instantaneous. Her heart rate increased, and her fear spiked. "I-I don't know. My husband is out a lot, so I don't know when he'll be home."

THE BLOODY MASSACRE

159

I stayed silent, and just as I expected, she looked at me hopefully. "Would-would you stay with me? Just until my husband comes home."

I smiled at her. "Absolutely. No woman should go through this alone. How about we get some takeaways and eat before going back to yours. Pad out our time a little more."

Her response was to smile in relief and nod. I grinned back and turned the car around to fulfil my promise.

After all, everyone deserved a last meal.

It didn't take long to pull into McDonalds and order. After, I took us to an abandoned parking lot and pulled up. We divided up the food. She took a while to eat, but slowly her fear ebbed, and she was able to dig in. I nibbled at mine, strategically moving it around so it looked like I was eating more than I was. Vampires could eat, but we couldn't digest so I'd need to throw this up later. Slowly Sarah calmed down, and by the end of her burger and milkshake, she was almost smiling.

"Thank you for that. I can't remember the last time someone took me out to eat."

I looked at her curiously. I knew her husband was cheating on her, but I didn't know he was that useless. Reason number 8000 I liked my men without a pulse.

"Doesn't your husband take you out?" I asked, feigning innocence.

She sighed and looked at her hands. I watched as she played with her wedding ring, lost in thought. "He used to be great, taking me out and all those nice things. Things changed though when he got a promotion at work. He started staying out late at night and not answering his phone. It wasn't until I found lipstick marks on his white shirt that I figured out what was happening."

She looked up at me with a tired smile. "You probably think I am an idiot for staying, but it is so hard to leave. I'm staying for the memories of the old him, and the life we built. I do want to leave eventually though. I owe it to myself."

I squeezed her hand, and she met my eyes. "I know you'll leave him, and who knows, the day you do may be sooner than you think."

She looked at me like I had hung the stars. I internally rolled my eyes at her, though I supposed she didn't know what I meant. I let go of her hand and used mine to find a napkin and wiped off all the grease. I knew I was going to pay for that later, but I'd do anything to have a little fun.

Once I was clean, I put the car in gear and backed out. It was only because of my vampire reflexes I could drive, but who cares. All that mattered was the plan was working, and I was one step closer to being able to taste her terror and her delicious blood as I gulped it down. If I was lucky, I might be able to bathe in it first, but I knew Raphael didn't like wasting a single drop. It'd just depend on who could convince who, and I knew I was very persuasive.

"Let me know if I'm going in the right direction. He should be long gone by now." I was so glad I wasn't a Fae since the Light Fae couldn't lie unlike the Dark Fae who were closer to Demons.

"Go back to the street you were on before. We were about six houses away from it when you pulled over."

I nodded, doing a fantastic job of acting like I didn't. We remained in silence until I parked outside her home. My gaze wandered to the bushes where Raph and I had messed around to her screams, and I couldn't help but feel another wave of desire wash through me. With any luck this would end with a bang once the cattle finished squealing.

We got out of the car, and I locked it up. I didn't really need to, but I needed to keep the game going as long as possible. We walked up the pathway to the door, and I internally scoffed at the little awning. It looked so idyllic, but thankfully I was about to change that.

She unlocked the door and stepped in. It took her a while to realise I wasn't following her. This was one of the more annoying sides to being a vampire; you could never show up to

THE BLOODY MASSACRE

a party without an invitation. She sent me a quizzical look, and I forced the annoyance off my face.

"I was raised to never enter a house without express permission."

Realisation dawned on her, and she gave me a soft smile. She was rather pretty for an older woman, with a sprinkling of freckles and crow's feet pulling at her eyes. Her hair was cut short and dyed to hide her natural greys, but she still held a youthfulness about her that was refreshing.

"Come in, Levana. My home is your home."

A surge of magical power washed over me, and I sighed in contentment as it fizzed and popped against my skin. I had never worked out why I couldn't enter, but guessed it was something to do with a house being designed to protect the living and I wasn't one of them anymore.

I offered her a smile and slowly stepped over the threshold. There was no resistance or shocking sensation, so I grinned and walked in. Sarah smiled at me happily before turning and walking away, not realising that she had just uttered the words that would lead to her doom.

Chapter Four

My hands shook as I filled the jug. I knew I was safe in my home but knowing that man was so close and had ill intentions unnerved me more than I cared to admit. Levana was a sweet girl, and her presence helped, but I couldn't stop the way the hair at the back of my neck stood up, and the shivers that danced down my spine when I thought about what could have happened.

"Do you need any help?" Levana asked, and I turned to give her what I hoped passed as a warm smile.

"No thank you dear, you have done enough for me today. Go have a seat and I'll bring your tea out to you." She looked like she wanted to protest, but instead did as I asked.

I needed a few minutes alone to collect myself. I didn't want to think about everything, but those thoughts came unbidden. I could've ended up being just another statistic while my husband never knew what happened to me. A surge of sadness swelled inside me, and I reached for my phone. With shaky hands, I composed a text to him and sent it off. I had no idea about whether he would see to it, but it eased my soul a little to know I was trying.

THE BLOODY MASSACRE

The jug popped, signifying it was done. With deft movements I finished making the tea and carried them in. My hackles rose as I automatically searched for spiders. They liked to hide, lurking in dark corners. Ever since my dream my phobia had increased tenfold, and I didn't know how to control the fear.

"Thank you," Levana said as I passed her the cup.

If she noticed my hand shaking, she tactfully didn't comment. I walked over to the couch and sat down after placing my cup on the stand. Levana daintily sipped her tea, and for the first time since I met her, I paid attention to her looks. Her hair was long and shiny, and coloured a deep black that that I wasn't entirely sure was natural. It was out, but it still looked stylish. Her outfit was a pair of black yoga pants that hugged her figure and a tight dark purple tank top. A twinge of jealousy sparked inside me, and I shoved it down. I wished I was like her, young and gorgeous and shapely. The voice in my head taunted me, saying if I looked like her my husband wouldn't cheat on me. I knew that type of thinking wouldn't help anyone, but I couldn't help it.

Jealousy was human nature.

We sipped our tea and filled the silence with meaningless chatter. Worry gnawed inside me as I fretted about whether my husband would come home. Even more, what would happen if he did. She was gorgeous, and he already had a wandering eye.

"Are you okay, dear? You seem a little quiet."

I forced a smile and nodded. I wasn't going to tell this young thing what I was thinking, especially when she had been nothing but kind to me.

She looked like she was going to reply but was cut off by a familiar engine. My heart and hopes soared, and I looked out the window eagerly. Lyle's white car parked on the street, and my heart sunk. He wasn't going to be happy parking there, but there was nothing I could do to fix it now. When three doors opened, I frowned. Along with my husband, two of the most attractive men I had ever seen stepped out. Much like Levana they looked more supernatural than human, with their beauty being almost celestial.

I hastened to get up and shuffled to the door. My mind was swirling, sending all my thoughts flying. I reached the door before they did and opened it, plastering on a hostess smile.

"Lyle! Wonderful to see you honey," I said, internally wincing at the extreme chipperness in my voice.

Lyle grunted and shouldered me inside as he walked in. He turned around and nodded towards the men. "Sarah, this is Leander and Raphael. Their car broke down and so I gave them a lift so they can wait here before the tow comes. Invite them in and fetch us a beer."

I flinched at his tone but didn't let my smile fall. "Of course, dear! I'd be happy to."

I returned my attention to the men again. "Please come in and take a seat."

Their eyes glimmered with something I couldn't quite place. "Thank you for your hospitality. We appreciate your kind welcome."

I was momentarily dazed by Raphael's smile before I controlled myself. The boys stepped inside, and I shoved away the nagging feeling of dread that arose. Faint alarm bells were ringing, and it took conscious effort to drown them out. They smiled politely as they passed me and once alone, I took a few calming breaths. I was just on edge today after everything that'd happened, that was all. I needed to focus on the fact my husband finally came home when I asked, instead of thinking about the darkness that eclipsed the good of my day.

Finally ready, I walked past the lounge and into the kitchen. My mouth formed a small o when I saw Levana standing by the counter with three open beers before her. She gave a closed-lipped smile when she saw me and stepped back.

"Sorry, I didn't mean to overstep. Just figured I'd help out."

My surprise wore away and I walked over and took the three beers in my hands. The outside was slick with condensation.

THE BLOODY MASSACRE

"Thank you, now go have a seat. It won't do for us both to be out here."

She squeezed my arm and sashayed into the room. I followed, feeling uncomfortable in my own skin. I needed to pull myself together and be the hostess my husband expected.

The two strangers greeted me with small nods as I walked into the room, but my husband didn't bother looking up at me, too engrossed in his conversation with Levana. The green-eyed dragon reared its ugly head again as I watched him admire her, his eyes drinking in her beauty almost feverishly.

I didn't bother making conversation, just sat down and kept drinking my tea. It was a little sweeter than I remembered, but maybe that was just my bitterness infecting it. The group all chatted and laughed, and I joined with a fake chuckle every now and then. My anxiety was so bad I was sure I was going to vibrate out of my skin. To compensate, I gulped down the tea, hoping it would steady me.

Slowly, my vision started to swoop and turn fuzzy at the edges. I noticed Lyle slurring his words and narrowed my eyes in concern.

A cool hand on my arm shook me out of my thoughts. Levana had her hand on me, and her pretty face was crinkled in concern. "Sarah, are you okay?"

"I don— don't know what's ha-happening. Vision.. . swirling. Body feels stiff." The world dipped around me, and I struggled to keep my thoughts straight.

Levana's concern melted away and it was replaced with a cruel smirk and wicked gleam in her eye that was deadly enough to cut glass. "Good. I was hoping it would kick in soon."

Alarm bells screamed in my mind, and I frantically tried to look at the other men for help. They just chuckled darkly, and I swear I saw one of them grow fangs. Lyle was unresponsive in his chair, which made the panic grow inside my chest. My limbs stiffened like they were filled with drying concrete. Dark fuzz blurred the sides of my vision and I looked at her desperately, pleading with her to have mercy. Before the darkness finally took me, she leaned over, her painted lips hovering just over the shell of my ear.

"Oh Sarah, you naive little cattle. You should be more careful who you invite inside your home; you never know what monster you're letting in."

My eyes burned with unshed tears, and I had enough sense to feel a few slides down my cheeks. I heard her low chuckle and sensed her moving closer, and fought the urge to scream when she slowly, tauntingly so, licked it up.

She roughly turned my face to look at hers and whispered something to me, but I couldn't quite grasp it before the world turned black.

CHAPTER FIVE

As soon as the potion dragged them under, I looked at my beloveds and nodded. They leaped into motion, with Raph getting the chair as Leander picked up Lyle's hefty form. How he got multiple women to sleep with him was beyond me, but at least no more idiots would be suckered into it soon. Anticipation pulsed through me as I watched as they were dumped in chairs on opposite ends of the room. Their arms were tied around the back using rope and some handcuffs we brought with us before we tied each of their legs to the legs of the chairs.

I stepped back to admire their work. They did well, but something was missing. A sly smile crossed my face, and I strode to the male cattle. My nails sharpened into claws, and I cut through his shirt and down his pants, causing him to moan in pain as my nails nicked him. Oh well, that was nothing.

"Take his clothes off while I work on the female. Cattle don't get to wear clothes in this household."

Raphael nodded and did as I asked. Affection swelled through me as I watched my devoted man work. It was hard to find someone who shared your brand of psycho these days. Sighing I sauntered back over to the female. I had noticed her looking at me all night, so I thought it was time I did the same. I gave her clothes the same treatment, though I allowed her to keep her panties on. Her sagging skin and boobs were on full display. I especially like the way the bright red of her blood stood out against such a pale colour.

"Her skin would make a fantastic purse, don't you think?" I asked, gently stroking the bleeding spot.

"It would. Do you want us to leave her back and abdomen alone then?" Leander asked, and I hummed my agreement.

"I do. I've grown a little attached to her and would love to always keep a piece of her with me." I stared at her skin in silent reverence and gently smeared the blood around, my mind already imagining it strung over my arm in a bag or hung up with all my others along the shelves Raph built for me.

I gracefully slinked up and looked at my boys with a blinding grin. "Get the boiling water, then we can start."

"One step ahead of you darling," Leander said, holding twin buckets of steaming water.

I watched the steam twirl into the air like a ballerina as he put one in front of the male cattle before doing the same with the female. I stepped over to the light and plunged us into darkness, with only the small lamps casting some of my beautiful shadows away. Taking my cue, the guys pulled the buckets closer and forced their feet in. The mania rose in me as I imagined how their skin would blister under the unrelenting heat. I allowed them to sit in it for a while before saying, "awaken" in a loud, clear voice.

The effect was instantaneous. Their shrieks soaked the air and mixed with their delectable terror. It was a delicacy; one I could consume for a century and never tire of it.

"What did you do?" the male cattle screamed, his face blotchy and the veins in his neck bulging out.

"You can see what we did. We drugged you with a magical potion, tied you up, stripped you, and put your feet in boiling

THE BLOODY MASSACRE
169

hot water. It's not rocket science, swine," I replied, watching him closely to see his reaction.

"Mag—you are out of your mind! Get rid of these buckets and untie us!"

I shrugged. "Okay, Leander, Raphael, take the buckets away."

They didn't hesitate and as soon as they were free, I moved closer to inspect the damage. Their feet were bright red, with a layer of burned flesh barely holding onto the layer underneath. Discoloured yellow blisters littered the detached, leathery layer, and I stared at them closely, trying to decide if I wanted to pop them or let them remain.

"You are psychotic!" I rolled my eyes at the male cattle. Clearly, he was an idiot if he didn't understand this was just the beginning.

To prove my point, I squatted in front of him and ripped the leathery layer off, causing him to scream loud enough to cover my moans. I pushed up again and shoved the piece in his mouth, allowing him to taste the pus as it oozed into his taste buds. I snickered as I heard him gag, before turning on my heel and sauntering over to new prey. Silent tears were streaming down her cheeks, and she looked up at me, her eyes pleading for a mercy I'd never grant her.

"Oh Sarah, what a day you've had. And here you thought being stalked was your biggest problem." I sighed dramatically and squatted next to her.

In reminiscence of earlier, I reached out and squeezed her, this time wrapping my hand around her damaged foot. Her scream was so delightful that she forced me to squeeze harder, making the pustules explode. I wrinkled my nose at the disgusting texture and wiped it on the floor, leaving a yellow stain in my wake.

"It's a shame you know. If you had been more aware you would've seen him following you and that could have saved, you. Well, if he was human. Sadly, for you, Leander is anything but human, aren't you babe?"

170   MULTIPLE AUTHORS

Leander walked over, a cold imitation of a smile on his lips. "Yea, it's almost like you haven't been sleeping or something. Nightmares been plaguing you?" he asked, injecting false sympathy in his voice before it gained a teasing lilt. "Perhaps dreams about spiders laying eggs inside you while you're awake and can feel it?"

Her eyes widened and another heavy dose of fear wafted from her. "H-how do you?"

"How do we know? My wife here is incredibly good at what she does you see. Whether that is gaining an insipid, desperate woman's trust or plaguing her with nightmares using her magic while her other husband eats her out. She is good at everything."

I bit my lip as memories of that night flooded back. That was so hot; one of the hottest experiences we'd had in a while.

"Who-who are you?"

"I believe you mean what are we," Leander said, turning to look at Raph who was amusing himself by drawing the tip of a knife along our captives' arms and down his torso.

Instead of replying he just let the redness of his power seep into his eyes. His fangs extended, and he looked at the female cattle like he wanted nothing more than to stick them inside her. My pussy fluttered at his actions, and suddenly I wanted nothing more that the hurry this up so we could get to the fucking part.

To make sure he understood, he smirked and sunk his fangs into her husband's neck. The loud slurping sound was heard by all, and rivulets of blood ran down his neck and down his naked body. I was a little curious why they didn't comment on their nudity, but I suppose they had other things to worry about. A little disappointing, but I was nothing if not adaptable.

Catching on, she let out another ear-piercing scream. I chuckled and stepped back, allowing her to watch the show as I took my time sauntering over. I could feel her revolution and pure, unfiltered terror flowing from her, so to sweeten the deal, I gently dragged my sharpened nail along his upper arm. I made

THE BLOODY MASSACRE

171

her see what I was doing, how my hands explored where I wanted. I wanted to give her a visual to go with all the thoughts and questions she'd had. He was definitely cheating, and I wanted her to see what it was like for another woman to touch her man.

I looked over my shoulder and met her wide, scared, eyes. There was something else there, a glimmer of defeat and despair that just sweetened this situation even more for me.

I let my hand drag down his back and curl around his dick. Despite the stress it was under, he hardened at my touch. I met the cattle's eye as I worked it, causing her pain to grow to a crescendo. It was so addicting, but I had other things I needed to do. So, as soon as my lover took his fangs out of the cattle's neck, I took my sharp nail and sliced it straight through the base of his shaft. Oh, the scream that reverberated around my mind like my own personal symphony. I'd treasure them forever even after their corpses were long since gone.

I winked at the horrified woman and stood up. The male was still screaming, so I decided to shut him up by shoving his own appendage into his gaping jaw.

I leaned in so my hot breath teased the shell of his ear. "Since you like your cock being sucked so much, figured it was only right for you to go out that way," before pulling away.

I looked at my men fondly. "Now, what's the plan?"

Raphael shrugged. "We could skin them alive, or we could force her to cut her own husband's legs off."

"Or we could force him to eat her leg flesh." Leander added.

I tapped my lips. There were a lot of options, but none felt... right. I had invested a lot of energy into this, so I wanted a payoff.

"You boys play with them a bit. I'm going to think." I walked to the couch and curled up, ready for the entertainment.

As per usual they didn't disappoint. I watched, entranced, as Leander mind controlled the male to slash at his own body with a knife. The ingenious bit was he was to feel everything but never scream. Truly a masterpiece.

I watched eagerly as his skin turned more red than white. It was beautiful watching the rivulets fall, like they were bloody stars falling from their entrapment in heaven. The man's face was frozen in agony as he carved away at himself, creating a red pool under him.

"Please... you don't have to do this," the female cattle said, and I turned to look at her lazily.

"I know I don't. But it is really, really fun. Now Raph can you do me a favour honey and make her shut up? She's ruining my thinking time."

Raph didn't reply, just turned to her. He knelt down and forced her to look him in the eyes. His mind control Feet being listed in was always so beautiful. He favoured control, so this was always expertly done. "You are going to shut up and only speak when spoken to. I want you to bite on each of your fingers hard enough to break them in two."

I clapped, ready for my bloodlust to be fed. She looked up at him desperately, but her hand raised despite her attempts not to. I watched; my heart happy as she bit hard down on her hands. It didn't take long for the satisfying crunch to fill the air. The bloody appendage landed in her lap, and I barely got enough time to see the tendons spilling out before she was onto the next.

I looked at my man playfully. "A little gruesome for you, isn't it Raph?"

He looked at me with a fond expression. "I figured I'd show off to you a little. See how riled up I can get you before I turn you into a quivering mess."

I bit my lip and gave him the eyes. He winked at me before turning to Leander. "I have a fun game. Let's have Sarah ask him questions about his feelings and infidelity, and for every time he says something that hurts her, she stabs herself."

Leander lit up like a fucking Christmas tree. "Oh, fuck yea. Have her show him just how much cheating hurts."

THE BLOODY MASSACRE 173

They shared a wicked look before kneeling down to look each of their captives in the eye.

"You will not try to escape. You will stand there and do exactly as I say. Nod if you understand." She did, and he went to work undoing her restraints.

There was the small issue of her feet being blistered, but she'd figure out a way there. I had confidence in my cattle.

Her feet gave out on her, and I watched as she crawled. Ahh there we go, I knew she could do it. Her face was painted with her pain, and I just smiled more. There was beauty in pain, much like there was death, and I sometimes thought I was the only one who saw that. When she finally made it over, Leander pulled her up by her hair, making tears leak from her eyes. Raph gave her a knife which she took with shaking hands and held it with the stumps of her fingers.

"Here is how the game will work. You'll ask him a question, and if his answer causes you pain, you'll stab yourself then him in the thigh. You'll keep doing this till we get bored or one of you bleeds out. Oh, and you have to ask at least five before we will consider stopping." Leander said, shrugging.

He tore the man's bloody dick from his mouth and threw it across the room. He gasped and looked at his wife with so much fear and sorrow that I almost stopped plotting just so I could watch this.

With a shaking voice, Sarah asked her first question. "How long have you been cheating on me for?"

He averted his gaze, and muttered, "off and on for ten years."

She made a small whimper and looked at him with pure heartbreak. Before she could reply, she held the knife as best she could and plunged it into her thigh. She grunted at the effort, before pulling it out. I swear I saw a hint of satisfaction in her eyes as she slammed it into her husband's thigh with more force than she did her own. I considered commenting, but he deserved it. I squealed in excitement when the knife twisted on the way out, making his pain oh so much sweeter.

"Who have you been cheating with?"

He sighed and looked at her pleasingly. I knew he wanted to not answer and was fighting it, but he had no choice. "Everyone you know. Including your sister."

This time she really did put extra swing into it when she stabbed him, and as a reward I gave them my full attention as a mist of blood clouded in the air.

This carried on until she asked the final question. Both their thighs were filled with gashes and gushing a thick stream of blood. I could see them turn pale, so I knew we'd have to be quick.

"Do you still love me?" She asked, her voice cracking.

He sighed and after a tense silence, finally spoke.

CHAPTER SIX

"I did, once, and I do have some love for you, but not as much as before." Exquisite agony rolled off her and I leaned in closer, utterly transfixed.

She let out a sob and slammed the knife into her thigh. Ugly sobs escaped her, and I watched her buckle under the immense pain she was under. She took a moment to collect herself before pulling it out. She his eyes and held his gaze as she slammed the blade into his mangled flesh.

He howled in pain, and tears raced each other down his face. I could only imagine the agony they were enduring as both the physical and emotions laid waste to their psyche. Finally, I understood what I was going to do. She loved him, despite all this, and she was bordering on hysteria. I was thinking of having them play Russian roulette to decide who died and how, but right now I just wanted to bask in their agony. They were already close to being dead, judging by their paleness, so it would only take a nudge and then the grim reaper would do the rest.

"Sarah, tell him how his answers made you feel. Explicitly." I commanded, a faint threat lurking in my tone.

I watched as she looked up and met his fuzzy gaze. "I love you, still, after all these years, even after all the pain you've put me through, I still love you. I will always love you because you are my husband, but right now, I also despise you and hope you fall into the cracks of hell where you will burn until nothing of your disgusting soul is left."

Despite the disorientation and weakness in her voice, I could tell they landed right in his heart. Now, I was going to make sure they were the last words he ever heard.

I nodded to the men, and they immediately jumped on him. Their fangs descended and they drained his blood, not letting a drop out. Right before he was about to die however Leander leaned in and whispered something I couldn't hear. They pulled back and Raph pulled out a lit match. I glowed with a gorgeous glowing aura as he placed it on the other man's skin. He screamed, he wailed, he begged as it was pulled along his mangled body. Black lines of burnt flesh were left in its wake until he reached his eyeball. With a smirk, Raphael stabbed him in the eye, and the other man howled at the fire greedily burned his retina and robbed him of sight. We all knew he was almost dead, so for one final touch, he let the fire climb onto his head where it grew and began to consume the rotten meat.

Leander doused the fire, and I wrinkled my nose at the stench of burned meat. Sarah was faintly sobbing, and I looked down at her with pity. I considered dragging it out further, but the moment was passing. Instead, I knelt down next to her and met her exhausted, emotionless eyes.

"Any last words?"

She mustered a weak glare. "Go to hell, bitch."

My smirk widened. "I'll give your husband my regards. Or maybe I'll fuck him like so many women have before."

I didn't give her a chance to speak before pulling my fist back and thrusting it through her chest, right where her heart is. She gasped, a pathetic sound really, as I wrapped my hand around the squishy organ and pulled back. Her eyes were wide as they

THE BLOODY MASSACRE   177

stared at it, and in case she could still comprehend, I lifted it up to my lips and took a hearty bite. It was slightly chewy, but the blood was sweet on my tongue. I watched as the life finally left her eyes and she slumped back, as worthless dead as she was alive.

We basked in the post-death silence before I threw her heart away and looked up at my men, lust and thrill sparking in my mind.

"Let's take her skin and get out of here. I've had my fun."

Leander slipped away to find me a photo of the couple; one of my traditions which I'd add to my death shrine. Once he was back, I grinned and we left, but not before I took her ring.

She wouldn't be needing it anymore.

* * *

By the time we sauntered into the vampire clan's base, I was feeling untouchable. This was the most fun I'd had in a long time and felt a hundred years younger. Unfortunately for me, my father was not feeling the same. He was standing in the cavernous foyer with the rest of the clan fanning around him and trailing up the steps. The abandoned building was huge and nestled in the bad side of town. No one ever suspected a thing when they went past, just as we liked it. Next to him, Callista stood, her body encased in a bright red dress. When I reached him, I crossed my arms and waited for him to speak.

As usual, he stared me down before finally answering me. "You have turned someone without their permission which is a direct violation of the laws sent by the Protection Agency, and if that was not bad enough, you left bodies at the scene of the crime. What do you have to say for yourself?"

I tapped my fingers on my lips before tugging the lower one down with my index finger. I topped off, and I was left grinning. "That I had a fantastic time and would do it all over again."

Whispers erupted around us, and my father sighed and pinched the bridge of his nose. When he pulled them away, he looked at me with a steely glare. "Then it is settled. You, Levana

Josephine Di'Charmine are banished from the Di'Charmine Clan.

My world froze. I stared at him in absolute shock as I tried to wrap my head around what he was saying. There was no way he was actually kicking me out. I was his daughter, his blood. My mother would be turning in her grave at the very idea of it. The more I thought and the more the conversation rose to a crescendo, the more a burning anger stoked my insides. I created a wall around my mind and met his stare with a venomous one of my own.

"You have already lost my sister; do you really want to lose me too?"

He did not budge, in fact, the only thing that changed was he tilted his chin up a little higher. "You are bringing unwanted attention to us. At least your sister is doing something worthwhile with her time."

I hissed and bared my fangs, my hackles rising. Fine, if he wanted to ignore our blood relation, two could play that game.

"Fine, but first, before I am officially kicked out, I want a hug with my father, if that is not too much hardship."

The steel in his expression softened and he nodded. "Very well, after, you will be banished."

I sauntered over and met him in the middle. Looking up, I memorised the faint wrinkled vampirism mostly smoothed over and the bright red of his eyes. He pulled me into his arms, and I melted against him. He held me tight, and I leaned into the safety he provided.

"I love you, Levana, just remember that, but I cannot put that love above the safety of everyone."

The emotion in his voice caused a lump in my throat, but I cleared it away.

No weakness.

"I know, Father. I love you too. You do what you have to do, and so will I."

"Wha—"

THE BLOODY MASSACRE

I plunged my hand through his back and again wrapped my hand around it. I pulled it out with one tug. Leander appeared behind him and twisted his head off, before throwing it away like a cork. My father's sense of betrayal filled his eyes and his pain filtered through the air until the magic keeping him alive blinked out and he turned to ash. My own heart ached, and Leander wrapped his arm around my waist and pulled me close while Raphael scooped up the ashes.

I looked up at the shocked faces and let them see a glimpse of the monster inside. One by one they dropped to their knees and bowed towards me in respect. By law, since I was his only blood and, still technically in the clan, I was the next in charge. Raphael joined me and together we watched as my kingdom bowed to their new queen, one who would reign terror down on anyone who opposed her and would lead my subject towards a new age, one filled with blood and debauchery, and I'd do it with my men at my side.

This morning, I had woken up a princess, and now, I was a queen. I knew some would oppose me, but I was ready, and they'd all meet their end if they tried because I was a warrior and would make sure no one opposed me and live to tell the tale.

The only thing left to do was to keep living, to keep exploring my dark cravings and feeding them. The clan was going to grow more powerful with me as a ruler and with me at the helm, days like mine would be normal,

Just wait and see.

.

About the Author

Arianna started out as a paranormal why choose author, before venturing into contemporary. She is a coffee fiend and love devouring and creating new worlds. When she isn't drinking unhealthy amounts of coffee and writing she is bingeing TV, working and gaming. She is super thankful to you for reading her work and hopes you enjoy.

To stay updated on all her work, join any of her social; medias found in like linktree elbow. Afterglow will eventually have a sequel, so keep your eyes out and stay safe!

HER DRAGON KNIGHT

Elise Whyles

Phoenix Voices Anthologies

CONTENTS

Chapter One #

Chapter Two #

Chapter Three #

Chapter Four #

About the Author #

CHAPTER ONE

K adriye stared at her reflection in the looking glass, her dark hair had been washed and brushed until it shone. Delicate braids circled her head decorated with the elegant jewels Ambria had woven into them. From somewhere, Ambria had produced a small box full of cosmetics and set to work. Kadriye had to admit, the other woman had done a good job, her face was flawless, her eyes large, innocent looking.

She rubbed a finger along her lower lip, removing the small amount of lipstick before she got to her feet and turned. Laid out across the bed, her gown waited for her to dress. Dark greens and silver wove together to create a unique style. Lifting it, Kadriye blinked, her heart pounding, the stitching looked like dragon scales.

Her eyes burned with tears; her stomach dropped to her feet. Trembling fingers traced over the scaled stitches, the memory of Raqir's dragon form teasing her. Across the room the door swung open, and she dropped the gown. She turned her head, recognizing Ambria stepping into the room and closing the door.

THE BLOODY MASSACRE

"It will look stunning on you," Ambria pointed to the dress. "I spoke with Bea; she was going to ensure everything was in readiness for your entrance." She stepped closer, rubbing Kadriye's arm, her eyes reflecting her own emotions. "There has been no word."

No, no word. I have to believe something happened. Or perhaps he simply came to know he was not destined to hold my hand any longer. Kadriye offered a weak smile. *He deserves to have--*

"You must never think such a thing." Ambria squeezed her hands gently. "You are his, Raqir would not have stood by you if he were not in love with you. You must trust me, the man I know, the man you know, would not abandon you. I know the nature of the man, my friend."

Kadriye nodded, Ambria's words held some truth. No man would go to the lengths Raqir had gone through, but if she were to put her full trust in Raqir, then there had to be an explanation. She shivered at the dark thought weaving its way through her mind, her chest tightening painfully. If Raqir had fallen...No, she would not entertain such a thought.

Ambria smiled and picked the gown up. She held it open, slipping it over Kadriye's hands and lifted it to slide it over her head. Letting the fabric fall free, she pulled Kadriye's hair free and turned her to begin lacing up the side. Kadriye stood, hands folded in front of her and stared at the looking glass against the far wall.

It had been so long since she'd seen her full reflection, even distorted as it was. In the place of a half-starved girl, stood a warrior. In her face she recognized her mother, the gentle slope of her nose, the curve of her jaw. Gone was the pallor from her tanned features, instead there was a warmth, a depth to her skin she'd forgotten about.

"You are stunning." Ambria tucked the last length of lacings into the fold of her dress and stepped back. "A true *sdorwali*."

Kadriye turned her head to meet Ambria's eye, a frown tugging gently at her brow. *A what?*

"It is the title given to the wife of the holder of the Staff of *Sdorwal*. Raqir's in line for it, a true dragon master." Both women turned to the looking glass, matching smiles curling their lips upward. Kadriye reached up to take Ambria's hand, squeezing it as she wallowed in the silence for a moment.

A timid knock drew her attention, smoothing the front of her gown down, Kadriye crossed the room and opened the door. Bea stood, her face pale, a look of unease on her face.

"A thousand pardons, my lady, but the guests we were to expect tomorrow have been spotted again. They'll be here before the moons have set. Everything is in readiness for you. Xerolik insisted I come to tell you."

Kadriye smiled at her friend, patting her on the shoulder as she walked by her. She heard Ambria join them. Ambria and Bea fell into place behind her, as befitting their position as her servants. Bile rose to choke her with each step she descended the stairs to the hall. Gathered in the room, her counsel stood huddled together on one side of the room, Raqir's dragons on the other side.

Tapping her fingers on the stair railing, Kadriye stared at the two groups and shook her head. Waving Ambria forward, she made a quick sign.

"Lady Kadriye would speak." Ambria called out over the hushed conversations. "My voice is hers, her words, her thoughts. To ignore me, is to ignore your queen."

Kadriye rolled her eyes at the words and shook her head but straightened. Regardless of title, she was but one voice in the counsel. Wiping her sweaty palms on her dress, she paused, allowing Ambria time to get into position. Her motions weren't as smooth as usual, but Ambria ignored the fine tremble in her hands.

"Today we hold court for those who have been accused. Justice will be served, with a clear mind and a willing heart. No one, regardless of position or relation will be spared. We must stand together, to show those who have wronged us we are

THE BLOODY MASSACRE 187

stronger." Kadriye paused, searching through those gathered, relief flooded her at the open, though emotional expressions on her clan. "There are some who close in on us, they will be treated politely, firmly, and be sent on their way. We are allies with Karul, with the dragons who have offered us shelter, food, and healing, against a common foe. Know this, I will not turn from my people and should anyone attempt to interfere with our clan, they will be reprimanded."

Aware of those gathered, Kadriye stepped off the last stair and headed for the door. She opened it and stepped out into the silvery light of a full moon. Glancing upward, Kadriye recognized the hint of red around the moon.

CHAPTER TWO

The blood moon has begun, her mind supplied the truth. Nodding to herself she turned to walk along the repaired boardwalk winding between the two stone temples. Shrubs and flowers had been planted, giving the area a warmer, more peaceful air, a stark difference to the mud and debris filled space her father had lorded over. The foliage brought to mind her mother's love of gardening, and she smiled to herself. *Yes, it was the right path, Momma would be proud.*

Behind her the sounds of footsteps eased the discomfort wrapping itself around her. The sounds of armor rubbing against itself, the clank of swords told her she was not the one who had been summoned before the supposed king, but rather the one in control.

Guards armed with spears lined the recently replaced stone walkway leading into the courtyard. Her heart thundering in her ears, Kadriye walked calmly along the stone to the steps leading up to the platform where her high-backed chair had been brought. Stepping onto the platform, Kadriye could make out the fury and disgust in the voices coming from the opposite side of the courtyard.

THE BLOODY MASSACRE

Swallowing hard, she inhaled a deep breath to calm her nerves and stepped forward. Each footfall behind her offered a hint of calm, a reminder she was not alone. Head held high she walked around the chair and stepped up on the dais to settle into it. For the first time she looked out at the area.

Around the edges of the space, she could see the first attempts at planting foliage, small shrubs and trees encircled the half-circle. Spaced equally throughout the space in a staggered design, the pillories and gibbets had been secured from their previous location. Several flat stones had thick metal rings were laid out in the middle.

At the end of chains, men - if they could be called such - hunched over. Kadriye counted each device, her stomach twisting. Every cage was filled, every chain occupied, the tormentors more numerous, thus the need for the tethers.

"How dare you defile my throne!" Gurak's voice filled the night air. "I will see you punished for your treachery, you worthless --" He cried out at the sudden jabbing of a stick into the gibbet he stood in.

"Hold your tongue, traitor. Our *sdorwali* has not granted you permission to speak."

Kadriye wiped at the smile curling her lips. Confident her expression was masked, she nodded. The shuffling steps of her counselors had her straightening in her chair. A glance out of the corner of her eyes revealed her advisors stood lined up to her right. Ambria stepped forward, striding forward to stand at her left hand.

Ambria bent down, her lips close to her ear. "You need not fear them, Kadriye. We all stand with you. Where would you have us begin?"

Kadriye rubbed her chin, nervously shifting. Her fingers moved fluidly, her signs clear along with the clicks and snaps of her language. *I would hear each complaint against them. My people deserve to be heard.*

Ambria nodded and turned, waving Xerolik forward. "Bring in the first complainant."

Xerolik gave a brief nod and stepped forward. "My lady, I would speak if it pleased you?"

Kadriye glanced at Ambria who offered a raised brow but remained stoic. She waved him closer and gestured for him to speak.

"I am Xerolik, kin of Gurak, and I would ask for justice for my sisters, my mother, my nieces." He glanced out over the prisoners. "For it is they who have suffered greatly at the hands of the monster who stand caged."

"You worthless--" Gurak cried out again, a slim guard stepping forward to jab him roughly. He twisted, spitting and hissing at the guard. Two others stepped forward, further bindings in hand. They reached through the bars, grabbing Gurak and pulling him back so the third could wrap a gag around his head. They ignored his struggles, his screeches as they hurried to complete their task.

When they stepped back, Kadriye breathed a sigh of relief. Those on the other side of the courtyard's walls would be able to hear him and it would be disturbing. Glaring at Gurak as he clawed at the gag, she nodded to one of the guards who grabbed his wrists and shackled them on the outside of the cage.

"A traitor to our lord!" Grexor jerked in the pillion, the heavy wooden structure creaking with his struggle.

Kadriye turned to Ambria. *Send in the next person. If the prisoners continue to lash out, please see to it they are all silenced for the duration. There are a great many claims to be heard.*

"Freak. Look at her. Waving her hands about like some child. Weak. You're all weak for following--" Kadriye stood, reaching out to grab a spear from one of the men on the platform. She traced from her chair down to stand in front of her brother. Staring at him, she tapped his prison with the spearhead. Grexor shrank back when she smiled, fear rising in his eyes.

THE BLOODY MASSACRE

Turning the spear in her hand, Kadriye drove it into the ground between his feet. The staff quivered, stilling when she grabbed it. Holding her brother's eyes, she snapped it off the broken end close enough to his groin to make him sweat. She patted him on the head as she would a pet and turned away. Her steps measured, she walked among the prisoners, pausing to study each before moving onto to the next. Silence hung heavy in the air as she climbed the stairs and took her seat.

I am ready for the next clan member. Kadriye hid a smile at the fear among the prisoners, the stench filling the air around her. *Aye, you should be scared. Very scared.*

CHAPTER THREE

P ale orange streaks danced along the horizon as Kadriye stood. Her back cracked with the slow stretch of her body; muscles twinged in protest from hours of sitting. The men before her still struggled, their muffled voices filled with rage and hatred. There could only be one ending, but she loathed the idea of raising a hand against another person. Not once in the hours since she'd heard from Xerolik had any of them admitted to wronging the clan. No, every time they opened their mouths, it had been to spit out insults and crude remarks.

She turned and paused at the sight of Dramin hurrying toward her. Anger and disgust twisted his features as he strode passed the guards to stop in front of her. A fist over his heart and he spoke. "My *sdorwali*, the guests we have been expecting are at the city gate. I have posted two of my men at the western wall, and two more will take to the skies. Should I bring them forth?"

Kadriye sighed, her shoulders hunching under the weight of her exhaustion. She glanced away for a moment, her eyes skimming the horizon. Nodding, she patted Dramin on the shoulder and watched him hurry away.

THE BLOODY MASSACRE

193

A gentle nudge had her twisting to look at Ambria, a glass of steaming cider in her hand. "Drink, it appears our day is not yet done."

Taking the glass, Kadriye sipped at it as she watched Dramin lead a procession of men toward her. There was no indication Bruja, or the other queen was with them, rather it was soldiers and one man who wore a more elaborate armor.

Who is it?

"He did not give a name," Ambria whispered. "But from the insignia on his armor, I believe he may be a high-ranking member of the king's guard."

Could it be the king was unhappy with my response?

"If he were, it is hardly a concern, *sdorwali.*" Ambria chuckled and stepped back to her place beside Kadriye.

"My lady, I present--" Dramin bowed and turned to the group of men.

"I would speak with your leader, not a dragon who does not know his place." One of the guards stepped forward, his hair pulled back from his face.

Kadriye met his stare, her fists clenched at the lack of warmth within his gaze. A subtle glance at Ambria and the other woman gestured for the guards to move forward. They pressed in around Kadriye and Ambria, at the ready should anyone make a sudden move. Smooth, familiar the handle of her visenthor filled her palm. Wrapping her fingers around it, she inhaled a calming breath.

"You are rather rude, a pitiful habit." Ambria sniffed. "You are guests in our city."

"And you should learn to kneel before a king." The man lashed out with his staff.

Kadriye grabbed the back lacings of Ambria's tunic, sending her stumbling back. She traced forward, her weapon swinging down, splintering wood with a crack. Jerking it upward, the side blade sliced through what was left of the man's weapon with ease. A smile curled her lips up as Kadriye stepped closer, pressing in on the man. Eyes locked with his, she caught the back of his knees with the edge of the battle head and jerked forward.

"We are done kneeling." Ambria straightened her tunic. "Speak for your master and then get out of our queen's city."

"Dorstan, do not anger them." His tone biting, the man strode forward, as if his words were a royal decree. He held a hand up, the other soldiers standing at attention, hands on the hilts of their swords.

Swinging the weapon in her hand, she stared at the man kneeling at her feet. Dismissing him with a flick of her hand, she rested the handle on her shoulder and turned to walk away.

"My lord, they should show a modicum of respect."

"It is ok, for now." Striding forward, he stepped past his men to stand in front of Dorstan. "I am Hemat, King of Dreken. I have come to speak with Kadriye, daughter of Engryd."

"For what purpose?" Xerolik stepped forward, arms crossed over his chest. "Our *sdorwali* is a busy woman."

"It is for her and me to discuss." Hemat sniffed at him. "Go and bring her to me."

"We are not bound by the laws of Dreken within these walls." Xerolik waved a hand about. "Here, only our mistress gives the commands. You may be king in your fine city, with your courtesans and your pretty boy soldiers. Ah, but here, you are of no more importance than anyone else. Nay there is no truth in that - for those who scrub the floors and serve the food hold more value than you - vampire."

"I am the king, and you will--"

Kadriye couldn't say who moved, but she hid a smile when her guards had the kings' men disarmed and on the ground before Hemat could speak. She turned her head to Ambria and winked. The other woman grinned and stepped forward. *How would you like to handle the situation, Kadriye? His men threatened you; the dragon warriors will not take kindly to such an act.*

THE BLOODY MASSACRE   195

Licking her dry lips, Kadriye glanced from Hemat to the others. *They were not invited, but I would not alienate them. I would know what he wants.* Hemat studied her, his eyes following her hands, a look of pity on his face. *Then he can take his pity and his rude soldiers and get out.*

Ambria nodded and raised a hand. Switching to amphurnian, she turned to the dragon guards. "Our dragon mistress would know what the fool wants. Then, if she be displeased with his words, we may strike. The guards remain outside, we will hear what he has to say in the Chamber."

Dramin gave a quick nod. "We will see they do not trespass."

Kadriye agreed with a clap to his shoulder, lifting her skirt, she walked across the platform, down the steps and headed for the hall. Ignoring the scuffling of bodies behind her, Kadriye kept her grip loose, comfortable on her weapon as she hummed under her breath. There was a worry of what the king would have to say, but in the hall, she would control the interaction.

CHAPTER FOUR

A roar from above drew everyone's attention. Fumbling the visenthor, she caught it before it hit the ground, her eyes taking in the dark shapes above them. Beneath her feet the ground trembled, as if an earthquake had unleashed itself upon the land.

"Kadriye," Faint, Ambria's voice held fear and anger.

Whirling to see her friend, Kadriye eyed the king as he whirled to watch the dragons above. *There must be more of his forces.* Kadriye signed with a hard look at Hemat. *There is no other reason for the guards to go on defense.*

Ambria nodded and rushed to intercept the king. Kadriye stalked toward them, her claws digging into the palms of her hand. Dagger in hand, Ambria pressed it against the king's neck, looking at Kadriye.

If you do not wish to have your forces destroyed, you will tell me exactly how many followed you.

"Everyone ordered to attend me, is present. If there is an army it is not mine." Hemat jerked in Ambria's grip, he stared at Kadriye through narrowed eyes. "Perhaps the treachery is yours."

THE BLOODY MASSACRE 197

"Dramin," Ambria called to her friend. "What do they say?"

"There is an army approaching from the south," Dramin raced forward, slightly out of breath. "A great host. From the east there are three dragons approaching. They will see the army shortly. I will take two of Ambria's trained soldiers and intercept them."

Kadriye looked upward, inhaling a deep breath. She froze at the faint but familiar scent swirling around her senses. *Send a scout to the south, they will pose the greatest threat.*

Dramin and Ambria shared a look, then Dramin darted off, transforming quickly as he took to the sky, two other dragons following him. Ambria shoved Hemat aside, her attention on Kadriye. "My friend, your eyes."

Kadriye reached up to press her fingers to her skin. Expecting tears or something blood, she met Ambria's eyes. *What?*

"What manner of creature are you?" Hemat demanded, staring at her. "Your eyes are glowing."

Kadriye shook her head, waving aside his words with a flick of her hand. Her ears picked up the faint sound of a beating heart. Turning toward it, three dragons appeared in the sky followed by the rising sun. Her heart leapt in her chest, was it? As if aware of the dangers of the sun, one of the dragons hovered above them as the largest of the trio circled, the sunlight dancing across green scales.

Raqir. Kadriye mouthed as the dragon descended, landing with an earth-shaking thud nearby. He twisted his massive frame to peer at Hemat, stepping carefully until he was between the king and Kadriye. With a rumble, he shifted, facing Hema. There was no doubt he was prepared to do battle, his legs were spread to brace his weight, his hand rested on the hilt of his sword.

Kadriye gaped at the wounds encircling his wrists hurling forward to take a hand in hers to study the wounds. Her anger stoked, licking at her control, she traced over the wounds with a shaky finger. Someone had kept him, had hurt her lover. She barely heard Hemat's voice when he spoke, her focus on the wounds on Raqir's wrists. Looking up, she met his eyes. Cheeks burning, she ducked her head, she stepped back.

"I demand to speak to the leader of this...this--"

"Who are you?"

"I am Hemat, King of--"

"Ah," Raqir interrupted him. "An errant fool who forgets his people. Who spends his time wallowing in the decadence of court and his wives' warm cunts. There are none here for you to show interest in."

"I will speak with the clan leader," Hemat stepped forward. "It is my right as king."

Kadriye tapped Raqir's shoulder, drawing his attention. *I meant to meet with him inside. Unfortunately, there is an army marching upon us from the south and the judgment to be passed upon Gurak.*

Raqir brushed his knuckles over her cheek. Warmth flooded her body at the touch, memories stirred. She pushed the images aside and focused on the discussion in front of her.

"He is the king, perhaps it would be better to simply hear what he has to say, so he may depart." Raqir squeezed her shoulder and stepped back to allow her to stand next to him. "So king, speak."

"I will speak to the--"

"You are in the presence of our Sdorwal and Sdorwali, so spit it out." Ambria groused, shouldering Hemat aside. "Or shall I take a guess? Your wife ran back to tell you of some great sin in your world and now you have come to demand justice."

"It is true, Bruja did speak to me of the events which transpired. She explained, Kadriye drank a man to death but there were circumstances she only learned of after the event. However, there is no punishment to be dealt, it was a case of self-defense. It would only become a matter of concern if she began to suffer the hunger."

"Then why are you here?" Ambria demanded.

THE BLOODY MASSACRE   199

"It is my understanding, Kadriye is akin to Bruja. A woman of breeding and --"

"Her lineage is of no concern to the likes of you. Get to your point." Raqir stepped forward, towering over the vampire.

Kadriye stared at Hemat, a fine tremble racing through her body as she played the options in her mind. Was there something about her bloodline which made fools of others? Was her blood to be tainted forever? There could only be one reason the king would have made the journey here, and it had nothing to do with goodwill.

Stepping forward, she stopped right in front of Hemat, aware of Ambria scurrying to be able to see her hands. *I can assume what it is you desire, King of Dreken. Once you learned of who my ancestors were, suddenly my clan became far more interesting. A blood tie to your queens, perhaps it would garner you favor in light of the circumstances. Here is what I believe. You came to offer a place within your court, perhaps within your bed. There is nothing you have, I desire. King of the vampires, you may be, but you are of no more value to me than Gurak - or any who would make slaves of my people. I am* sdorwali *of the* Zamphurna. *I have no desire to leave my people or be your broodmare. You may leave. We have a battle to prepare for.*

"*Sdorwali,* the army is here." Dramin dropped from the sky to a crouch. He straightened and pointed to the southern wall. "It is like the ocean, endless."

Kadriye whirled around, all thoughts of the speechless king gone. She looked to Raqir then bent to pick up her visenthor, resting it against her shoulder, her mind raced in circles. With a firm nod she turned to Ambria. *Death to Gurak and his followers.*

The punishment is to be carried out immediately. All who are unable to hold a weapon are to be taken to the caves. Then we stand at ready for war.

About the Author

Canadian Paranormal Romance author Elise Whyles, the author behind the Forsaken series, relaunching in 2023 as The Dark Immortals. Sizzling stories of love, redemption, and forgiveness amid the sprawling backdrop of her Immortal beings' worlds.

Elise lives in the Canadian Prairies with her husband, son, and their furbabies. When not writing, she's an avid reader, and crafter.

RABBIT

Nicole Brown

Phoenix Voices Anthologies

CONTENTS

Chapter One   #

Chapter Two   #

Chapter Three   #

About the Author   #

CHAPTER ONE

Brenna muffled her screams. She could hear the blade of the machete scrape the side of the metal building. She couldn't run back into the woods. The traps the killer had laid out already killed her friends. This was supposed to be an enjoyable weekend. Now everyone is dead.

"Hey Rabbit," Henry called out. "I know you're in there. I just want to play!! Your buddies weren't much fun. They bled out too fast. They didn't fight like you."

Tears streamed down Brenna's face. She had to keep it together. But her thoughts kept going back to her friends.

"Rabbit!" the monster yelled. "Don't make me come in there! The crazed man began to pull on the door."

Brenna wedged the door behind him to go away. But fright kept her quiet. Sitting in total darkness, her hiding spot was now her grave.

Henry continued to slam into the door until the frame started to give way. "I'm going to skin you alive, Rabbit."

Brenna could no longer hold on the screams. "Go away!!"

"Yes! Fear makes the meat tender." Henry said with a stutter.

THE BLOODY MASSACRE

205

Brenna sat in a puddle of her own pee. Dirt and grime stuck to her legs. She tried to search for a weapon.

"Damn it!" she yelled. She couldn't see anything. Brenna grabbed a shovel laying on the floor. She backed into the corner, as the door finally gave way.

"I can smell you, darling. Did you wet yourself?" Laughter coming from the demonic man.

Brenna stayed huddled in the corner. Henry swung the machete toward her head. She brought the shovel up to protect herself. The metal banging together made her hands burn. The pain shot up her arms.

"Get away from me!!" In a heated rage. Henry went took another swing. Brenna kicked him in the groin, He dropped to the ground. The weapon is still in hand.

"You killed my friends!" She landed another blow. This time, he dropped the machete.

Brenna started to run, but he grabbed her by her ankles. Knocking her off her feet. She falls face down on the ground. He jumps on her knife to her throat. He was so close she could feel the heat of his breath. His tobacco split slid down her face. The crazed man started making minor cuts in her face.

"Help me! Somebody help me!" Brenna screamed.

He held her face like a love lost love.

"Sweet, sweet rabbit. It all will be over soon." He raised the knife.

Something or rather someone kicked the man off of her

"Alex?" Alex is still alive? But she thought he died in the traps.

Alex knocked Henry to the ground. "Get off of here!!" Henry had a confused look on his face.

Alex repeatedly pounded Henry in the face. Brenna wanted to jump into Alex's arms.

"We don't have time for that." He grabs her hand and pulled her back towards the woods. Brenna pulled back. "What about the traps?"

Alex yelled over his shoulders. "We don't have a choice. Now come on!"

Brenna heard Henry yelled in the distance. "RABBIT!! RABBIT!! Noo! Come back!"

The two ran blindly into the forest.

"Alex," Brenna cried, "Alex! I need to catch my breath!"

Alex didn't slow his pace. "Come on!"

Brenna was on the verge of throwing up.

"Watch your step," Alex said.

Brenna saw a shimmer of a tripwire.

"Just a little bit more than we can rest." Alex cautioned.

Brenna had no clue where they were headed. She only knew she wanted to leave this place. She saw a light-up ahead. Is this nightmare over? They were back at the cabin.

"No!" Brenna yelled. "We can't be here!!"

Alex turned and faced Brenna. "Welcome, home rabbit."

Brenna's world turns black.

CHAPTER TWO

"Rabbit, Rabbit". Wake up. It was Alex slapping her in the face. Everything was blurry. *What's going on?* She couldn't feel her hands. Then she remembers Alex covering her nose and mouth with a dirty cloth.

"Alex, what's going on?" Out the corner of her eye. She saw Henry walking up behind Alex. Henry knocked Alex to the floor.

"Why did you hit me so hard, boy?!" Henry glared down at Alex

Alex turned and faced Henry. "You were going to kill her! We just found her and you trying to kill her!"

Brenna didn't understand what was going on. The two men stopped arguing and turned to face Brenna. Henry stepped forward as they had never met. And that he murdered all her friends. Well, all except Alex.

"Well howdy, Rabbit, it's been a long, long time. I'm your daddy and you already met your brother Alex." who said this? It's implied but write it out.

"Brother? No, My parents are Mark and Grace Larson," Brenna said.

Henry grabbed Brenna by the face. "No! We are your family, Rabbit."

"Stop calling me Rabbit. My name is Brenna," she said through sobs.

"Your name is Rabbit! And this here is your brother, Antler."

"I don't understand?" Brenna looked at the men, confused.

The look on Alex's face changed. "The people who raised me renamed me Alex. But I never forgot who I was. Antler."

"I don't know you people. I am Brenna Eve Larson. My parents are Mark and Grace."

Henry pushed Alex or Antler out of the way and screamed in Brenna's face. "Your Name Is Rabbit!! Your mother was my life, her name was Doe. I am your father and this here is your brother!"

She couldn't believe what she was hearing. She remembered the times she and Alex spent together. The kiss they shared. How he would kiss her neck and her stomach. She felt sick.

She spat at Alex.

"If you knew, how could you? How could you, Antler!" Brenna said through gritted teeth.

Alex just smirked." I had to play the role. But you were tasty."

Brenna lost it. She began rocking back and forth in her chair. "Let me go! I'm going to kill you!"

Alex slapped her hard across the face. "Just because it took a long time to find you, doesn't mean I won't slit your throat."

"I won't say anything!" She pleaded. "I just want to go home"
"

Henry laughed. "Baby girl, you're already home. I was surprised you didn't recognize the place when you walked in."

Brenna remembered walking through the cabin and Mariah laughed at the old picture. "This kid looks like you." It was a child no older than one, holding a stuffed rabbit sitting on her mother's lap.

"Your mother Doe was the sweetest woman. She had a lot of fire. That fire gave us Antler and you. Your brother had that

THE BLOODY MASSACRE

209

spirit like me. You were different. As much as we tried. That spark wasn't in you. I tried to beat it out of you. Even your brother burned your little fingers. You only cried. Your mama hit Antler so hard. He was knocked out for days. I thought she killed him. He laid in the corner right over."

A memory flashed through her mind. She saw a pile of dirty clothes in the corner. She thought she heard it moan.

"So my mother knocked my so-called brother out, and you just left him there?" Brenna said.

"The boy had to learn. But when he returned to school, he told his classmates. They called DSS. The state took you away. Your mother died of a broken heart." Henry actually had tears in his eyes.

Brenna laughed to herself. 'Now you feel sad.'

Henry rushed to Brenna. But stopped short. "Don't test me Rabbit."

The whole time Brenna was rubbing the tips of her fingers. She remembered the tiny scars, but not how they happened.

It was Antler's turn to speak. "Rabbit, I know you don't remember much. You were so little when they took you away from us. I tried to give you hints early on. I would leave you presents on your doorstep. But your so-called mother would throw them in the trash. I even found an old dead opossum. Left it right where you find it before you would leave for school. You used to enjoy playing with them. What did you used to call them?"

Brenna stopped crying, "Stinky Kitty."

Henry clapped his hands together. "Boy, I think she is finally starting to remember. We'll knock those rocks out of your head before long."

Antler walked over to an old chest. He pulled out an old blanket. It smelled of musk and decay.

"Brenna," Alex said in that loving way he would call her name. "Sorry, Rabbit. This belonged to our mother. She kept it until she died. Small bones were falling from the blanket. She even kept Stinky Kitty."

Vomit rose in her throat and began to fall out of her mouth. "Why would you keep that?"

"Mother was hoping you'd come back." Antler said easily.

I managed to run away. But you were too young. You would forget us if we didn't find you.

"When you and your little friends rented the cabin, it was fate," Henry said.

"It wasn't fate, Alex drip shit Antler told us about the place!" Brenna said.

Henry just shrugged his shoulders as he spat on the floor, "Whatever."

CHAPTER THREE

B renna felt the knot come undone. She held her breath. She knew she couldn't run through the woods. She noticed there was a truck in the back of the house. It was properly Henry's. The cars her friends drove up in were gone. She needed keys. As if Henry was reading her mind. He tossed them to Alex.

"Son, go get the gear. We need to burn and dump the bodies."

Alex catches the keys and heads outside.

Brenna began to cry again. They murdered her friends. "How could you?"

"Rabbit, you may not understand now, but you will. Your friends were a distraction. You're more than you ever know. You gotta kill the fear," Henry said.

"What if I don't want to be free?" Brenna needed to keep his attention until she could plan her next move.

"Baby girl, once you taste it, you'll never be the same," Henry said.

"I call bullshit," Brenna spat.

Henry walks over to Brenna and rubs her head. "You wait and see."

Henry pulls the machete from his waistband. He drops it on a nearby table.

Brenna sprang forward. Grabbing the knife from the table. Quickly slicing Henry's neck. He couldn't even cry out for help. He bled out on the floor. Brenna slipped behind the door. When Alex walked back in. He saw his father on the floor.

"Daddy!" Antler ran to his father's body.

Brenna took the blade and stabbed Alex between the shoulder blades. Alex's body fell on top of Henry's. Brenna let out a primal cry. She was free, freer than she had ever been.

She was Rabbit.

About the Author

Nicole Brown is from a small coastal town on the beautiful beaches of North Carolina. She is the proud mom of two wonderful boys. Her oldest son serves in the military and her youngest son is in his first year of college.

Nicole has been writing for as long as she can remember. Her imagination and creative is top notch. She is stepping out of her comfort zone now and wanting to publish her work becoming an official author. The Bloody Massacre Anthology is where she will have her first work published for the world.

This is the first time you will see her work in black and white, but it will not be the last!

A Soul's Decay

Harper Shay

Phoenix Voices Anthologies

CONTENTS

Chapter One	#
Chapter Two	#
Chapter Three	#
Chapter Four	#
Chapter Five	#
Chapter Six	#
Chapter Seven	#
Chapter Eight	#
Chapter Nine	#
Chapter Ten	#
Chapter Eleven	#
Chapter Twelve	#
Chapter Thirteen	#

Chapter Fourteen #

Chapter Fifteen #

Chapter Sixteen #

About the Author #

Chapter One

"Fuck, Lily. Where are you?" The harsh voice, along with the clanging of plastic dishes hitting the hardwood floor, caused me to shrink back as sensations of unease filled my head. "What a mess." I heard him grumble before his voice rose. "Lily, you better answer me before I send out a search party for your ass."

"I'm over here," I groaned in reply. "In the closet." I knew he'd over-react once he saw the state I was in, but the light hurt my eyes. The crickets' chirps pierced my eardrums, and despite it being a hot July morning, I couldn't stop trembling. It felt as if I was sitting in a meat cooler and my fingers were bordering on frostbite.

The heavy wooden door was flung open, and my body relaxed as the rest of Brom's build materialized and blocked the light from sneaking past the frame. His eyes widened as they lowered huddled in the far corner of the closet and buried under a mountain of blankets that seemed to barely take the edge off the chill that burrowed into my bones.

"For the love of—" Brom stepped into the space, and I groaned as the artificial light from the room behind him hit my eyes. "We've been searching for you everywhere. Why are you in the closet?"

"I think I'm getting sick." I shifted and tried to sit up, but the weight of the blankets made it difficult. "Maybe it's the flu. I just can't get warm, and my body is reacting like I have a hangover without the fun that comes before the consequences."

"Should I take you to the doc?" The worry in his eyes bled into his movements as he lowered his broad body with caution to study what he could see of my face. His brows scrunched up and his lips twitched.

"No, I'll be fine," I replied with effort. "I'm sure it will pass by tomorrow and I'll be back to my normal self."

"If you aren't, you better know that I'll carry you into the doctor's office myself."

"Brom, honestly. Quit fussing." I straightened my back against the wall and the fluffy warmth of the soft blankets slipped from my face. "What is it you need?"

"Huh?" He looked at me, confused.

"You said you were looking for me everywhere." A soft chuckle slipped out.

"Oh, yeah." He exhaled and ran his hand through his thick, blonde hair. Passing his wife, Sam, had taken a toll on him, making him look older than his thirty-two years. I couldn't imagine the strain her loss had put on him and his poor son, Corbin. He was only two when the sickness took his mother away from him. It's strange to think it's already been three years since that horrible day. Brom cleared his throat, and I noticed he was now standing again.

"Sorry, what did you say?"

"Another stranger has arrived, seeking the witch who can save his soul."

"Another one? And what's this crap about a witch?" Using the wall for support, I let it guide me to stand. "Who the hell is telling shifters I'm some kind of witch?"

THE BLOODY MASSACRE

"There's a group keeping him busy near the entrance to town. Let me take you to him, and with any luck, he'll give you answers to your questions." His arms fell, and he straightened his spine. I could see his thoughts churning as he looked past me and got lost in the past. No doubt he was reliving the last day his wife was alive. I saw the moment reality collided with his memories and his eyelids closed, hiding the pain of his past.

A battle waged inside me, and all my pain faded into the background. I desperately wanted to ask him if he was all right and if I could do anything to lessen his pain, but I realized that if I brought up what he considered weakness, it would make his feelings worse. There would be a day, hopefully soon, when he would reach out and let his pack brothers and sisters help carry his heavy load. For now, he only continued to punish himself for something he couldn't stop.

With a deep exhale, I threw the blankets off me and untangled the fabric from around my legs. The last thing I needed was to fall on my face. My foot was trying to remove the last of the remnants when a rustling noise distracted me from my task. My head jerked up, and I saw the apology in Brom's eyes.

"I'm sorry, Lily. I can see you aren't feeling well." The remorse in his voice dissolved what remained of my impatience, and I went up to him.

"It's fine," I replied with a softness only given by a mother or a lover. "I'm fine, besides we need to figure out what this stranger expects from this *witch*." I ended my statement with a gentle smile, and he bowed his head in resignation.

"Very well, but I won't have you walking into danger. Don't leave my side," he demanded. I rolled my eyes. "Lily, I mean it."

"Yes, Dad," I mumbled as I walked past him out of the closet. Snagging the bottle of painkillers and the half empty water bottle next to it on the side table, I continued to the front door. "Well?" I looked back at him as I popped two pills into my mouth and chased them with a big swig of lukewarm water.

He still stood in the closet's doorway. I creased my brow. "You coming?"

Chapter Two

As I made my way to the entrance of town, I heard a threatening growl. The depth of that sound touched the part in me that sensed the shifter's pain. It was demanding and threatened to paralyze the human that housed it. The enormous pressure in my chest, a crushing weight filled with hunger, stole my breath. This poor creature craved the blood of all that stood before him. The human half feared losing himself before he could be subdued.

I ran towards the sensation and even though the closer I got made the pressure unbearable, my feet didn't slow. If I did not reach him within the next few seconds, there would be no saving him or the crowd surrounding him.

"Get back," he roared. "Where's the witch? If you don't bring her to me, this will be your end."

I cleared the trees as the enormous man collapsed to the ground. His body curled in on itself. He was trying to hold on. All his energy being eaten up by the fight. I slowed and halted at his disheveled appearance. The t-shirt that clung to him was full of blood and his hair damp with sweat. My lungs filled with air as my eyes slid closed and the air heated around me.

I could feel the filth seep from his skin. He was battling the oily taint that swirled in his soul. He was so saturated by it I could see it circling the whites of his partially open eyes. Like jaundice, a tinting of the bleached outline of his orbs. However, this corruption entered him. I could feel its hold and the fact that it refused to let him go. The man's body twitched as he rolled to his knees. His fingers curl in the dark crown of his bowed head.

"The witch, now!" His rage magnified as the demand ripped from his dry lips.

Rooted to the spot, I stood at least fifteen feet from this shifter and all I could think of was the immense pain he must be in. His white-knuckle grip threatened to free him from the obsidian strands that were covered in days of filth. My feet moved of their own accord, and I kneeled before him on the cold ground and rested my hands over his tense fists. His body vibrated as it held in the darkness, fighting with all he was about to have it.

The strength his soul still carried was astonishing. Any other creature would have crumbled under the weight of the anguish he suppressed. But at last, his strength had waned, which was the reason he had sought me out.

Just then, in my awe at his endurance, his pale-yellow eyes looked into mine, and I froze at the fear he refused to show with his body. Then I realized I had no choice. I would relieve him from his burden, but I was positive it would cost me more than sore muscles and a chill.

My back bowed with the taint of his soul. It was too much, too great for my own soul to swallow. How had he held on to his humanity for this long? Muscles tensing under my palms, the heat from his body almost scalding my flesh, I pulled the darkness from him with every deep breath I took. No other shifter I had treated had this much anger and ferociousness. The amount of strength it had taken him to hold out this long, just draining away as the rage left his system and exhaustion

THE BLOODY MASSACRE

stole him from consciousness. All the rigidity melted away as he slipped under the peaceful blanket of sleep.

Panting, I looked around to find Brom and his expression of disbelief. That amazement shifted to fear when his face twisted, and his foot lifted to get.

"What?" I felt so confused. Nothing felt right, as the rage brutalized my insides and stole my ability to focus. The last thing I remembered was Brom reaching for me as I felt my body give out. The hard muscle that stopped my face from meeting the pebbled ground, a muffled voice I tried to hold on to, and the warmth that ran down my face, were the last sensations before I followed the stranger in sleep.

CHAPTER THREE

The traces of copper and dirt filled my mouth and I swear I'd swallowed the desert. "Water." My voice cracked as razors lanced my throat. Air and the absence of spit, a punishment for freeing the feral beast from the human. I knew this last incident would have me on my back for a while.

The whisper of footsteps came closer until they echoed throughout my head, bouncing, and ricocheting against my skull. My lids pressed tightly together until a cool smooth object pressed against my lips.

"Here, drink this." Raspy and low, the voice that spoke was not a familiar one, but my parched throat desperately sought the soothing liquid as my tongue slid across the rim of the glass.

While my skin was itchy and my muscles twitched, I swallowed the water until the last drop disappeared down the rehydrated passage of my throat. It didn't solve all of my aches, but the desert that lived in me now felt more like the sand after a rainstorm. Quenched and nourished until the sun beat down on it again.

The strange presence remained close, and I wasn't so sure I wanted to open my eyes to see who it was hovering so close.

THE BLOODY MASSACRE

The give of the pleather chair in my bedroom quickly answered the question of where the stranger would be when I gave into my curiosity. My interest peaked, refusing to wait any longer and my eyes slowly opened, blurry shapes and colors covered my vision. Blinking hard, the fuzzy images fading into clarity as shadowed eyes look down at me from the side of the bed.

Eyes hidden by furrowed brows and long dark lashes, pursed lips surrounded by rough dark stubble, and thick fingers gripping one of my water glasses welcomed me back to the real world and my new reality. To my right sat the man whose taint I absorbed, and he did not look impressed.

"Thank you," I wheezed. "Where's Brom?"

"You mean the big blonde lumberjack?" His gruff voice sent tingles along every nerve in my ravaged body and pooled in my core. His impression of Brom wasn't that far off, but his tone made me frown.

I tried to raise myself to sitting. Hoping my headboard wouldn't fail me, I pushed back and up with my palms, and my elbows almost buckled with the weight of my body. Weak from the purging of his soul, that's all it was. I'd be fine in a few hours. No need to worry, but worrying was all I did nowadays. "You don't seem all that grateful for your humanity," I mumbled.

"Oh, that's not the issue," he grumbled back, turning to place the empty glass on my side table, giving me a good view of a savage scar on the column of his neck. It couldn't have been more than a few months old, the skin still mottled and inflamed at the edges. I wondered what caused the marring of his otherwise smooth skin. And how badly something like that hurt him. His eyes connected with mine and the anger that permeated from the deep brown pupils hypnotized me.

"Well then, what *is* the problem?" I replied with a little snark. You'd think he'd be excited and thankful for the relief he must feel from the purge.

"You're just a girl." What I now knew to be confusion drifted from his expression as his lips drooped with his reluctance to come to terms knowing that a girl, not some witch or all powerful being, had saved him from damnation.

"So, you're upset that a female could help you. Too proud to admit that you, a powerful shifter, couldn't beat whatever this thing is on your own?" I turned my head in disgust. His dismissal of me caused a pit to open up and thorny vines to coil around my heart.

You're being stupid, Lily. Let it go. He's not the first Shifter to struggle with yours being a Sin Eater.

"Wait, no. That's not what I meant." He leaned forward. "It's just that you are so young. I pictured someone with your type of ability to be aged with experience."

"So, you're upset that I'm not an old crone?" Interlacing my fingers in my lap, I examined a hangnail on my thumb. It was better than looking at the pity I was almost positive was taking over his expression. Calloused fingers gripped the side of my chin as he forced me to look up and face him.

"No, that's not it at all." His eyes read my pain, but he didn't release me. "You should be living life. Falling in love. Being consumed by someone who can treat you like a queen. Not taking on this sickness for others and spending your free time in bed."

"Don't pity me," I whispered. "It is what it is. There's no giving this thing back and no ignoring it. It's who I am. There's no sense in fighting it or being angry with the hand I was dealt. Those emotions are just a waste of time and could cause an innocent's death."

"Oh, well, you're awake." Brom interrupted the conversation as he strode into the bedroom. The man quickly dropped his hand, and I focused my attention on Brom. "You had us worried."

"Lilllllyyy!" His squeal could be heard before his small body shot through the doorway and ended up on my bed. "Boing, Boing. I'm like a kangaroo, Lily." I chuckled and reached for

THE BLOODY MASSACRE

Corbin as his feet left my mattress and he was momentarily suspended in the air.

"Corbin, what do you think you are doing, mister?" I lay him on his back and started to force high-pitched giggles from his lungs as I mercilessly tickled his sides. He tried to squirm out of my hold while he also tried to catch his breath. "Oh, no you don't." I rolled behind him and pulled him into me. My arms wrapped around him in a hug, but his laughter stopped when he got a look at the stranger in my room.

"Who are you?" Corbin pushed at my hands, trying to evade my hold. The stranger was more interesting. I let go and sat upright, pulling the loose hairs from my mouth.

"Hi there, Little Man. My name is Nocs," he said, extending his hand out to shake Corbin's much smaller one. Corbin looked at it as if he was determining whether it was safe, which I could understand, but after a beat of silence, he gave in and shook the man's hand with exaggerated eagerness.

"What are you doing in Lily's bedroom?" His little mouth was notorious for asking big questions and my checks grew hot as he continued his interrogation of Nocs. "You're not married. Daddy says only married people should be in a bedroom together."

"Corbin," Brom interrupted. "That's enough now. Nocs is keeping Lily company while she gets better."

"Oh, sorry Daddy. I forgot." He looked from Brom to Nocs, a deceptive look of innocence on his face as he surveyed the newcomer in my room when what came out next had me mortified. "Daddy said only married people share the same bed. My bad." Corbin looked at me and the smile on his face reflected his intelligence. He did that on purpose. He was so good at picking up on my emotions. He and I have been bound in a way that was indescribable since his mother passed and my ability came to life. It was like his broken bond with his mom transferred when her death triggered the Sin Eater in me. It still haunted me that her death was responsible for the ancient secret to surface in me. Why couldn't my ability have emerged before Sam got sick? I would never comprehend why she had to die, and I will forever feel guilty.

"Alright, Corbin. Go watch some cartoons in the living room while I talk to Lily and Nocs."

"Okay, Daddy." Corbin kissed my cheek, bounced off the bed and smirked at Nocs before disappearing into the hallway.

That little boy made my heart swell. His curly blonde ringlets bounced like springs as he fled from the room with the promise of talking cats and bunnies dancing across the glossy TV screen. Corbin had always been a joy, the sunshine that broke through the storm clouds. He was our reminder of his mother, a miniature of our lost Sam.

There would never be a day where I didn't think about how I could have saved her life. If only my ability had surfaced in time to devour the sickness that had snuck into her body and slowly stole her from us. But this world had never been fair. Like my little buddy, my mother was taken from me when I was young. I never knew who my father was but losing her to the actions of cruel human children when I was six had left me all alone. No more would I feel her arms wrap around me. Now she lived in my heart alone.

Brom, fifteen found me at the base of a tree. Scared and too weak to change from my raven form back into human, he scooped me up and took me home. I had a broken wing and he nursed me back to health. He gained my trust and coaxed me out from behind the safety of my feathered disguise. The shifters of this beautiful town had raised me and even now, at twenty-three, still watched over me as if I were born to each and every one of them.

But Brom would always be my savior. An overprotective big brother who acted more like a helicopter parent than anything else. It breaks my heart every single day, knowing I couldn't save his love and give him the future he and Corbin deserved.

THE BLOODY MASSACRE 231

The worst part was that Sam's death broke through the barrier and released the Sin Eater I now housed. And with every new day, every breath, I fight for our shifter brothers and sisters in her name. She was the beginning of the darkness and I swear with everything I am, that I will be its end.

CHAPTER FOUR

"Lily?" Brom grabbed my upper arms. "Where do you think you're going?" Like waking from a dream, I stood in front of him, halted by his grip. With no recollection, I had gotten out of my bed to follow Corbin.

"I have to use the bathroom." The words formed and spilled out, and I lowered my head so he couldn't see the heat of embarrassment tint my face. Lost in Corbin's innocence fascinated me. It drew me to him with the intention of assessment. How did this tiny human survive his pain? My soul felt the loss of all those I hadn't been able to help, those whose souls had been destroyed by ailment, and eventually had to be put down to deliver them from further destruction and suffering.

From the corner of my eye, I studied Nocs' expression. A slightly tilted head, soft lines shadowed the corners of his deep eyes. He was still trying to figure me out. What he didn't understand yet was that I wasn't worth his interest. I filled my lungs with air, absorbing the reaction to his curious look, and felt the results ripple through my body. The gentle rhythm of my heart quickly began to race, and like a flight of butterflies dancing in the summer sun, one escaped the safety of my beating organ and

THE BLOODY MASSACRE

found its way to my stomach. Bumping against the sides and tickling my insides. The effect trickled lower and awakened a tingle between my legs.

Nocs studied me with deliberate heat and as I gasped with the sensations that flowed through me his eyes sought mine and, in a flash, I looked away before he could notice my returned interest. I was no good for anyone in my state. Plus, the heat in his glare wasn't from desire but suspicion. He still couldn't come to terms with the fact I had sensed his frailty before pulling the crippling illness to the surface and freeing him and his beast before he snapped.

The unique thing about him was that he had concealed just how close he was to turning feral. The fear and humiliation he partnered the darkness with should have descended into the monster more rapid and unforgiving, but he'd caged it until the very moment I released his soul from the torment he was barely surviving. Nocs' strength, stubbornness, and golden aura made me recognize his animal was a wolf, and that's not all. His soul concealed a secret he had kept hidden.

I could see it all now, like a memory. His memory? His shame? Nocs was an alpha, the leader of a pack he's vowed to protect. That loyalty had become a part of him and the thorns of that promise had saved him from a life of slavery. He just hasn't accepted the truth about his status and authority. Although I was a raven shifter, it's all I could do not to bow at his feet. The amount of power I felt from him could mean he bears the ability to control all divisions of shifters. Like the King of the jungle, there was a good possibility he could be a Crown Alpha. But only if he accepted this reality.

A hallucination. Maybe the hope for a connection. Never have I seen or felt the emotions or memories of another shifter, and for it to be one from another breed of shifter just didn't make sense.

"Did you hear me?" Brom's irritated voice breaks into my thoughts and I felt lost. *What did he ask me again?* All I could do was look up at him in confusion. But he looked at me like I was a stranger. He no longer gave off the aura of concern. He seemed to be heading closer to frustration, maybe anger.

"Sorry, Brom. I got lost in my head for a minute. Maybe I just need more recoup time, but first I need to use the bathroom."

"Has this become too much for you?" His fingers tightened around my upper arm as he whispered through his teeth. His expression was scaring me, like he wasn't himself at that moment. "Dammit, Lily." The heat of his fingers as they jerked away from my skin left a burning sensation and a numbing feeling slid under my skin to soothe the intensity of his touch.

"I'm fine, Brom. I just need to rest." My vision blurred with the emotion I held back. I couldn't show weakness, or he would know, one hundred percent, that I was lying.

Studying me, I saw the exact moment his thinking cleared, and he came back to himself. I could see the remorse in his eyes the moment before he straightened. Turning, he yelled for Corbin, pulling him away from a show filled with entertaining puppies in uniforms.

"Do we really have to go, Dad? It's just getting to the good part."

"You heard me," he replied with an open hand stretching towards his son. "We have more people to visit and the day's schooling to complete."

Corbin didn't question his father again. He sprang up from the floor and ran to his dad. His little hand sliding into the much bigger one, and the love I felt in that gentle contact erased my unease from our unusual confrontation.

"Bye, Lily." Corbin turned his head and smiled. "See you tomorrow."

"Bye, buddy. It's a date." I smiled back at him, lost in his innocence once more. Brom stole one last look at me before they left the house, and me, with the Nocs.

CHAPTER FIVE

Knees pulled into my chest; I sat in the dark staring into the dark of my living room. Nocs said nothing before he too walked out of my house, leaving behind a residue of his emotions. He had been curious, and he received no answers when he was here. I could also sense he wanted to stay to flush some from me, but decided just then wasn't the best time.

My chest felt heavy, thoughts tangled themselves into tight balls, and I was so tired. Like most nights after an expulsion, I was to wound up to find peace in sleep. The twisted emotions of the tainted shifters always haunted me. And until my soul fully consumed their sins, I remained the one trapped in their phantom memories.

But now, instead of feeling like a zombie, my anxiety has crested, and I felt the darkness creep under my skin. This was the worst of them yet, and I was trying to comfort myself through the truth I concealed. There would be a day where I'd need to trust someone with the truth, because there was a very good possibility I'd need to be taken down. This darkness was past sin. It was an evil that remained in the darkest part of the soul, festering until I could no longer contain it. Even now, I could feel the swell, the pressure against my head, and the weakening of my heart.

My body jerked and my legs flew out. I must've fallen asleep. The question was, what woke me? I didn't remember dreaming. A chill, like icicles gliding across my flesh, hovered in the air and my ears throbbed from the quiet in the room as I desperately tried to hear anything besides the booming of my heart.

After my heart rate decreased, I rose to make my way through the darkness to the bathroom down the hall, and as I dropped to my knees, I shielded my ears to defend them from the loud screeching of metal rubbing against metal. Then a low, menacing growl replaced the sound, and I held my breath as the haunting sound faded into a whimper. I was petrified, but I couldn't hide. With my pulse jack hammering against my veins, I jumped to my feet and ran to find the creature responsible for the wounded plea.

The sound penetrated through the exterior walls and poured pain into my heart. Something or someone was injured, but the more I focused, the more it felt like a record skipping in my head. Pushing through the front door, my senses were startled into high alert. The chill seeped into my clothes and the hair on the back of my neck lifted. I spent hours searching around the outer perimeter of my house with no luck, every twig and leaf that rustled in the dead of the night causing my heart rate to spike and my breath to catch in my throat but no body or evidence of anything injured was there. Exhausted, I finally gave up and went back into the house slumping, back into bed. It took more time than I'd liked, but I finally fell asleep.

***

I grumbled nonsensical words into the empty room as I tried to awake, slowly forcing my reluctant eyes to open. The clock

THE BLOODY MASSACRE

read seven in the morning. Great, I got just under three hours of sleep total. It would be a highly caffeinated day.

My muscles groaned, so tense from both my body's exertion and the anxiety that plagued me. Last night's adventure gradually reemerged and the slow tingle that ran across my skin, followed by every hair standing up on end made me shiver and want to wrap myself tightly into my comforter, hoping the cocoon of cotton material would protect me from all the bad this world still sheltered.

Of course, this wasn't an option, and I needed to get my ass out of bed and into the shower, one of the not so simple ways to prove to the people of this town that I was okay. This time my muscles felt like they might snap as I stretched my limbs above my head, a mark on my arm catching my attention as my eyes truly opened from slumber. Confused, I pulled back the covers to expose my body to the day.

I shouldn't have talked myself out of the safety of my fabric shield, because when I whipped the covers back, a vision of death greeted me, and I couldn't hide from what I was seeing.

The cream sheets were caked in dry mud and crusty blood. Examining my legs, small cuts decorate my smooth olive skin. Crusty and pasty spots speckled the tops of my feet and when I sat up, feet resting on the floor, it came to my attention that my fingernails were chipped and some beds held traces of the crimson liquid as well.

Frozen, trapping the scream in my head. *What did I do?*

CHAPTER SIX

Sitting balled up on the floor of my shower, I watched as the water swirled down the drain in a rusty mixture of earth and gore. Staring into the whirlpool of evidence, I sought answers to a night that refused to reveal its secrets. Coffee-colored strands plastered themselves along my arms like slithering snakes while my world closed in around me. The steam from the boiling water tried to shroud my sins behind the glass sheets, but they denied me the refuge I strived to reach.

Hues of black and purple peeked through the bronze of my skin, creating footprints of the night's events. I had to have fought something. There could be no other excuse for the location and severity of the blemishes that peppered my otherwise flawless skin. My wrecked nails, all jagged and torn, made me feel as if I clawed my way from the Earth's core to flee from my demons.

It's difficult to describe the feeling of being alone. But, if I had to explain the emptiness I felt at that moment, I would tell the inquisitor that I hovered above an endless pit. The darkness beckoned me, and I found no relief from the constant weight that threatened to pull me down. The abyss wanted to control

THE BLOODY MASSACRE

me, seep into every molecule and devour my soul. A phantom that would squeeze my heart until I think I might just give in and save myself from feeling any more pain. But I'd go on, for Sam, for all those out there that need me more than I needed peace. One day, it would wrap me up and carry me home. This world and I would reach a truce and I would.

slip away into the forever, eyes closed and soul at rest.

Lost in a world of fear and confusion, I didn't hear the door open until the wood hit the linen closet door and even then, my body refused to react to the intruder. I remained immobile as strong arms lifted me up and a solid chest became my resting place. Cradling me like a wounded child, the man's muscles flexed with my weight, as he brought me from the numbness of the water to the cruelty of the chill that clung in the air.

A groan escaped from deep in my chest, and I tensed in his grip. I realized there was no way to hide my having been being held by an unknown man, and yes, that's right, I was covered in only my bruised skin and dripping hair. There was no way to hide my embarrassment and as my skin began to heat, its shade morphed into a rosy hue. I squeezed my eyes shut tightly and concentrated only on my breathing, my body barely shifting as he moved towards my bedroom, holding me firmly but gently in his arms.

A nest of messy bedding lay on the floor, all but the fitted sheet, tainted by the remains of a secret even I wasn't privy to. He halted before setting me down in my reading chair. Moments passed slowly and there was no way for me to define the time in which he left me shivering. The cool air caused my damp skin to react in tiny bumps before a soft cloud of fabric was wrapped around my unprotected frame.

His body seemed to slide against an invisible boundary as he lowered himself to his knees before me, and his caramel eyes, smooth silk swirls of tenderness, cured my paralysis... Nocs was in my house. And even more concerning was the gash along the side of his face that wasn't present yesterday when he left.

Without my permission, my hand reached out and my fingertips traced along the healing wound. He stopped breathing and his body went rigid at my touch. The tension released when his body shivered as my fingers continued to the back of his neck and winded themselves in his inky strands.

"Lily," he whispered as his own fingers softly pulled my arm down. "What's going on?"

Caught in a trance, no words could describe the emotion that rolled through me as his eyes tried to uncover my secrets. Warm waves of compassion spread through my chest crashing into the walls of my heart. The emotion promised to erode the barriers I'd built to protect myself from loss. A pressure built behind the cage of my ribs while my defenses were battered and the temperature between us rose. I clung to his hair like a lifeline, thinking he was the strength I needed to fight off this unwanted reaction. "Lily." His lips moved, but I heard nothing. The emptiness that tried to swallow me up started to disappear, overridden by the intensity of our connection. "Stop." His lips moved again, and pain creased his forehead. Eyes squinting as he tried to forcefully remove my fingers from his hair. As if the pain in his eyes was a switch my fingers released, and he shifted away from me.

My hand remained suspended; sharp claws covered in liquid crimson. Dripping from the tips and dancing around my fingers like fluid shakes. All I could do was stare at the curved razors as Nocs' blood began to dry on my skin. Wiping the back of his neck, Nocs also seemed stunned by the stains that covered his palm. Slowly lifting his gaze he looked more surprised than upset at the assault. "You're a bird shifter," he mumbled. Nodding, I silently acknowledged his statement.

"I'm a raven shifter," I replied numbly. "Is that a problem?"

"No—" Pausing, he searched my face for what, I don't know. "I just figured you were a wolf shifter. Your energy is strong."

"Is that a good thing or a bad thing?" I asked, snapping out of whatever mental paralysis my body was trapped in. Dread

THE BLOODY MASSACRE

took over and my reaction to his nearness, and the urge I felt to claim him, appalled me. Stomach churning like a boiling pot of thick stew, I stood from the chair and rushed back to the safety of the bathroom; the four walls not enough until the lock slid in place, and I sank to the floor. Stuck in the horror of my partial transformation, I mentally berated myself. What was wrong with me? Was the ability to liberate others changing me? Was I losing my own soul in the process? Was there a darkness lingering inside me waiting to twist me in its grip?

CHAPTER SEVEN

D amp cheeks and puffy red eyes reflected back at me through the mirror. Cool water ran over my fingers as they rested at the bottom of the porcelain sink. I wanted to erase the image that stared back at me; defeated and drained from the mental battle.

I had to figure out what was happening. There could be no denying the changes in me. I either needed to stop aiding shifters or prepare for whatever was happening. I splashed the cold water on my face and jumped when a forceful knock shifted the bathroom door. Racing to dry off my face and wipe away any signs of my distress I headed to open the door but froze when a figure flickered into sight. A small gasp caught in my throat at the intrusion of this particular guest. The anxiety quickly faded, and I jerked my finger up to my lips, signaling the new arrival to stay quiet. "I'm going to the bathroom," I spoke through the door.

"Are you okay?" the deep voice pushing its way through the hollow wood door. "Yeah, I'll be out in a couple minutes," I answered leaning against the door, my eyes focused on the being who was returning my stare.

THE BLOODY MASSACRE 243

"Okay, but if you're not out in the next few minutes, I'm coming to get you and this flimsy door won't stop me."

"Fine, but you won't need to damage any of my property." I listened as his retreating steps got quieter the further from the door he got. Once I knew he was far enough away I slowly moved towards the being that had magically appeared.

"Why are you here?" I whispered through my teeth.

"I can feel the darkness surging through you like an electrical storm." He spoke from underneath the cover of his hoodie. Dark and ominous was his only feature. He never showed his face, which wasn't rare for a Reaper. "I thought you might appreciate a little assistance with the backlash of your gift."

The mythical being that now stood before me had made his existence known shortly after my first soul cleansing. I had been sick and weak afterwards and basically attached to my toilet as I expelled all the things in my stomach. Shivering on the floor, thinking I was hallucinating, he appeared.

I was too weak to be scared, too exhausted to think he was anything more than a dream, and shortly after I found myself curled tightly on the cool tile, the phantom covered me with a blanket from my bed, and I disappeared into darkness. He remained close by as I slept and when I awoke, there he was, a mystery hidden by a dark hoodie and jeans.

Since then, he had found his way after each event. Speaking in riddles, I made sense of what he was. Each time he would talk in his toneless voice and share bits and pieces. One of the first facts I had figured out was that he was a Reaper. And like a puzzle I slowly put the full picture together, or I thought I had.

"How is it that you sense these things in me?" I questioned, even though I knew he wouldn't fully explain his connection but only gave me snippets instead. "I mean, you never showed up before my gift emerged and now you pop in whenever you want, leaving me with no privacy. Seriously, what if I was in the throes of passion and bam, here comes Mr. Reaper with his disregard for space and boundaries?"

"You are a Sin Eater. I am a phantom of death." His statue-like stance and deep voice always made me feel like I was in a horror movie. The soul stealer never moved a muscle or changed his deep tone. His presence always felt like a heavy blanket, one drenched in a pool of water and thrown on top of me. The promise to crush me, make it too difficult to escape him. "We exist on the same plain and our abilities run parallel to one another. We devour the evil that contaminates this world, but my ability allows me to soothe your pain by exorcizing the very cause of your discomfort, allowing you to continue your work. Without me, you would perish quickly."

"Wait," I demanded, stepping towards him. This was more information than he had ever shared before. "So, what you are saying is I am dying, for sure?"

"I am doing all I can to prevent that outcome, but yes, your body is weakening with every extraction you partake in." I reached my hand out to pull back his hood, but before my fingertips even grazed the dark fabric he looked up. I inhaled loudly; eyes transfixed to his face. "I can't allow you to pass from this world too soon." His voice softened along with his black eyes. "You are the key to this world's survival, to your kinds' survival."

This Reaper was dangerously beautiful. I had the inkling that I could go as far as him being deadly. This creature before me was a monster, one from nightmares and folklore. But his face was chiseled from the time of gods and even though he had empty eyes, I could see he too had a soul. A softness buried deep, but existing in a creature charged with the responsibility of death. My hand remained suspended in the air between us as I remained torn between continuing the path to his face or lowering it to my side.

"Your face," I said in a soft whisper. "How can such beauty hold such a dark gift?"

"That's ridiculous coming from a creature such as you," he replied, his voice gripping me like flannel sheets. It wound

THE BLOODY MASSACRE

around me, the warmth coaxing me into a drowsy state. My mind telling me to curl up and fall asleep. "You are the beautiful creature being forced closer to death in order for your kind to find salvation. You are a Lilith. Your namesake was a demon of night, powerful and cunning. She bowed down to no one. The difference between you and her is you hold a gracious soul full of compassion and love for all things. This is your weakness and the reason for your decline."

"Are you referring to religion?" I gaped at him in disbelief. "You think I'm a demon from the beginning of time? You're crazy."

"Is it so hard to believe?" he scoffed. "You have an angel of death standing before you, and you think the existence of demons is ridiculous?"

"Maybe not so much that, but the notion that I have demon in me, yes."

"Do you even know who your parents were?" He lifted an eyebrow.

"All I remember is my mom was a very loving parent and I never knew my dad, but I believe they were both Raven Shifters like me." I shrugged off the sadness that filled my heart as if I lost my mom yesterday. "Why are you asking about my parents?"

"I, of course, didn't know them personally, but I'm guessing one of them was a descendant of Adam and the other of Lilith."

"Woah, what the hell are you talking about?" I stepped away until my back hit the bathroom door. *This guy had lost it.*

"Lily?" Nocs' voice, once again, reached me through the door. "Lily, what's going on in there?" The handle jiggled as he tried to come in. "Lily, talk to me." His demand came with a more frantic attempt to enter the room. "If you don't talk to me and tell me what's happening, I'm going to break down the door."

"Shit," I mumbled. "You need to go before he sees you." I felt the panic resurface at the thought Nocs would uncover one of my biggest secrets. The Reaper's hand jutted out and found its way to the center of my chest. The immediate burning sensation stole my breath and I let free the scream that boiled up my throat.

The door buckled with Nocs' first attempt at ramming the door. I flew forward into the Reaper, and I looked up in painful surprise. He smirked at me, and I thought I saw a flash of fang. "I think it's time you share your name with me," I demanded in a hoarse voice. "Dipping your phantom claws into my soul and not sharing your name seems rude."

A white light blinded me as the burn turned into a white-hot flame, and splinters flew like confetti across the bathroom floor. "That's my cue," he whispered. "You can call me Colin." With his final words and Nocs' grunt, from behind, the Reaper vanished.

CHAPTER EIGHT

The bathroom door shattered into massive wood splinters around me, and on the other side was a furious Nocs. Chest heaving and a low growl escaping his sealed lips. "What the hell is going on?"

I slowly turned to face him and found not only anger but great concern on his face. "Nothing, I was just cleaning up." The jade of his eyes intensified, glowing like hell fire. Nocs was reacting to my lie. And I knew he was aware that I had not spoken the truth, but I stuck to it because how could I explain Colin to him? How could I explain any of what was going on with me?

My legs felt weak as I did my best to hide what Colin had done before vanishing into thin air. The one reason I refused to share my secret with the Shifters I kept close was because they would make me stop using my gift if they knew my health was dwindling each time I used it. But Colin has made it possible to continue saving those in distress. It not only freed the Shifter I cured, but the families attached to them and any person their feral nature may have been targeting.

The point was, Colin absorbed the worst of the impact the sins inflicted on my own soul. His choice to pull those from me made it possible to recover sooner and move forward, but he could heal no lasting damage, so I would continue to decline if I didn't stop soon. But I couldn't. As long as Shifters were being infected, as long as they were fighting the instinct to go feral, I would not stop. My conscience would not let me leave them to suffer.

"I know you're lying, but I'll let it go. You don't know me." Stepping over the remains of the door he came closer. With cautious movements, slow and planned, he made his way to my side and without thinking, I braced my hand on his chest to keep him from getting any closer.

A jolt ran through my palm and up my arm, warming my hollow insides and causing me to wrench my arm back with the feeling still bouncing around my insides. "What was that?"

"Not sure," he stated, confusion etched on his face, before switching back to his previous concern. "Like I said, you don't know me, but something is going on with you. I don't feel comfortable leaving you alone."

"You're being ridiculous," I replied with a dry chuckle. "You owe me nothing. You're not my guardian. We know nothing about each other. Why would you feel compelled to protect me?"

"It's a feeling more than a conscious thought," he replied. "A tugging feeling that I should stay close."

"That's odd. Don't you have a family or pack to control?" Before I could stop myself the words spewed from my lips and not in a kind way. They rolled through with anger. I wasn't a child and most important, I couldn't let him get too close; to figure out what I've tried so hard to hide away from everyone around me. And these feelings and reactions I keep getting from him could be nothing good, right?

He grimaced when the words lashed out at him, and then his face softened. An inner battle waging brought an emotion of

THE BLOODY MASSACRE   249

resignation closer to the surface. "Very well, I will leave you be." Without another word, apology, or sign of his own reaction to our closeness, he walked through the slivers of wood, out of the bathroom, and out of my house, slamming the front door for closure.

Placing my back against the wall I used the structure to slide down to the floor, curling my knees into my body and bowing my head. This was painful, but I couldn't get a grasp on why. For one, he's a Wolf Shifter, and a powerful one. Me, I'm a Raven Shifter. I had no future, and I'd come to terms with that fact, but there was something about him, something dark, but beautiful. Whatever it was, it called and I wasn't sure I could fight the tug towards him.

* * *

I came to with a cry. Sharp claws tearing through my abdomen. Teeth sinking into my throat. Thick warm liquid created rivers that flowed and emptied onto the earth below me. Pain racked every inch of my body as I fought with talons and tried to rip my attacker to shreds. But there was nothing on top of me, no resistance against my retaliation.

Sweat covered my skin, and I inhaled a deep breath as I choked on the air that fights to enter my lungs. Scratches and pitch from the forest floor covered my feet. Drying blood decorated the edges of my torn clothes. The talons that protruded from my fingertips had split open the skin of my knees. Noticing that I still remained in the same place Nocs left me in the bathroom, I stood, walking gingerly on the soles of my feet to make my way to the vanity mirror. I lowered my head and cried. My hair was a nest of matted curls and bits of pine boughs. I couldn't make sense of any of it.

What was happening? Was I blacking out? Was my raven losing her mind? She hadn't spoken stating any concerns like these, but something was happening to her, maybe to both of us. It's past time I figured out exactly what's been changing, and if there was anything we could do to stop it, to reverse any damage that I've done to myself or my animal, because of the sins I'd stolen.

CHAPTER NINE

T he warm water of the shower was not a comfort, so I quickly cleaned the injuries I found along my skin, doing a thorough job so they didn't get infected. After drying off and dressing in my favorite comfy gray joggers and an oversized light pink hoodie, I bandaged the bottom of my feet so there was some cushion when I walked. I then braided my hair and put on one of my slip-on fuzzy shoes. Taking a deep breath, I headed out on one of the many trails around the town. I needed to find a clue, any clue to what I was involved in.

Lost in my own thoughts, I took a path that led me into the heart of the forest. Birds chirped amongst the tree branches and furry creatures scuttled across the forest floor. But I halted when a familiar voice reached me from further down the path. "What do you mean, you saw her in the woods last night?"

"She was feeding on a fox, in her human form, but her talons were out and when she lifted her head at a sound her eyes were black."

"I was concerned about this happening." Anger tinged Brom's concern as he spoke with Nocs.

"We have to help Lily." Nocs' words were a plea. I assumed he got the message to stay out of my business, but I guess he'd choose to not listen and go to the one person I thought would be on my side.

Forget what they were doing, the information they were discussing had me frozen. Thoughts and images returned like an electric shock. This explained a lot. All of my bruises and scratches. The only good news was I was only going after forest animals, not other shifters.

Nocs' head shot up when a twig snapped under my foot as I tried to reverse and turn back. His eyes meeting mine, another vision hit me. Nocs and I, fighting in these very woods. Darkness blanketed us from the town's ever watching eye. Blood covered my lips as he appeared through the thick trees and spotted me feeding on the small fox. Him grabbing my upper arms in his massive fists and me twisting, arm coming up and a sharp nail slicing through the skin of his throat and face. I exhaled and my stomach dropped. I caused the cut I saw earlier. He didn't even say a word.

It was then I realized he saw me to discover if I remembered my actions that night. Nocs wanted to know if I was aware of the disturbing things I had done. Discovering I was ignorant to my shift in behavior, he'd become concerned and that's why his protective side showed up.

He didn't point me out to Brom, but that didn't matter. Apparently, there was a secret about me that I hadn't been aware of, but he knew, and he didn't share. Two days he had been here. And in that time, he was figuring me out. The images in my head and the disgust at my actions crippling me as I tried to run back to my house. It had to be a lie. There was no way I could have done those things. Could I? Helping shifters was the only thing keeping me but if I was part of the danger, the town would need to put me down. I couldn't fix myself like I could the others. There would be no future hope for my soul.

THE BLOODY MASSACRE 253

I fought with every step to banish the dark thoughts as I got closer to my sanctuary. But twisted up in the murky depth of my memories and haunting images, or were they hallucinations, I could see a clear image of Nocs laughing. His smile brightened the moment, and chased away the clouds, filling my heart with light. With a touch of his hand, tingles spread to all the places that attraction haunts. A palm on a belly domed with child. A tear rolling down his face. Lips locking and penetrating the agony in my soul. This wasn't my story; it never could be. According to Colin's predictions and knowledge, I was doomed to an ending without love. Torn from a future filled with the pitter patter of little feet and late-night cuddles. I would never be a mother, a lover, a wife. Family had been taken from me once, and this was only a cruel joke meant to push me off the ledge.

I fell at the base of my front steps, and before I could stand and wipe off the dust someone grabbed me from behind and covered my mouth. "This is for the best, Lily. I am sorry it has to end this way." His hot breath sent chills up my spine and goosebumps covered my body as if they were armor that would protect me from the man's evil intentions. "I wish there was another way. One where all your dreams could come true, but sadly that will never be a possibility. You're longing to free all Shifters has become a curse for you. This creature and its gift you house have condemned you to a world where only you exist. Alone, hungry for vengeance, and the end to all things you hold close to your chest. You will kill anyone who gets too close. Any loved ones you wish to protect would be massacred. Bloodshed would be your only goal."

Trying to scream through his palm, the oxygen became too thin. I felt dizzy. My energy was waning, and I didn't know if fighting would matter. But I had to try, I wanted my dreams to be fulfilled. I wanted to hold them close and protect them from him. Put them in a place where no one could touch them, but with his final words I knew I wouldn't have the chance.

"You are too powerful. With the creature inside you, you are practically invincible. Once she takes over, there will be no you. In order to make sure all you struggle to preserve stays the way you hope, you will need to be destroyed before it's too late," Colin whispered into my ear from behind. "I have been sent as your executioner."

Panic promises to seize my muscles, but my heart continues to beat so hard I swear it will shatter my ribs into little splinters. I couldn't breathe, and I couldn't figure out if it was due to the hand blocking my airway or the hysteria my body was trying to fight off. My vision began to darken at the edges and all I could see was a tunnel of light in front of me, all other things appearing before me blurry and out of focus.

My ears pick up murmuring that reminds me of humming. For all I knew, Colin was telling me exactly how he planned to get rid of me. My thoughts cautioned me of the forthcoming pandemonium, pounding against my skull. Visions come and go as all things become numb and I begin to drift away into a world of nothingness.

CHAPTER TEN

I remember nothing after calm stole me away. But when I came to, the dampness of the structure I found myself in produced a chill that began to enter my skin and bury itself into my bones. The only warmth I felt was a burning in my gut, more like a warning than a flame.

It grew until my insides felt like they were boiling, and my nails sharpened into razor sharp points. The Raven Shifter side of me wanted to emerge and protect me, but I hadn't shifted in weeks and my body was aware of just how weak it had become. But I continued to concentrate on what my body was telling me, and it wasn't the raven that wanted out. Something deep down was pushing to be released, but my mind and normal functions remained compromised by something unnatural. A drug, maybe?

The mattress I rested on was lumpy and missing a sheet and blanket, but no matter how cold I was, I couldn't move an inch. My brain yelled at my muscles, but I couldn't even get my finger to twitch, leaving me trapped in an immovable shell. Frustrated with the circumstances, my mind screamed but the room remained silent. The only thing working were my eyes.

But the only things I could see were stone or concrete walls with soggy moss attached to the surface, and iron bars that framed a darkening sky.

It felt like I lay there paralyzed for hours. My anxiety didn't allow me to close my eyes. I felt like I was slowly going crazy in the sinister, oppressive darkness. My insides buzzed when the sharp sounds of shoes clicking on the floor shattered the stillness of the room. There must be a hallway connecting to this space. Closing my eyes before it got too close, I kept my breathing slow so whoever it was would think I was still knocked out.

A figure stopped before me and darkened my lids further. Whatever light snuck through was stolen as soon as they stepped into the room. The air became heavy, and death hovered in the air, bringing the chill to unbearable levels. My nose hairs began to freeze and breathing became more difficult. So, challenging that coughs emerged from deep in my chest as I lay there struggling to fill my lungs. A deep, evil laugh echoed throughout the room, forcing me to open my eyes. I needed to see my murderer. To see their face and know the evil that would be my end.

"Well, look at that. You're awake." The stranger's voice was gruff. Like a bass in a choir, his tone rumbled through me and my fingers spasmed. "Can you feel it, the magic of my voice waking your body?" Without the ability to use my tongue, I remained a statue, staring at him. "Aw, yes, you haven't got the capability of speech just yet. It's fine, it will return in time. Until then, I will be the one who talks."

I grumbled, the words tripping over one another and coming out like a jumble of sound. He might be another beautiful man, but a mysterious glow surrounded him that suggested I pay close attention to his words and ignore his dark good looks.

"My name is Draven Wulfric. I am known as a raven hunter, but that hasn't been my role in many years. Now, let me make sure you understand, I did hunt your kind, but now I am more of a tracker for hire. But this unique job has brought me to a revelation. You are a unique case. The product of a Raven Shifter

THE BLOODY MASSACRE 257

and a Fae Shifter. That's not enough of an oddity. Throw in a descendant of Adam and Lilith and bam, we have us a Sin Eater bound to destroy not only herself, but the whole Shifter race."

"Fucking—" The word comes out on a growl. "—let me go!" It was coarse and dry, but my voice raised into a scream and the ground rumbled with my anger. "You can't hold me here."

"But I can." He smiled down at me with sadness in his multi-hued eyes. One minute I saw a deep blue that shifted into a purple, transforming them into a ripple on a lake. If his energy was any indication, I would have to say when pissed, they shift into red tones.

"That's what you think, but something is coming, and I don't think you're strong enough to defeat it."

"Oh, yes, that, that's why you've been hunted for so many years," he replied with a smirk. He must have thought he was funny. "But we will keep you around just a bit longer."

"You're a fucking monster, worse than me, I bet," I spit out the statement.

"There's a good chance you'll never find out." He folded his hands behind his back. As he straightened his posture with the new stance, his height made it almost impossible to look up at him, but I twisted my neck just enough to see his eyes light up. "But we thought you'd enjoy some company. It gets pretty lonely here and we wouldn't want you to spend your last few days alone, so we brought you someone to fill your time."

"What are you talking about?" I growled. "I'm a prisoner. Since when anyone cares about how a prisoner on death row feels or spends their last moments?"

"We can leave you in here alone, if you choose?" He raised a brow and studied my reaction to his question. "Or you can accept our generosity and enjoy time with the friend we've managed to acquire for you. It's as simple as that. It's solely up to you how you want to take up your time, but if I had to choose, I'd pick the second option. So, what will it be?"

"What will you do with this friend if I choose to spend my time alone?" I asked, curious.

"We'll dispose of them." He shrugged, like killing a person was no big issue. "Is that what you wish for, to be alone?"

"No, I'll accept your second option."

"Very well," he said and looked behind him to someone in the shadows of the hallway. "Bring him in."

Another captive was brought into the room with us, but they aren't happy. I could hear them trying to escape the hold of the two guards. I heard the grunt as they forced him to the floor.

"Here is your companion for the duration of your stay with us." He turned and left. A door creaked as he walked away and disappeared from the room.

"Thank God you're alive," he uttered in a weary voice.

My eyes widened. "Nocs?"

Chapter Eleven

How the hell was he here? Why had they taken him? To keep me company before they killed me. With the cause for my sluggishness starting to dissipate, I wiggle my fingers and toes. Soon the muscles in my limbs released and I pushed myself up off the bed and sit up.

Nocs had been dead weight on the floor, but as more of my movement came back, his body began to unfreeze as well. He grumbled and swore during the time it took for him to stand, but once he could, he walked over, rested on his knees before me and checked every inch of my body with his piercing eyes. I noticed the crusted blood still staining his neck and began to mentally chastise myself for hurting him.

"How did they manage to snatch you up?" My voice cracked. I needed water, my throat felt like a dried-up riverbank. Even my own saliva refused to pool in my mouth. "You're a powerful shifter, so why did you allow them to take you?"

"First, that Draven guy is pretty tricky. He came up to me. I didn't realize he wasn't a part of your shifter town population. And second, I felt your distress and when he reached to grab me, I didn't fight. I used my own hidden gift of persuasion and once he confirmed that you had been nabbed by his accomplice, I allowed him to put me under," he grumbled. The gravel in his voice told me he was as dehydrated as I was. "No way was I letting you face these two fuckers alone."

"Very valiant of you," I snorted. "I'm not exactly a damsel in distress."

"You could have fooled me," he retorted. "There's something happening to you and if you're not gonna share then I'll just have to hang around to figure it out."

"It's your choice." I stood and with slow steps, made my way to the barred window. "You do know they plan to kill me?"

"It's one of my theories, but why would they have a reason to kill you?" He lifted his muscled body from the floor. "You're saving the shifters. What could make them want to get rid of their salvation?"

"Well—" I gripped the bars and glanced over the terrain. "According to Colin, I'm what will be the shifters' destruction."

"That's laughable," he huffed. "How can you destroy us if you're the one saving us from becoming feral? That doesn't make any sense to me whatsoever."

"It's a long story. Maybe I'll share it sometime. That is, if we have time." I couldn't take my eyes off of the full moon. It took up most of the sky, and its brightness lit up the land with its eerie bluish glow. I teared up for a moment. Because of me, Nocs would meet his end trapped in a cage. He should run free in the forest, back to the pack he was born to lead.

"I can feel your sadness, you know." He shifted until his chest pressed into my back. I wanted to lean on him for support. The comfort would do me some good but raising my spirits to have them dashed against the rocks at the bottom of this mountain would be pointless. We had to figure out how to get out of here, and if it can't be both of us, then I needed to make sure he was free before they took me. "Please, Lily. Tell me what it is so I can help you."

THE BLOODY MASSACRE

"Nocs, we are strangers." His big hands rounded the sides of my shoulders, and he drew me back against his chest. A tear betrayed me as it rolled down my cheek. "You owe me nothing. All I am trouble for you. Can't you see that?"

"Lily, you might be too young to understand our connection, but I know you can feel it." His breath rustled the loose hairs around my forehead. Without warning he placed his lips on the top of my head and exhaled a slow breath through his nose. I closed my eyes, because I both knew what he was talking about and enjoyed his affection. But the issue with this was that I was marked for death. Whether it be by Colin and Draven hands or the Sin Eater's obsession with absorbing all the darkness for itself. "I am here for the long haul. This is not something I can walk away from."

"Tell me something. And no lying to me please," I said softly. "How did you get the cut on your face? It wasn't there before."

"I don't fear you, if that's what you are asking?"

"No, I want to know where it came from," I demanded, voice still calm.

"The night before, I found you in the woods feeding on a forest creature," he started, paused for a breath, and continued. "You were in human form, but your eyes were midnight black, and your talons were buried in its chest. I walked up to you, but it wasn't you. You lashed out with your claws, and I didn't move fast enough. You ran off."

"So, my suspicion was correct; I caused you harm." It was a statement, no tip toeing around the truth. I was a danger. Something had found a place in me, and the sickness was what it craved.

"I'm telling you the truth, Lily. I'm not afraid of you." His hands slid down my arms and he moved to wrap his around my middle. He pulled me tighter to him. "I am here for you, no matter what you are."

We stood there, connected, but my mind was far from him and his comfort. His beautiful promises couldn't even hold me in this moment, my thoughts wouldn't allow it. I drifted away on images of destruction and blood. Maybe I would be strong enough to fight back. The possibility that the Lilith blood wouldn't twist me into something other, different, was so far from what my heart wanted and what my soul held. I was a caregiver, not a killer. But with the Sin Eater's power, my soul might not be pure enough to stop what I felt was building up inside me.

Chapter Twelve

Trapped for days in the small stone room, we survived on the minimum given to us. A cup of water and sometimes crusty bread that Colin had shoved through a crack in the door. We passed the time by learning what we could about one another. Nocs was the son of a widowed mother. His father was killed before he was born. A pack run gone horribly wrong. But he told stories of how the pack came together to help his mom raise him in the pack and teach him their ways. He knew at a young age he was stronger and faster than most of the full-grown members, but he hid his uniqueness from everyone but his mother. She died two years ago, and his secret remained locked safely inside her heart and mind when they burned her shell and set her soul free.

His pack had an alpha, but he was aging quickly. With the sickness that compelled Shifters to veer towards their dark side, the alpha had sickened with the loss of so many of his pack. That's when Nocs chose to seek the *witch* that held the power to free him from his demons. He felt a draw to our town and now he wasn't so sure it was only because of my energy but because he felt the link we share like a heartbeat. The closer he got to my location, the deeper and louder the sound resonated within him.

I had a difficult time comprehending his journey. No one else had ever stated that I was some beacon. I asked him questions about how he made it so far, considering the shape he was in. How he knew about me.

The last question was simple, word of mouth. The Shifters that had been cured by the witch spoke of where she lived, in the town made up of all types of paranormal creatures. I was their only hope.

He couldn't explain any further about the draw he felt when he set out to find me. Nocs said it was like a shared umbilical cord. The closer we got to each other, the stronger the compulsion to find and get.

I shared little with him because there wasn't much to tell. Not sure if I should reveal how my mother died, but I figured he opened up to me, so it was only fair to do the same.

In as much detail as I could remember I spilled the story that was hidden deep in my heart. My mother decided it was time to teach me parts of being a Raven Shifter, so she shifted and took off into the air to prove how freeing our wings were. I remained on the ground, where I stayed glued until the police pulled me away. They thought I had been abandoned, but they didn't see the dead Raven laying at my feet. Wings broken, and a bloody mess where her head should be.

When she was flying up into a tree, kids from the nearby playground decided it would be fun to throw rocks at the black bird to see what would happen. She couldn't dodge them all at once and one hit her wing and she fell from fifteen feet onto the sidewalk, breaking one wing with the collision and the other from the rock hitting her. I bawled and ran up to her, but before I could get to her and pick her up, the children surrounded her, and they laughed and prodded her damaged body with a stick. As I pushed my way through the little bodies a boy lifted his leg

THE BLOODY MASSACRE

and brought it down, crushing her fragile bird skull and killing her in front of me.

All I could do was stare at her broken body as an adult scattered the kids. I started screaming uncontrollably and no one could console me until paramedics and police showed up. I was injected with a sedative by one paramedic and taken to a home where someone from Ash Creek noticed I wasn't human and adopted me. I've lived with the Shifters and like his pack, they showed me how to survive.

Brom was my foster brother, and he has been protective of me ever since. When he married Sam, I moved in with them, staying until I moved out on my own. When Sam passed away everything changed, and my ability emerged.

Nocs listened and made the right choice not to console me during or after I shared my story. If he would have tried, I know I would.ve shut down and stopped speaking. We not only shared our stories, but we also shared our loss and pain.

Things between us began to change and a friendship grew. At night it was so cold that we curled up together for warmth, and in the darkness of the night, under the watchful eye of the moon, we grew closer physically, as well.

CHAPTER THIRTEEN

Limbs tangled, clothed in our filthy clothes, content to be alive, to be with each other, if only for one more day. We had become more secure with each other and found it comforting to be near the other. We took it as far as touching and caressing each other's skin. There was nothing sexual, but we had crossed the line of intimacy with our conversations and how we affected the other's heart and soul. Nocs even managed the hard task of making me laugh.

We'd play games to pass the time; twenty questions and truth or dare were the recent ones. Draven and Colin hadn't informed us of their plans; they hadn't even shown their face except to grant us the right to nourishment.

We laid on the mattress on the floor one night under the window. The partial moon showed its light across Nocs' face and sparks of yellowish amber danced in his cocoa-colored eyes. He had been smiling at me as we gazed at one another.

"I'm sorry you're in this mess. But I don't just feel bad for that," I said softly. "I'm grateful you are here also, because I don't think I could have made it this long alone."

THE BLOODY MASSACRE

Nocs brought his hand to my face and cupped my cheek. Before another breath left my lips he leaned in and kissed me softly on the mouth. "I won't leave you or let anyone hurt you." He kissed me again. I kissed him back and the hunger in the kiss grew. Rolling on top of him, I sat up with my knees on each side of his hips. Gripping the edges of my shirt I lifted it over my head and dropped it on the floor next to us.

His palms gripped my hips. "Are you sure?" He asked, hesitation infusing his normally strong tone. I didn't speak, just nodded my head, and leaned down to kiss him. His hands ran up my back and stopped below the strap of my bra. Unlatching it, he followed the elastic band across my ribs and ran the material down my arms. I sat up to make it easier for him to remove the barrier. Discarded and thrown somewhere in the near vicinity, Nocs used his big hands to lean me forward once more and as our lips met my legs wrapped around his hips as he flipped us, so he looked down at me.

His smile was brilliant and sweet, and I felt right with my decision. If we were bound to die here, at least I'd feel something other than fear and emptiness before I left this world.

He maneuvered himself backward, loosening my grip on his hips and began trailing his lips from my collar bone to my chest. With the energy building, teasing his tongue over my nipple, he trailed lower and made his way down my belly as he eased my pants and underwear down, using his feet to push them off of my feet.

The feel of his hands and tongue on my skin was almost too much. I reached up to guide his shirt off and when he took over, my greedy hands started to work at his pants. Frantically I tried to roll them past his hips, but again he beat me to it. Once we were bare against each other he lay his weight on top of me and kissed me deep. As he rubbed his body against mine, I spread my legs wider and braced my heels on the back of his legs so I could increase the friction.

I whimpered as his thick length ran across my tender lips, back and forth until I became slippery and wrapping his fingers in mine, he slid into me. Slowly, he buried himself deep and stopped. Pulling back so he could look at my face, he smiled before returning his lips to my nipple.

Nocs' hips rotated and his tongue teased, both sensations lit me on fire and made me burn. My core tightened and the friction grew as his own patience snapped and he thrust into me hard. I screamed before he could cover my mouth with his hand. He pumped into me faster, harder until our bodies began to move up the mattress with the force of the thrusts.

He lowered his hand from my mouth and circled it around my throat to quiet me. The pressure of his palm was just enough to control my volume, but not enough to hurt or cut off my airflow completely. He fucked me until my orgasm released and sent me flying, and he continued through my release until his cock swelled inside me, his back arched and he gritted his teeth through his own climax.

Easing himself from my body, he turned me to my side and rested behind me. Sweaty bodies curled together, we fell asleep, under the light of the moon, naked and uncaring of what would come next.

***

Thankfully Nocs woke before either of our captures visited us the next day. We dressed, oh how I wished I had the option to shower and put the mattress back on the rusted frame. Luckily the mattress was bigger than a twin, but it would have been more comfortable for Nocs if it was a California King, but somehow, he made do with the double option we were given. My skin heated as he looked at me and smiled. Understanding my shyness, he brought up the idea to play tic-tac-toe using the dirt between the stones on the floor. He made our first time after

THE BLOODY MASSACRE   269

sex a simple and comfortable stage. The day passed by with ease as we came up with new things to soak up the time.

The only way we knew how many days and nights we had been stuck in this room was by the rise and fall of the moon. I could tell the phases called to Nocs, but he fought the need to change and stayed with me. The partial transformations that hampered him the last three nights was an amazing sight. Sharp teeth and claws lengthened as patches of fur sprouted across his skin, but all he did was close his eyes, patiently taking minutes to breathe through and reverse the process. He had this control over both sides of himself and I felt safe knowing his strength.

We lay on the mattress, wrapped around each other, my hand rested on his chest and his fingers traced lines up and down my arm while we absorbed the silence and enjoyed the feel of skin on skin. Our breaths in sync along, with the rhythm of our hearts, we exist in this space, together. Not knowing when our time will come, we just soak up all the time we are allowed.

The door opened, thinking it was time for our daily rations, I sat up and prepared to make my way to the door, when Colin stepped in with empty hands. "It's time for you to clean up." His smile was wicked and filled my stomach full of rocks.

"She's not going anywhere," Nocs said as he stood and placed his body in front.

"Do you think you're gonna stop me from taking her?" Colin stepped closer; a cattle prod braced in his hand. A gasp escaped me, and my fingers gripped the back of Nocs' pant legs. "I'd like to see you try."

Nocs tensed and I knew he was ready to charge the crazy Reaper. Before I could plead with him or stop him with my grasp on his pants, he bulldozed straight for the man with the manic smile. Colin didn't blink, he held out the wand and when it came in contact with the stubborn wolf shifter's skin, it lit up and he jerked. The deep growl that filled the room wickedly reacted Colin's face. As if he too could transform, the Reaper's mouth opened, teeth lengthening into sharp spikes, and he struck Nocs repeatedly with the stick until he crumpled to the floor and the smell of singed flesh permeated the room.

I bolted up from the mattress and rushed to get to his side, but before I could drop down next to him, the cell door swung open wide, and Draven reached out and grabbed me. Picking me up with no issue, he flung me over his shoulder, circled the back of my legs with his arm and marched out of the room and down the hallway. I hear a deep laugh and the door of the cell slam shut before a boom rattles the metal door. Killer growls, muted, but undeniably Nocs', echoed through the hall behind us.

I fight, wiggle, and try to beat my fists into his back. I pinch and force my locked knees to move. His grip was too tight and he laughed at my attempts to free myself before he got me to the place, they had chosen for me.

Draven set me down, hard, on my feet. Pricks of pain shoot through my ankles and I tripped backwards, falling on my ass in the middle of an open shower stall. There were only rock walls, a removable shower head, and a circular drain embedded in the floor. Whatever this was, it wasn't a standard shower stall. It was massive and open, and unless my eyes were deceiving me, chains with manacles were hanging from bolts on the ceiling.

"Are you ready to get clean?" Draven smirked as he looked me up and down. "I bet you have a beautiful body underneath all that filth."

"We will see. She looks a little bony to me," Colin retorts. They walk towards me, menacing, but in slow movements as if not to scare me. These two were crazy. No way would I just let them watch me shower. I would fight and fight I did.

"You can make this easy or hard," Colin muttered.

"I'd much rather you made it difficult," Draven's voice dropped to a deep octave. I saw the moment the images in his head filled him with desire. "The fight is the best part. I like to break my victims. The fractures in the strong willed makes the screams so much sweater in the end."

THE BLOODY MASSACRE 271

My eyes grow large. All of my muscles tighten and freeze for a quick second, but then a switch is flicked and something inside me forces me to move, to run, to save myself. I jump up and vault over the decaying bench to my right, my eyes pinned to the entryway. My only mission: reach the hallway. I wasn't fast enough, and my agility was shit. What did I expect when I had been starved, fed just enough so I didn't fall into a coma?

Colin grabbed my swinging arm as I was on my way down from the pitiful jump. I thought my arm would detach from my shoulder joint. I came down hard and Colin placed a knee on my back. With my arm pulled behind me and my chest being pushed into the hard floor, he bent down to speak close to my ear. "You better behave if you want him to cause minimal damage to your sad excuse for a female body. If not, you may end up missing a few pieces."

Air left my lungs when he pushed off of me to stand and he pulled me up with him like a rag doll. Being dragged across the floor wasn't all that comfortable, but the panic I felt as I tried to catch my breath held priority. Rough motions greeted me when the air finally gained permission to fill my lungs, and the sting of the clang from the manacles being clamped shut tightly around my wrists, spurred my fight response and I kicked with all the energy my body held. Draven laughed.

With my arms suspended over my head all I could do was brace myself from any assault sure to come from these two crazy animals. Draven removed his shirt and laid it over the broken bench before he walked towards me, hand reaching into his back pocket. "The fight is my favorite part." The glint from a knife in his hand brings me pause. His finger slides slowly across the blade as he looks from me to it, and the sinister look in his eyes makes me wonder if he planned to stab me to death or enjoy my pain and make it slow with cut after cut. He stepped closer. "Now let's see what's under all of that dirty fabric.

CHAPTER FOURTEEN

With every step closer my mind filled with images of my death. "Wait," Colin ordered. "We need to call the others. They'll want to witness her cleansing, along with her passing."

"Then hurry," Draven growled. "I can't wait much longer to taste this bitch and see just how tainted her soul has become. Sure, she might be a Sin Eater, but I'm a Soul Eater and hers holds all the magic and darkness of the past. Her blood smells sweet and her body calls to me."

Colin closed his eyes in a frown and for frozen moments Draven's sole focus was on me, examining my reaction to all the things he said. I tried to remain calm, at least on the outside. I'm almost positive, by his statement, that what's to come is a prequel to my end, but I made a promise that I would fight. Even if I have no chance at survival, I'd still go down swinging.

"They're on their way, you can start," Collin broke the stare's intensity, and Draven continued his walk in my direction, knife out and ready to slice.

Without a word from him he began to shred my shirt and pants to remove them and leave me hanging with a bra and

THE BLOODY MASSACRE

underwear covering my skin. That didn't last long though. The knife blade ran up one side and down the other before it found its way under the fabric of my once pink boy shorts and separated the cloth from my skin, splaying my bottom half. The blade then ran across the thin patch of hair that protected the skin of my lower most sensitive parts and up my stomach, dipping into my naval before it created a thin red trail up to the space between my breasts.

"Have you ever sketched a naked human body?" Draven asked. His warm breath heated the skin of my collar bone. The pressure against my chest released as a snap of fabric echoed between us. He had cut the center of my bra and now I was naked before him, minus the fabric that hung on my shoulders, and the many bodies that had popped into the room. Reapers. They were the only creatures that could manifest from nowhere. "I enjoy tracing on actual skin. To map out muscles, tendons and sensual body parts is an art in itself."

I refused to look at him as I focused on a chipped rock on the wall behind all the bodies. He fisted my hair and pulled my head back, so I had no choice as he continued to talk while slicing my bra straps, letting the item fall to the floor. I no longer cared for what he had to say. His words were only taunts and I didn't want to hear his voice anymore, so I continued to focus on the chipped wall on the far side of the room.

"We have brought you all here to witness the purification and destruction of a Lilith descendant," Colin's voice boomed in the room. "We have found an offspring that also seems to hold the blood of Adam along with the gift of a Sin Eater. She is the most unique creature we have come across in our centuries of hunting. This is our chance to figure out just how powerful Lilith's line can be."

"Are you ready for this, Little Birdie," Draven gripped the flesh of my ass with one hand as he stepped to the side and ran the knife blade back down the center of my abdomen and circled my inner thigh. I continued to ignore him as I forced myself back into the memory of Nocs and I sharing our bodies, and the emotions that followed. I sank into the feeling and everything else disappeared until pain ripped through me and escaped in a scream.

A howl shattered the expression on Draven's face and the angry wolf banging his massive body against our cell door upheaved with the Reapers. "We will try this another time. Call upon us in a week or two once you get the beast under control." I saw one of the other Reaper's mouths move in slow motion and Colin's angry glare aimed towards the shower door. No doubt he had a plan for controlling Nocs. Draven squeezed my breast with angry fingers. He was pissed that he'd have to wait to inflict any more pain on me. "Also make sure you keep that hunter away from her in the meantime. He looks like he wants to eat her alive." The same Reaper demanded.

Draven's lip curled. "That Reaper isn't wrong." He raised his opposite hand to his mouth, stuck out his tongue, and licked the red liquid from the blade. "You taste like heaven mixed with lust and darkness. Who could resist that kind of temptation?" He released my bruised flesh and stepped away from me. The loud banging from Nocs trying to escape, to get made my ears ring. The Reapers began to disappear, their fear obvious.

I could feel Nocs' anger and fear for me. Closing my eyes I relaxed my body, knowing he was reacting to my energy, my fear and anxiety. The whimper of an injured dog chased the last crash, and everything went silent once more and ice-cold water rained down on me from the waterfall shower head. I looked at Colin, "Can you remove the manacles so I can wash myself?"

As soon as the request left my mouth my arms fell as the locks released and I moaned. Pins and needles raced across the nerves as the feeling returned to my limbs. I attempted three times to reach for the bar of soap on the shelf to my left, and eventually I realized I had to wait until all feeling came back. I shivered through the shower and felt like a queen when Colin handed

THE BLOODY MASSACRE 275

me a flannel nightgown. Feeling like myself again, even if there was a chance, I had hypothermia.

I gasped at the cell door in amazement. The thick metal panel had been dented outward. Warped to fit the shape of a huge wolf. I hope Nocs didn't knock himself out with his attempts. This time Draven held the electric baton when we entered the room. The Wolf Shifter lay naked on the floor. Chest heaving while he tried to calm himself. "Your turn mutt," Draven taunted. "I hope your girl here likes the scent of wet dog."

There was no way they'd get Nocs in a shower. Even as exhausted as he was, he was in wolf form. But he didn't fight when Colin revealed his own stick. Nocs looked at them and didn't fight. He followed Draven out with Colin at the rear. "We won't hurt him, Lily. He's just getting a shower." Colin shut the door behind him, and I plopped myself down on the mattress and started to count.

Chapter Fifteen

Only a few minutes passed before a human Nocs was thrust through the doorway. A small glass of water and plate of stale sliced bread was shoved in before the door was shut and locked.

Wrapped in a blanket, his hair dripped water along the stone crevices. "They didn't give you any clean clothes?" I asked when I kneeled beside him and placed my arm across his back. He turned slightly so he could look at me. A bruise followed the left side of his jaw and blood had crusted in the crease of his lips. "What did they do to you?"

"Well, nothing until they made me shift back with their electric stick," he grunted in disgust. Then once they chained me up, they decided it was the perfect time to beat it into my head that you were off limits. I am here to keep you company, not for sexual enjoyment."

"How did they know?" I almost choked on my embarrassment.

"Lily." He placed his hand on mine resting on the floor. "You aren't all that quiet. It's kind of hard to hide your pleasure." He grinned and I reddened.

THE BLOODY MASSACRE   277

"Well, then I guess companionship is all I will ask of you from here on out." I lowered my head with the weight of his sacrifice. My life would never be my own. Choices would always be taken from me, and love, well I'd have to love him from afar without the physical intimacy. Wait, what? Love? I squeezed my eyes tightly at that revelation, yes, I had to admit it to myself, I loved Nocs.

"Fuck them," Nocs swore. "If I die loving you fully, then I will gladly go to my death knowing we shared something pure and good."

"Nocs—" I started, cleared the emotion from my throat and continued. "I can't ask you for that type of sacrifice. It's not right."

"It's not a sacrifice if it's true and I want it too." He caressed my face as tears escaped through my lashes. He shifted himself closer and placed the sweetest kiss on my lips. It was soft and so full of the love he spoke of. I melted into him. With great difficulty we made love in the darkest corner of the room. He held me tight and kissed the thin pink marks left on my skin from Draven's knife. He swore to whichever God would listen that the hunter would meet a grizzly end.

With hands clasped together and lips tight to mine, he loved me until the moon began to fade and our bodies were slippery and sated. With every whimper that left my lips, every scream that built up in my chest, he absorbed them as he controlled my orgasms. I rode him like a wave. My hips rotated as I looked down at him and when my inner muscles began to clench around his rigid cock, he stole the breath from me with his fingers around my throat so I could not give us away. We came together that time and it didn't matter we weren't having protected sex, I wouldn't be around long enough to bear the child in my vision anyway.

I allowed myself to feel in the shadows. To absorb his love. The fact we were not even the same breed didn't faze either of us. Our hearts were connected and if, by some miracle, we survived this evil, I would gladly have winged wolf pups. It wouldn't matter although that's not what we would create. I would think the stronger breed would attach itself to our child.

The dim light from the window and the heat from his body wouldn't grant me my plea for sleep. Once he passed out, I was trapped in my sadness. There was no way I'd let Nocs end here. He made it believable when he spoke of our love not being a sacrifice, but his others depended on him. This wasn't about us. The Shifters will need an alpha once I'm gone, and he's the perfect wolf and man to guide them through this sickness.

If they come for me again, maybe I'd must activate my Lilith blood and pray to the Sin Eater to aid me in destroying them. The mix of those two should be enough to protect Nocs and the rest of the Shifter community. The problem is that I don't have a clue what will happen or my soul. Hell, I don't even know if I could pull it off. I hiccupped through my tears and Nocs, on instinct, pulled me in closer. His hand on my hip calmed me with his circular motions and I fell asleep.

***

Weeks passed and my body thinned with the lack of food. Nocs began to worry about my health, and I shrugged it off. He had lost muscle mass, so he took it upon himself to exercise when I napped during the day. He stayed strong while I grew weak and sickly.

"You need to take care of yourself better. I know a good chunk of your weight loss is due to lack of nutrients, but I think if I give you my half of the food every other day, we can get you back to good health." He talked as he ran his fingers through my thinning hair.

"No, if either of us is going to get out of here, it's going to be you," I declared. "Either way, my end would be sooner

THE BLOODY MASSACRE

than I deserved. Housing the Sin Eater was my death sentence anyway."

"It can't be your end," He stated, as anger entered his tone. "There's no way I'd find my soul mate just for the Gods to take her from me shortly after. I will not let it happen."

"It's not your choice. It's fate." I watched the wolf work its way into his eyes, but I stood my ground. "I will protect you until there is no me left. So, love me while I'm here and move on when I'm gone."

The door opened and in a state of undress we both looked in its direction. It was the middle of the night, they never came. "You fucking fool," Colin snarled. "We warned you not to mate with the demon."

"Demon?" I scoffed. "I'm no demon."

"Well, in the next few days I guess we will all find out." He came towards us, but he wasn't alone. The group of Reapers poured into the room behind him, all carried a cattle prod. I stood and backed up against Nocs.

"You won't hurt him," I growled.

"You bet your bony, demon, sin eating ass we will." He pulled me away from Nocs and I turned and flung myself onto his back. "Lily, we don't want to hurt you just yet. Get off." I looked over at Nocs, surrounded by Reapers, but he locked eyes with me, and I saw he was ready to free the wolf. My talons shot from my fingers and pierced through the meat of Colin's shoulders. He roared and turned fast. I flew across the room but landed on all fours.

"Shit. Draven, get in here!"" He shouted. Next thing Draven stood before me, eyes sparking with anticipation.

"So, your Lilith blood has been activated," He stated. "You should see the endless pit in your eyes. Looks like we are doing the purification now."

"Don't fucking touch me," I barked. My voice was deep and hoarse.

"Sorry Lily, but today is your day to die." He pulled a weapon from his side and raised the silver gun and pulled the trigger. Something sharp pierced my shoulder and the blood fog that surrounded me evaporated and filled with shadows until my eyes refused to stay open.

CHAPTER SIXTEEN

Coming to I found myself tied to the wall. Whispering could be heard, but I couldn't pinpoint the exact direction. "She's with child. How could you let this happen?" The older Reaper's voice was clear in my ears. Pregnant?

"Well Bash, she's going to die anyway, so the child will perish with her," Colin retorted.

"You don't understand," Bash started to explain. "She is with child and her Lilith blood has been activated. If we survive the night, it will only be because she is too weak to fight back. But she is already transforming."

"Lily? Lily?" Nocs whisper yelled. "Are you okay? Are you awake? Come on Lily, wake up." I didn't speak, I looked around in hopes I'd find him somewhere nearby. My eyes found him pinned to the wall like a butterfly. It looked as though we were both trapped. He screamed at me, so he knew I heard the words. "I won't let them hurt you or our child. If I have to let the darkness in again, I will save you, my heart." I shook my head back and forth and mouthed a *"No"* in reply.

"She's awake. We need to start the cleansing right away," Bash pleaded. "Get her strung up."

Nocs fought his bindings, but these men were smart. The chains were too strong for him to get free. This would be my one chance to save him. Neither I nor our child wouldn't be ended easily.

Colin held me while Draven untied my ropes. The dragged me back to the torture shower where they got the manacles around my wrists, but they got little further than that. Once Draven unveiled his sharp blade Nocs lost his shit. The beast fought and pain shot through my body with his panic and rage. This felt like when he came in town. This wasn't just Nocs, this was the sickness as well. How is that possible?

"Lily," Nocs roared as his muzzle lengthened. "Let them out." Our onlookers may not have understood what he was saying, but I knew exactly what he was saying.

I closed my eyes and prayed to the Sin Eater to meld with my blood and gain the power needed to save my family. Electricity answered my plea and my body arched with the power that shot through me. I looked up in time to see Nocs' beast break free from his chains and burning saliva spray from his mouth. The color in his eyes had disappeared and all that looked out at the world was foggy white.

I was so full of energy my body felt like it would explode. If I had seams, they would burst, and my insides would be splattered everywhere. I too began to fight, and the Reapers shouted to Draven to take care of me before I was free. Words meant nothing. The small knife Draven held wasn't anything more than a toothpick regarding the power that raged through me.

My skin burned and my eyes became clear as Nocs picked off the Reapers before they could evaporate and disappear. Heads and limbs flew, and blood and gore decorated the walls.

"If you think you will take my child from you, you are dead wrong," I screamed. "You have awoken the wrong beast, and she is pissed."

THE BLOODY MASSACRE

283

Draven and Colin stepped back and tried to run, but with the snap of my fingers they were lifted off the ground and suspended so they couldn't escape and Nocs couldn't reach them. *These fuckers are mine.*

I balled my hands into fists and the shackles holding me shattered into tiny pieces of shrapnel. I floated closer to the two trapped by my magic. Piss ran down Draven's leg as Nocs gorged on flesh.

"You think I would stand back and let you take my family from me?" I licked the face of the shaking Reaper. "You two are nothing but playthings. But now you will die knowing you awakened something more dangerous than the sickness and the Sin Eater. Lilith has come to claim her beasts and anyone who stands in her way will pay the ultimate price."

"Lily, you know me," Colin stuttered. "You wouldn't hurt me."

"Shut your fucking mouth you coward," Draven muttered. "She's just a bitch in heat and now she's a bitch with a litter. This whole world is in danger. Hey Witch, you wanna fuck before you kill me? At least I can go out on a good note."

Draven, always sticking his dick in his own mouth. "Close your eyes and imagine it, because that's all you're getting from me," I sneered.

With my hands held high I curled them into fists and the two men screamed and wriggled. Blood poured from their eyes and mouth until their insides joined the other gore on the floor and walls. What was left of them splattered on the floor below and I slowly lowered myself.

Nocs walked up to me in beast form and sat at my feet. I ran my fingers through his bloodied fur. "Now, let's go wipe out the weak and free our brothers and sisters."

About the Author

Harper Shay is a Paranormal/Fantasy Romance author who lives in Northern Minnesota with her husband and their teenage son. She enjoys reading, writing, music, the outdoors, and a good campfire. She is often lost in all different genres when she reads, but fantasy worlds are her favorite. She loves that she can join in the action and emotion of well-written characters. You can find her, most days, pouring out the characters and worlds that hang out in her head.

https://linktr.ee/HarperShayAuthor

Where the Dead Things Lie

E.R Hendrix

Phoenix Voices Anthologies

CONTENTS

Chapter One	#
Chapter Two	#
Chapter Three	#
Chapter Four	#
Chapter Five	#
Chapter Six	#
Chapter Seven	#
Epilogue	#
About the Author	#

Chapter One

Coraline

As I pace in the small kitchen of my studio apartment, my hands tremble, and my nerves flare. My skin itches as if I've caught a bad case of poison ivy, but I know what this is. It's the craving, the deep-rooted desire that's lingered in my veins for as long as I can remember.

My head tilts as I remember standing in my mother's kitchen as a child, staring at the warm blood as it dripped through my fingers. Watching as it gelled and coagulated against my palms. I recall the copper taste as it hit my tongue, the way my belly fluttered at the taste, how I became warm with the desire to drink more of it. The burning feeling that if I didn't get more, I would lose my mind. I watched as my mother lay bleeding out on the floor, her life pouring from the slit I cut in her neck. There was so much blood, it pooled under her head and spread out like a drop of ink on paper, it spread slowly over the shiny white tile before seeping into the grout and following those tracks.

My alarm blares on my phone, drawing me out of my daydreams and back to reality. That burning need is back. Who am I kidding? Honestly it never truly left. It only hides temporarily

THE BLOODY MASSACRE 289

until the need rises again in my chest. My pussy clenches at the thought of having another man beneath me. I shut the alarm off and make my way to the front door. I've been ready for hours, just simply waiting, biding my time until the darkness came.

I make my way to the elevator, riding it down before heading out the front door of my apartment building. Its front looks so similar to the other buildings surrounding it. Which is exactly why I chose it. It's indistinguishable, neutral, and blends. The Lyft waits at the curb, and I step up to the driver's door.

"Coraline?" The young-looking woman asks as she looks down at her phone before glancing out the side window at me. I nod my head before climbing into the back. "Where too?" she asks, her eyes are kind, I wonder what that feels like; to not have these twisted desires, the hunger for flesh and blood.

"Altitude please." I say in the fake voice I have adapted over time to make myself appear more normal. She nods once before pulling away from the curb. We reach the club within fifteen minutes, and I thank and tip her before stepping out.

The line is long as I make my way to the entrance. "Kyle." My eyes connect with the bouncer who I've taken home on more than one occasion just for this purpose. His smirk causes a dimple to pop out on his cheek as he waves me through.

The lights are dimmed but the multicolored lights flash around the space, allowing people to see each other and *me* to hunt for my prey. My eyes scan the floor, taking in all the details that most people miss. I found a few men that meet my profile. I study the way they look around, the women that their eyes are drawn to the most, or come back to multiple times. Seeing which one will be easier to manipulate. I watch to see what drinks they order, judging who's the most intoxicated. The process is time consuming but serves an important purpose.

Since tonight is a special night, I pay close attention to the males. Although I love females and often take them home with me when the need arises, a man is what I need tonight, to satisfy the itch that has buried itself deep under my skin. I resist the urge to claw at my own flesh, as the hunger courses through me, heating my blood and causing my heart to beat faster.

I make my way farther into the club until I can slide into a space by the bar to get myself a drink. Ordering my usual, I make my way to the dance floor. I despise dancing, but if I creep in the corner, it's more conspicuous than playing the drunk girl flailing about on the dance floor. I start my act, only having to wait five minutes before I get a taker. I feel him before I see him as he steps up behind me. His hands snake around my waist, grabbing my hips in a firm but gentle grip. Spinning in his arms, I'm able to get a better look at him, and realize he's one of the guys I had my eye on when I first arrived. My gaze slowly tracks over his body, making sure to appear slightly tipsy. I giggle softly while profiling him. Blonde hair, blue eyes, tall but lanky.

Perfect.

I take a step closer, moving to grind my body against his, sizing him up while not giving up the façade of dancing. He's eager to comply as his grip retightens around me and he pulls me closer to him. I can feel the outline of his cock as it hardens in his jeans. Not huge but it will be enough to work with. I sip my drink as I raise an arm in the air, really selling this basic white bitch routine as I sway against him. He smirks as he takes my glass from me and brings it to his lips. I cringe slightly at the backwash that is sure to now be floating in my drink before grabbing it back and downing the rest like a shot.

THE BLOODY MASSACRE

"I'll get you another one!" he yells over the music, and I nod my head as I continue to dance. He returns with two more drinks in his hands before handing one to me. I watch as he sips his drink, he watches me closely and I tilt my head as I stare at him. Being a serial killer and just an all-around sick fuck, I have the unique access in to the minds of the unhinged. Without logistics and morals to bog down my mind, I'm free to view people as they truly are. Which in this case has given me the ability to read people. I smile as I take a step back, bumping into the guy dancing behind me, spilling most of my drink on the floor.

"Shit!" I hiss, making sure to giggle and appear embarrassed by the action. His jaw ticks and I get the confirmation I was looking for. "I'll go get a new one." I say already walking away. Not wanting the fucker to drug my drink again. Fresh drink in hand I make my way back to my victim. "Ready to take this somewhere new?" I bite my lip as I let my dress strap slip down over my shoulder, revealing more of my breasts. His eyes drop before he subconsciously licks his lips.

"Fuck yes." He nods eagerly as he takes my hand and drags me through the club as if I will change my mind before we can get outside. "Did you drive here?" he asks once we're outside and can hear each other clearly.

"Nope." I slur as I stumble on the sidewalk, my six-inch heels hitting a crack. He catches me and laughs.

"You alright?" he questions but there is no worry or concern in his eyes, he's getting what he believes he wants. I smile up at him like he's my knight in shining armor.

"Yeah, I'm fine. Those drinks were just really strong." I giggle again.

He hails a cab before pulling me in and giving them his address. I cut him off. "Actually, take us to 4699 South Albacore Dr." I lean into the guy whose name I still don't know. Not that it matters he will be dead soon anyway.

"That your place?" His hand slides slowly up my dress, as he reaches for my pussy. I allow him too.

"Yeah, that okay?" I ask, even though it's not an option.

"Yeah, that's fine." He nods as though he's surprised and impressed by what he presumes as my enthusiasm.

The driver turns down my road and pulls to a stop at the curb. He pays before I take his hand. My turn to pull him into the apartment building and into the elevator. I push him against the wall before my lips are on his.

"Fuck!" he grunts as his back hits the wall and his breathe is cut short by my lips. I bite his lip hard enough to bleed, tasting the mix of blood and liquor on them. My hands slide down his chest until I reach the bulge in his pants, palming it roughly. "Damn. You like it rough don't you," he purrs, and it sounds like a bad porn script.

"So...Rough." I chuckle at my own joke which he doesn't catch onto.

The elevator doors open, and I pull him out and down the dark hall. His eyes widen as he takes in the dark space for the first time. "Ugh...?" He braces himself, dragging his heels.

"Sorry, the power must have gone out. But we don't need it for what we are going to do...do we?" My voice is seductive as I

THE BLOODY MASSACRE

lure him deeper into my trap. He seems to shrug it off and follow me. His dick convincing him it's okay. I open the door with the key and pull him farther into the cellar.

"Where are we?" he stumbles slightly through the storage room before I get to a trap door through the closet within the room. I flick the light, the harsh fluorescents flicker on, bathing the room in its harsh glow. I grab the mild sedative I keep by the door, before injecting it into his neck as he takes in the clinical space. He drops like a sack of potatoes. I might have given him a pinch too much. Oh well.

I drag him closer to the table before lowering it to the floor and rolling him onto it. I use the lever to raise the metal slab to where I need it. My fingers wrap around a knife on the shiny tray full of tools and cut him free of his clothes, then use the remaining time to strap him down to the table. Making sure there is no way he could get out of it.

I slowly undress myself, savoring the moments that are to come before stepping back and waiting for him to wake. A few moments later his eyes flutter open, and he seems confused and disorientated. I smirk.

"Well, hello." I smile as I come into his view.

"W-whats going o-on?" he stutters, his mind struggling to wrap itself around his current predicament.

I climb on top of him. My bare cunt lining up with his now limp penis. I rock my hips against him, causing him to harden slightly against me. When his eyes finally adjust as they connect with my naked breasts. They bob and bounce as I rock, and his cock hardens further.

"That's right. Get that cock nice and hard for me to bounce on." I rake my nails down his chest, causing blood to swell as the skin tears away. He hisses but his eyes dilate. Once he's hard enough I line him up with my opening before slamming myself down on him. His dick is rather small and even though I'm tight I can still hardly feel him. He grunts as he feels me against him.

"Fuck." He groans and I know he's already getting close. I roll my eyes as I continue to bounce. I feel his cock jerk and pull him out of me in time to spray his hot cum all over himself. So disappointing, I was really hoping that would have been better, but alas, another letdown. I dismount and lower my feet to the floor. Grabbing the hand saw off the table, I take a few steps closer to him. When his eyes meet mine, he smiles dopily before his eyes drop to the saw in my hand. I watch carefully to take in the fear that flashes across his face. He swallows hard. "I'm not really into blood play." He chuckles like this is all a bit of fun. I laugh too but not with him.

"Oh, really? But it's my favorite." And that's probably the most honest thing I've told him since we started interacting. I can smell the fear as it works its way through his body. The smell is sour as he sweats. He jerks his body hard as the cold metal touches his skin, but the restraints hold.

"Let me out. It was fun while we fucked but I'm over it." He growls as if he can intimidate me out of this situation.

"No. That's not going to happen." I tell him as I start to work the saw back and forth against his arm. His screams pierce the air and his blood drips onto the cement floor and heads towards the drain under the table.

"Fuck! Fuck! Stop. What do you want? I've got money!" he hisses as he pants to get his words out through the pain. I cover

THE BLOODY MASSACRE 295

his mouth with a strip of tape, muffling his infuriating please. The saw's teeth are sharp and eat away through his skin and into the muscle. Tears run down his face, and I can taste his fear in the air, it coats my skin like the condensation on a cold glass on a hot summer day. I lean forward, flicking my tongue out to catch the salty wetness before it hits the table beneath him.

Delicious.

I keep cutting until I make my way to the bone, his meat dangles there. I use both hands to cup the blood that pours from his arm. I bring it to my lips before gulping it down. His eyes are slowly lowering, and I know he's close to passing out. Grabbing a salt pack, I break it under his nose to keep him awake.

"Tsk tsk. Playtime's not done yet." I say as I use the bone saw to finish removing his limb. The tape I had put over his mouth is only partially blocking the screams, which is fine. The room is soundproof. His pathetic cries are more annoying than anything else. I filet the meat from the bone just like I would a chicken and toss it into the meat grinder that I have set up in the corner before working my way to his other arm. "Hope you're hungry." I whisper in his ear as he jerks his head back and forth.

I repeat the process with his other arm before he dies of blood loss.

"Well, damn. You lasted about as long as you did during sex." I roll my eyes as I use my fist to jerk his cock, forcing what little blood he has left to build up into it. It takes a little bit but I finally get him hard again. I straddle his hips before sliding him back inside me. I grind my soaking wet pussy against him. He's going to make me cum whether he wants to or not. I press my hips firmly against him, causing my clit to rub against his pelvis. Using his blood that I caught in a small bucket I pour it over myself, rubbing his blood over my tits and stomach. Moaning as I feel the now cool wetness against me.

"Yes! Yes!" I moan as I work myself as hard as I can. Next time I need a guy with a bigger cock. Right as I'm about to finish I slide my blade through his throat, spraying myself with the last of his blood, the warmth sets me off as I cum all over his now flaccid cock. I run my fingers through the blood, dragging it up my chest before sucking it off my fingers. At least he tastes good.

I smile as I raise the knife over my head and slam it down in the center of his chest. The blade sinks to the hilt as I bury it deep. I saw the blade back and forth as I cut down his chest to his sternum. I get the rib spreader and crank his ribs apart, spreading them wide enough for me to get my hands inside. I remove most of the organs, getting rid of the ones I don't need and saving the rest. I leave the heart for last as I marvel at the dark red color of this particular organ. Admiring the large, bulging veins and arteries that lead to and from it. Such a fragile organ for something that is the only thing keeping you alive. Slicing it free from its confinement, I hold it in my hands. Appreciating it for a moment more before bringing the still warm organ to my lips. I close my eyes as I take my first bite, savoring the flavor and the slight chewy texture of it under my teeth. My pussy clenches and tightens as another orgasm rocks through me. The feel of his blood sliding straight from the source, past my lips and down my throat making me feel more pleasure than this guy ever did. Still mounted on his dead body I rock my hips, using his body for friction and prolonging my pleasure.

They are always better when they're dead. No cheesy lines. *No talking at all.* Just the way I like it. The only downside is they don't stay hard long. Oh well, that's a normal issue too.

THE BLOODY MASSACRE

I finish the heart, making sure to savor it as much as I can. Rubbing the flesh between my tongue and the roof of my mouth, enjoying the texture before it slides down my throat. I lap at my chin trying to catch every drop of blood as it drips down my face and onto my bare breasts. It's still warm as I close my eyes, relishing in the tang and sensations coursing through my body.

I take my time removing the rest of his skin before separating the meat from the bone. Placing the muscle into the grinder, I watch as it grinds it up and spits it out, making it look like hamburger. I smile as I package it up and place it in the fridge with dates. Lastly, I wash my tools and gather the unuseful bits into a large sack to dispose of it.

Chapter Two

Coraline

I park in front of the little store before making my way inside with the cooler.

"Hey, Coraline. How are you?" Mrs. Winters asks as she steps up closer to me. I smile before responding.

"I'm good. The farm's doing well. So, I figured I'd bring you some meat." I smile again as I nod towards the cooler in my hands. She smiles wide before taking the container from me.

"Of course. Your meat is always a hit!" She smiles back as she takes it to the section with the rest of the hamburger and turkey meat.

I wait in her office as she quickly writes out the check before handing it to me.

"Thanks so much for your business." I wave as I make my way out of the store. Smirking at my little secret.

***

Not able to hold my desire back with how unfulfilled I had been the night before. I find myself back at Altitude the next night. This time choosing to stand back and play the field a little more, while the desire is more manageable.

THE BLOODY MASSACRE

My eyes are drawn to the far end of the room. The neon lights of the club flashing over his face briefly before flitting away. I find my eyes are drawn to his, their intriguing, the blank look in his eyes, there's a deep darkness that seems to match my own. By the time the strobe lights flash back to where he was standing, he's gone. My eyes flash along the club, not liking for my prey to have the upper hand. I move from my position on a high top table to float smoothly around the club, sliding between patrons while they grind themselves against one another. My eyes flick from one couple to the next, searching for *him*.

He's gone.

My hands tighten in a fist and I feel my nails stab into my palms, the blood that drips down between my fingers and over my knuckles causes my heart to race. The feel of the blood as it fills my palm before spilling from my hand causes moisture to build at my core. I groan as the sounds around me fades and all I can hear is my heart thumping in my ears. The high of the hunt combined with the rush of the blood causes my body to heat.

Needing more of it, I set my sights on a new victim. My fingers itch to enjoy the kill, last night was sloppy and rushed. It'd been so long that I was unable to wait or resist. I had lost the careful control that I require. That *will not* be the case tonight. My eyes scan the club again, looking for a man that fits my profile. He has to have blonde hair, and on the leaner side so he's easier to move. My jaw tightens at the image it produces. The reminder of how this all started. My eyes glaze over as the images paint themselves in my mind in vivid detail without my permission.

His blonde hair, so similar to mine, looks messy; like he's just woken up. I feel his warm hand as he covers my mouth and whispers "Shuushhh...baby." In my ear. "We don't wanna wake Mommy." His voice, stern but gentle as he shoves his hand up my Barney nightgown. My eyes widen as he pulls down my pull-up, before he slides his finger inside me. Pumping in and out of my private. It hurts so bad, it burns like fire as he forces another finger into me. I have no clue what's happening but then he touches something else and the pain eases slightly. I want to speak but no words come out, fear halts the words in my mouth. Why is Daddy doing this to me? My mind is spinning with confusion. What is he doing?

"Now be a good girl for Daddy and stay still. This is going to hurt but it will be over soon." He tells me as he keeps his hand over my mouth. Today is my fourth birthday, maybe Daddy is giving me some kind of gift? The pain goes away as his hand moves from beneath my jammies. But then I feel something warm and bigger pressed against me and as it starts to push closer, the burning is so much more intense than it was before. I scream into his hand as I feel my skin tear. Something drips down and onto my bed, not sure if it's blood or if I peed. My cries go unanswered as Daddy continues to push whatever it is, farther into me. My head thrashes back and forth. I can't take it anymore. It hurts too much.

"Ouch. Ouch!" My words are muffled and don't sound like what I'm trying to say. I try yelling for Mommy and beg inside my head that she will come in and fix my booboo, she always makes the pain go away.

Tears leak from my eyes, and I scream until my voice is hoarse and I realize Mommy isn't coming, that no one's coming to help me. Daddy moves the object back and forth inside me and the pain is now constant. It feels like it goes on forever until I feel something warm and wet inside me and I wonder if I'm peeing again. Daddy pulls away and leaves me lying there on my pink barbie sheets.

I didn't understand what was happening at the time, but I would soon learn that Daddy would come back and do that again and again almost every night for the next three years. Until I became too old and he no longer had a use for me.

An arm bumping into my side shakes me from my tortured memories.

"Excuse me." A short woman says as she tries to scooch in closer to the bar to reach her drink.

THE BLOODY MASSACRE 301

I slide over a little to make room. She gives me a gentle smile in thanks. My eyes remain diligent as I continue to scan the room. Two men stand out to me, their blond hair gleaming in the low light of the club. My palms sweat as I picture the knife firmly in my grip, the blade sliding through their warm flesh as I take everything I need from them. My thirst is growing and expanding within me, my desire eating up the empty expanse of my chest.

My chosen mark is a tall man who stands slightly off to the left of the dance floor. His eyes land on mine and a slight smile tilts his lips and his eyebrow raises as if in question. I bite my lip, turning my eyes seductive, telling him without words that I like what I see. His smirk only grows as his large steps eat across the distance between us until he's standing right in front of me.

"Hey," he whispers as he leans down closer to my ear. His voice is slightly raspy and deeper than I would have expected. My eyes slide across his body as I work my way across his broad shoulders and firm chest, before moving down to his trim waist and long legs. Yes, he will do nicely. He's got this handsome boy next door look to him that I'm sure in normal circumstances gets him whatever he wants.

"Hey, yourself." I smile as I run my hand over his chest stopping when I meet his shoulder, my grip tightens, and I use the leverage to lean up into his ear. "What is it you desire?" I let my words trail off as I nibble on the shell of his ear.

His head tilts back, getting a better look at me as he takes in my expression as if gauging my seriousness. He must see what he wants because his fingertips trail down my arms before reaching for my hands. "I feel like this is a trick question, but I'll answer honestly. I want those full lips wrapped around my cock. I want to bury myself so deep in your throat that tears stream down your cheeks and down my thighs." As if emphasizing his words, he runs his finger down my cheek the way a tear would. His eyes darken as he admits his desires, I watch the pulse point at his throat as it throbs in time with the rapid pulse I feel at his wrist.

I watch his tongue as it slides across his bottom lip as if in slow motion. I imagine what it would feel like sliding through the slick folds of my cunt.

"Only if you return the favor." I smirk as my eyes stay focused on his mouth, not even bothering to be subtle.

"Of course." He growls as he steps in closer to me, I feel the heat of his body as he presses against me, his stiff cock rubbing against my taut stomach. "Want to get out of here?" He nods in the direction of the back alley where there is an emergency exit. Now if I was a normal girl this would be sending up red flags right about now, but I'm not, so I don't give a shit.

"Yes." Is all I say as he uses his grip on my hand to pull me through the crowd.

Chapter Three

Lucian

I watch the bland, boy band fuck as he pulls her to the exit in the back of the club. I should have made my move but I'm not ready to reveal myself just yet. The desire to get her under me burns so strongly inside me that my cock stiffens, but it'll have to wait. I've held back this long without acting on it, what's a little longer. The anticipation will only make the moment I sink my huge cock balls deep in her sweet little cunt, that much sweeter.

I know he won't be able to satisfy her, none of them do. She uses them to please and feed the dark, twisted hunger that grows inside her but it will never be enough. I know because it's never enough for me. They are only temporary pauses in the long thread of need. Only stopping points along this lonely path of existence. The desperation to ease the ache never ends, only halts briefly. I stopped trying to resist it long ago. It's easier to feed the beast then to hold it off until it builds beyond your control.

My dick throbs in my pants as I wait for what's to come. It's almost as enjoyable as my own kills. Watching her fulfill every dirty thought that passes through that corrupt mind of hers. The insatiable thoughts of joining her, sliding in behind her and taking her ass. Breaching that hole I know has never been touched by anyone but our father. To fuck her while she fucks them, controlling them both simultaneously.

I long to feel the warm sticky blood as it dribbles from her chin and onto her lush, full tits. Using our victims' blood as lube to fuck her boobs so hard I leave bruises on her chest. I groan at the thought, stroking a hand down my thick shaft over my worn black jeans. I give it a tight squeeze before I follow them at a distance.

I watch as he pushes her up against the brick wall of the back of the club. His hands sliding down her full curves to her lush, rounded ass. He moans as he thrusts his cock against her pussy. She watches on, almost clinically, before she begins the act. Although she enjoys the fuck, she only enjoys it on her terms, taking her pleasure from them without their consent. Whether they find release in the act is inconsequential. She moans and although they are good, I can tell they're fake, having heard the real thing. She rocks her hips against his as she plays along.

"Get on your knees." He tries for dominant and command-ing, but it comes across as forced. She isn't weak like the usual girls he must take home. I can hardly see in the absence of light in the alley, but I can make out the sigh that causes her chest to expand before she slowly lowers herself down, allowing him this. His fingers thread through her hair and he tilts her head up, his lips move but I can't hear what he's saying. A moment later she's unbuckling and unzipping his pants before pulling his already hard cock free of its confines. She takes a few seconds to look at his cock before her tongue slides past her full lips to lick at the bead of cum that's already formed on his tip. Her eyes watch him closely as she opens her mouth wide enough to take him in. He urges her mouth farther down with the hand still in her hair. Her lips touch his pubes as she takes him as far back as he goes. Her eyes almost challenging as she doesn't even

THE BLOODY MASSACRE

gag. I smirk knowing I would make her gag. I would have her sputtering and drooling as my cock slid so far down her throat you would see the outline in her neck.

I observe as he thrusts his hips harder against her lips, trying desperately to prove himself and rise to her unsaid challenge. She hollows her cheeks and pulls her lips tight around him, his body shudders as she sucks his soul from his body, and I burn with jealousy. That should be my cock stuffing her mouth so full she can't breathe, not this pathetic excuse of a man, who can't even make her gag. I can already see he's struggling not to blow his load too soon. His head drops back and his eyes close and I long to slide my knife along his throat and bathe her in his blood, but I won't take the kill from her. No, she needs this.

Her hand reaches up and strokes his balls, encouraging him to end this short encounter.

"Fuck!" he hisses as his hips jerk, losing their rhythm as he unloads into her mouth. She smirks as she pulls back and swallows him down.

"Fuck. That was the best goddamn blowjob I've ever had." He runs his hands through his hair as he tries to regain his focus again. He quickly pushes his now soft cock back into his pants. Her smirk remains as she pulls him towards the end of the alley and out onto the sidewalk.

"My turn," she purrs. His smile ideotic as he follows behind her, thinking he's getting lucky. I smile to myself, knowing how similar we are, having mastered manipulation at a young age with the help of our father. We each like to play our own game of cat and mouse and at the moment, this poor fuck doesn't even know he's her mouse.

I vaguely hear as they talk about a ride, and she gives him her address. She follows him to his car, and I get on my bike, already knowing the address by heart, I beat them there.

Using the key I had made, I make my way into the utility room in the basement. Where at the back of a storage closet is a fake wall which hides the door to the room beyond. I remain in the utility room so I won't be seen. It's always pitch black. She uses it to disorient her victims before pulling them into the room beyond the closet. Five minutes later I hear her opening the relocked door as they shuffle inside.

"What's going on? You live here?" he murmurs bewildered as she continues to pull him further into the room.

"Yep, it's not much but it's home." She grunts, giving him a big tug before pushing him into the sterile white room, setup similarly to a mortuary. Complete with a metal table and all. The drain under the table makes for easy cleanup and I have to admit I admire her dedication and intuitive thinking.

"What the fuck is this?" His voice loses all its strength as the fear starts to sink in. He turns towards the exit, trying to get back into the storage closet. But it's too late, the door has closed behind him. The automatic lock, having already engaged, traps the stupid bastard inside. I smirk as I move closer to hear the muffled sounds of his confused voice coming through the door.

Needing to feed my obsession with her, I lower myself to my knees on the floor to the right of the door before sliding the small panel to the side. It allows me to peek through the hole in the wall and watch her. With each new kill, my desire to feed off her energy grows. To taste the depths of her depravity on my tongue. I *have* to watch her, to stroke my rock-hard cock until I cum over and over again as she forces the men to comply as she takes their last breath.

"What's wrong?" Her eyes slide down his body as the straps of her silk black dress drop off her shoulder to reveal her large, full breasts. His eyes drop as he takes them in. I can see the war battling in his mind. Not entirely sure about the situation, but not willing to give up the possibility of getting inside that sweet pussy, either. She takes another step closer and the dress snags at her wide hips before she shimmies slightly, allowing it to pool on the floor. Completely naked underneath, her smooth, bare pussy practically shines in the harsh lighting. I can see her cream glistening on her thighs as she aches for the kill. For his

THE BLOODY MASSACRE

blood. Her small hand slides down her soft stomach and over her mound until she pulls back her lips, exposing her swollen clit. I lick my lips, my throat burning with my thirst to taste her juicy cunt, to slide my tongue so deep inside her I can lick her cervix.

"I believe it's my turn now." Her hand reaches for his shoulder, and she pushes him to his knees before bringing her leg up and resting it over his shoulder.

Not able to hold back any longer, I take out my cock and start to work it. Wishing it was me in his place as he licks her from hole to hood. He makes a few passes before she's forcing him to the floor and riding his face roughly.

"Yes!" she moans as she suffocates him with her lower lips. My eyes close as I imagine what she tastes like. To have her perfect pussy smother me so completely, that I get high off the lack of oxygen. I've always had some sick desires, beyond the obvious ones I share with my sister, but I didn't know she would be my perfect match. We would feed our every desire within each other. My palms sweat as I stroke myself harder, my body heats to a fever as she unknowingly plays into my fantasies. Feeding my obsession for her with every thrust of her hips, egging me on with every whimper and moan while he mumbles and jerks beneath her as he fights for a breath. She lifts slightly allowing him the much needed oxygen.

Little Bitch.

Obviously she doesn't want him dead yet, but she only allows him one deep pull before she's sitting on him again. Her release, the only thought on her mind. She closes her eyes as she grinds against him, his hands lift to grip her hips trying to force her off so he can breathe.

"Fuck, make me cum," she moans as she pushes even harder against his face. I can hear his teeth clacking as he tries to fight for air. She lifts one final time, her cum spraying across his face as she moans, "Lucian."

My fist freezes mid stroke, I must have heard her wrong. It's impossible. She hasn't seen me since our father's funeral when she was fourteen, and I had only seen her less than a handful of times prior. Is it possible she has the same sick desires as me? *No... impossible.* But I allow my sick thoughts to convince myself it's true. At least for now, as I pull on my cock harder, milking the cum from my thick shaft. I moan her name under my breath as I empty myself over my palm and onto my shirt. I don't even give a shit; I know I'll come again and it will just continue to get everywhere. She always makes me come multiple times.

"Jesus Christ!" The idiot huffs as he tries desperately to catch his breath.

Without saying a word she moves lower, undoing his pants before bringing his flaccid dick to her mouth, working him up whether he wants it or not.

"Fuck. Stop." The little bitch mutters as she gulps him down. His cock still hardens, and she quickly glides it into her soaking wet pussy.

"I need it! I need it!" she pants, and I know she's not talking about his dick. She's talking about what comes after. The euphoria that is unattainable through anything other than the kill. The high you get from drinking someone else's blood, of holding their just beating heart in your hands.

I watch as she bounces hard on his cock, her face pinched as she chases her next release. Her fingernails dig into her skin as she roughly squeezes at her own breasts. The guy being completely forgotten, serving no purpose other than to fill her hole and her stomach with his blood. I can't help but think about how quickly I would make her come. How tight her snug pussy would hug me as she climaxed around my dick. The image of her bouncing on top of me as I slide my knife down her chest. Licking up her blood before bringing it to her mouth, forcing her to taste herself on my fingers. Watching as it pooled on my stomach, and I cut myself to mix our blood before we feast

THE BLOODY MASSACRE

together. I would paint her in our blood and cum before licking it off her body.

"I need more!" she growls, the disappointment clear on her face as he barely puts in any effort. Poor idiot doesn't know he just gave up his only reason for continuing to breathe. She leans forward pressing her chest against his, as she reaches onto the table to retrieve a small pocket knife. In a blink she has it open and is making the first little slit in his skin. He hisses but she continues, all the cuts are miniscule but enough to cause a bite of pain. It will enable him to bleed out slowly, so she can enjoy the torture a little longer.

"What are you doing?" After the third cut he sees the knife and figures out what's happening and starts to fight back. He's still inside her as he tries to buck her off. She groans, enjoying the fight. Finally bucking hard enough he launches her off of him. He scurries back until his back hits the table before he uses it to stand.

I watch as her head tilts, observing him to see what he does next. He launches himself at her, his arms swinging wildly until his fist connects with her jaw. Her eyes droop as she takes a slow inhale.

She changes the direction, putting the table at her back so she's able to grab the sedative discreetly before flinging herself back at him and jabbing the syringe into his thigh. He grunts at the pain. I can see from here as his eyes roll back within moments and his knees crumple beneath him, unable to support his weight. Using his arm she drags him over to the table and pulls him onto it before restraining him. Unwilling to wait, she continues with her tiny cuts. She gets to over a dozen before he finally wakes up.

"Ughh..." he groans, his eyes still closed .

"Wakey, wakey, Keith. Can I call you Keith?" There's a brief pause. "I'm going to anyway." She shrugs as she runs the dull edge of the blade down his chest, pressing just hard enough to cause the skin to blanch before blooming red.

"Why?" he slurs, as the drugs work their way through his system leaving him disoriented.

"Honestly, no reason other than you fit my profile and you were there." She says nonchalantly as she paces around the table.

"Fuck," he yells, "Help!"

Chapter Four

Coraline

My muscles jump and quiver with adrenaline and excitement. This is what I live for. The time in between each kill is just the commercials of my life, an interlude in the show.

I smile as I keep making quick little cuts. He hisses and mumbles still delirious from the sedative.

I place the knife down and switch it out for a bigger one. I drag it lower this time bringing the sharp edge to the tip of his soft cock.

"Definitely a grower and not a shower, ehh?" I tease, using my fingers to hold the tip before quickly slicing the sharp edge through his flesh. His scream tears from his throat seconds later as he registers the pain. The blood spurts from the wound and my eyes close as it connects with my body. Showering me in its warm spray, the contrast euphoric against my cooled flesh. I bring his head to his mouth, making sure to rub it against his lips. He whines and whimpers in pain mixed with disgust. He yells and screams as he fights against the binds, desperately trying to free himself. I toss his tip into the grinder before pouring alcohol onto his open wound. Enjoying the howling sound he makes at the sting, before using a large torch to burn the flesh and stop the bleeding. He passes out multiple times during the process, unable to handle the pain.

Knowing I want him to suffer more. I study my tools, which vary from actual tools to whips, chains and even tasers. I enjoy mixing it up.

While he's passed out I loosen the middle strap slightly before lifting his waist with a rounded support pillow, causing his hips to jut upwards into the air. Grabbing a very large strap on; I fastened it to my pelvis before crawling between his legs. I smile at the thought of pegging this man. I wait patiently for him to awaken before pressing the bulbous tip of the massive dildo against his tightly puckered asshole. His eyes widen in shock at the pressure and his eyes flash to me. Fear and horror painted on his face.

"No! God No! Please!" he begs, and I think this might actually break him. I stay very still, allowing his fear to build in the anticipation of what I'm going to do next. I remain motionless for almost five minutes. My eyes are locked on his as he sputters and cries, his body continuing to jerk against the straps before my hips slam forward unexpectedly. Breaching his ass while causing it to tear open with my harsh entry. As I pull back, I see his blood smeared across the dildo before forcing it back inside him. His entire body jolts as he tries to get away from the dildo, instinctively reacting to the immense pain. His cries fall on deaf ears as I feel the base of the dildo pushing against my clit. I can feel my orgasm building with each thrust of the huge cock. My pleasure building as I watch his tiny hole spread wide to accommodate the enormous girth, his blood being the only lubrication offered to him.

My thoughts flick back to my dad and how he would rub my clit while he fucked me, wanting to feel me tighten around him, not for my pleasure but to increase his. The thought sparks an idea. I reach to the table to grab some lube before I pour a liberal amount onto the rubber dick before sliding it back inside him.

THE BLOODY MASSACRE 313

After a few moments I can feel his hole slicken and his screams drop in volume. What remains of his dick starts to harden as I rub his perineum. His head thrashes back and forth in denial.

"No! No!" His tone, harsh, as if he can will his cock to soften.

"Oh yes. It's okay to enjoy it, Keith. To enjoy this huge thick cock fucking this tight little asshole." I egg him on, knowing that he's not enjoying it but his body is reacting anyway.

"No!!" He screams, his teeth biting into his tongue, the pain starting to soften his cock.

Oh no you don't.

I use my hand to stroke him, keeping his cock full of blood. His arms flex as he tries to push against the restraints. I feel his cock jerk and I know he's going to come. I let go of his dick and grab his hips to thrust mine faster. The stump that is all that's left of his tiny penis is starting to bleed from my rough thrusts, dripping down over the dildo. His eyes squeeze shut, and a long moan works its way past his lips as he comes harder than he had, even in my mouth.

When his eyes finally open, I can see the shame in them. I smirk. I remember that feeling all too well. The sight causes my pussy to clench and my clit to swell as I rock my hips three more times, until my body shakes as the orgasm works its way through my body. My legs twitch and my body goes limp, falling on top of him. Temporarily sated.

I catch my breath before unstrapping and putting the cock on the table, finally ready to end this. I work my way up his body, turning myself so I can face his cock, hovering my pussy over his mouth.

"Taste my cum." I command as I sit on his face. I'm surprised when I feel his tongue flick out, it hardly moves and I can tell he's given up. "Come on, a little more effort than that, will yah." I groan as he doubles his efforts. "That's it. You don't want any more pain, do you?" I encourage, and that's when I feel him really going at it. Long smooth strokes of his tongue as he slides it in and out of my pussy, gulping as he takes in all my juices. My cum spreading all over his lips and cheeks. He extends his tongue all the way, flicking it over my clit and I seize my opportunity. I lean back onto my knees, using the large butcher knife I picked up while he was distracted, to slam down on his throat multiple times before cutting his head clean off. It freezes his face in its previous position as the nerves are severed.

"Perfect!" I scream as I rock my hips against his outstretched tongue, holding his hair as I fuck his face. I lean forward, digging my nail into his chest as I race towards my peak. Unable to give a single fuck about anything else. My mind singularly focused on finding my release.

"Fuck. Fuck!" My moans echo around the small space. It feels so fucking good, but I need more lube, his tongue has dried out. I scoop up the blood that's now dripping off the table from his gaping neck and lift up enough to pour it onto his tongue, making it slick as I hump him towards completion.

I scream the only name I can ever remember, "Lucian!" The pleasure overtakes me, the feel of his blood slicking my pussy, drives me higher. I scoop up more and rub it around my nipples, squeezing them to the point of pain before bringing them to my lips to suckle. The added sensation prolonging my climax, it seems to go on and on as I fuck my victims decapitated head.

I dismount and slide his now useless corpse off the table. His body turning cold and blue from the lack of circulation. I listen as it hits the floor with a heavy thud. I get back up on the table, rolling around in the pool of blood that was left behind. Slurping it off the table and forcing it into my weeping pussy with my fingers, bringing myself to the edge before backing off and repeating. I needed this release in more than one way, the orgasms but also the kill. All that built up hunger screaming to break out, to taste the blood and hold someone's life in my hands. To have the control that I crave, that I desperately *need*.

I lay still on the table coming down from the high of the orgasm and kill for a half hour before I finally clean up and go through my usual routine. Once done, I make my way back

THE BLOODY MASSACRE   315

to my apartment and fall asleep to the soothing sounds of his screams replaying in my mind like a lullaby.

CHAPTER FIVE

Lucian

I watch her as she lays there, moaning and thrusting her hips in her sleep, and I know she's reliving the kill. I smile as I watch, taking in every little detail of her face and body while she lays vulnerable. I could have her right now, take her against her will, but I much rather have her come to me willingly... at least at first. I have been patient for so long, but watching her tonight has pushed me over the edge. It's time for her to reunite with her big brother.

CHAPTER SIX

Coraline

It's been almost a month since my last kill. My skin is burning, and it feels like it's stretched to max capacity. I try to go about my days as if everything is fine but it's getting harder and harder to resist the call, the need for that power of control that's hovering closer and closer to the surface each day. It's making it increasingly more difficult to remain in my normal façade.

Tonight.

I tell myself as I make my way to my job as a bank teller.

I let myself get caught up in the repetitive nature of the job, of counting the money and making piles before putting them in their rightful places. The mundane process of crunching the numbers and doing withdrawals. Before I know it, it's five and the bank is closing. I grab my jacket and wave goodbye to Carol as I make my way towards the exit.

The fresh crisp air hits my face and cools my overheated and overly sensitive skin. The chill clears my mind, at least for a moment, enough for me to focus on tonight. I need to come up with a plan of action and how best to approach the situation. I must tread carefully, if people continue to go missing from the same club it's not going to look good. And although the bodies are never found, thanks to them being consumed by everyone who shops at our local grocer, one can never be too careful. I don't want to end up in prison. Although the thought of getting the death penalty warms my body, I don't want to end this game too soon.

I make it to my car and drive home in silence, my mind too preoccupied with what's to come. I enter my apartment and strip down, eager to get tonight started. I shower and dress in something seductive, doing my hair and makeup to enhance my naturally big eyes, giving me a more innocent appearance. It's all part of the act; the game. I need the whole process, getting ready for the performance as much as the final act.

Deciding to avoid the Lyft this time I walk to the club instead and although it takes a lot longer, I enjoy the cool air against my flesh, it's like edging myself, building that anticipation and it has my core throbbing and my body humming.

I make my way inside and over to the bar without even bothering to look around. I thank the bartender for my drink and take my first sip. I can feel the fine hairs on the back of my neck stand on end, and goosebumps prickling along my arms, feeling the heat of someone's eyes burning into me. I close my eyes enjoying the sensations it's causing.

I slowly turn and my eyes are instantly drawn to the tall, dirty blonde haired man in the far back corner, his eyes barely visible in the throng of people. The golden glow so similar to mine that I suck in a ragged breath.

Lucian?

It's the first thought that pops into my head but I quickly dismiss it as I haven't seen my older brother in over twelve years. The last time I checked he lives in Ohio and is seeing some girl named Rochelle. My teeth grind slightly at the image that produces and I don't even feel shame, only ownership, despite the time and distance. Lucian will always be *mine*. We grew up together, until he moved out at eighteen. Being that he was

THE BLOODY MASSACRE   319

fourteen years older than me, I was only four at the time. But as I grew older, he would occasionally attend holidays with us. As my lust for him grew with age, I became disgusted by it and fought it for all I was worth. It wasn't until after I killed our father, that I gave into the hunger, into the sick desires I had within me. Killing him unlocked something inside me. Giving me the freedom to own what I wanted and I wanted him desperately. Not just to fuck me over and over, but to drink his blood and mark his flesh, to bathe in his cum and feast on his organs.

I shake those thoughts away, wanting to stay focused and not get lost in the thoughts of the impossible. I focus my eyes back on the man in the corner, his sharp jaw dusted with days' worth of stubble and his full bottom lip draws my eyes, as his tongue flicks out to run across it. I follow it further down, barely able to glimpse the harsh black ink that adorned his throat and cheek in the darkness of the club. I can feel my body heating again, the adrenaline of finding a victim surging through my veins.

Yes.

Tonight he will be mine.

I stand still, not wanting to make a move and spook the stranger off like I did the last time we were here. I won't lose him again. I watch him nod his head, as if convincing himself to make a move and I feel my insides squirm with glee. I don't feel much other than the need to fuck and kill, but in this moment, I feel the closest thing I have to happiness in a very long time.

He stops in front of me and his hand flashes to my throat, cutting my breath short and causing my pulse to hitch. He leans into my ear.

"I've been waiting a long time for this moment." He whispers cryptically.

"Me too." I say, forcing the air past my lips, even as it depletes what was left in my lungs. I've been waiting for him since the last time I saw him. His head tilts as he studies me and a smirk rises to his soft looking lips, revealing sharpened teeth. My eyes flutter closed, the image of him tearing into my flesh with those sharp teeth causes my pussy to drip with moisture.

"Tsk, tsk... Does that pussy clench for me? If I were to rip that scrap of a dress off, would I find that cunt leaking for me already?" he groans slightly, before leaning closer to my ear. "So alike, you and I." His grip on my throat loosens and I'm finally able to pull in a deep breath. The edges of my vision fill back in, but I remain still, letting him think he has the upper hand.

"Come," he commands and when I don't move fast enough, his fingers tangle in my hair and he yanks my head back. The pull on my scalp is painful and causes my nipples to harden beneath my dress. His other hand is forcing open my mouth before I watch him drip a large glob of spit between my lips and onto my tongue. I feel it as it slowly trails towards the back of my throat. "Swallow me down. Before this night is through, you will be swallowing everything I have to give and you will be begging me for more. Every sick and depraved thing you've ever thought about in that beautifully twisted mind of yours, is going to happen tonight, Coraline." I do as he says, loving the taste of the warm whiskey in his spit. I think he expects a reaction out of me by announcing that he knows my name, but all he's done is confirm what I wouldn't allow myself to believe.

"Lucian."

The smirk that rises to his full lips isn't one of surprise or shock, only pride. He drags me from the club and over to his bike. I mount the back behind him before he takes off at a speed that causes everything to blur around me.

Finally, after what seems like a relatively long time we pull up to a quaint little cottage. My head tilts as I take it in, it's such a harsh contrast to the image Lucian puts off, with his tattoos and rough exterior. It's flat out contradictory in its normality.

He dismounts the bike before turning to look at me. Although I've known Lucian since I was a little girl, it's been a very long time since we've interacted and I'm unsure what to expect from him. I don't trust anyone, and I certainly don't trust him.

THE BLOODY MASSACRE

Will he kill me for killing our parents? Is this all a setup for his revenge?

I eye him, watching his every movement, half expecting an attack. I keep my face purposely blank, not allowing him any access to my head. I can sense the darkness in him, could sense it since I first laid eyes on him the other night at the club. I just hadn't realized it was him at the time.

"You coming?" His smirk implies the double innuendo that I hadn't missed. The fact that he's making it openly known he wants to fuck me, with no shame or guilt or even hesitancy shows he's at least partially as fucked up as me. But how deep does his twistedness run?

"Depends...You gonna make me?" My voice stays steady but the challenge is clear as his eyes flash with a heat I can only barely make out in the light of the street lamp.

He steps towards me and in a flash my hand shoots out, the knife I always have strapped to my thigh embeds into his stomach. He may be the only person I've ever longed for, and he may clearly want to fuck me too, but that doesn't mean he isn't going to hurt me.

He slowly blinks for a second as the pain registers. Then he moans, long and low in his throat. I watch the blood drip from where the knife is jutting out from his stomach. My pulse thuds so loudly I can hear it in my ears as my blood rushes to keep up with it. I lick my lips, wanting a taste. My cunt throbs and drips in the same intensity as his wound. I twist the knife, not only to bring him more pain but to increase the blood flow. His hips thrust forward and I can see the massive bulge in the front of his pants.

He takes a step back, freeing the knife from my grasp before he yanks it out. He brings the sharp blade to his mouth to lick off the blood that clings to the silver before it drips down to the hilt and over his hand.

"We both know you want my fat cock inside you. I can force you and make you come if you'd like? Draw out this little game, but we both know it's my name on your lips as you finger fuck that pussy. As you slice the throats of all those men who look just like me... Just like our father." His cruel smirk is harsh on his lips as he makes these proclamations. But I feel nothing. No shame, no embarrassment, not even disgust in myself. I feel nothing but attraction. His harsh words fill me with desire.

"I do. Every time, since I was fourteen; the last time I saw you." I hold his eyes, so he knows I don't give a fuck.

"My dark and twisted other half. How I've wanted to fill you with my cum. To taste your sweet pussy tinged with blood. Whose? I don't give a fuck, but I will lick it from your flushed skin as I sink all ten inches of this thick cock inside you. I'll stuff you so full, you won't remember anyone but me," he growls. He still holds my knife, his wound is all but forgotten.

He yanks my arm hard enough to dislodge my shoulder from its socket as he tosses me over his shoulder like I'm nothing more than a rag doll. I don't bother fighting him as he heads inside the cottage that he must call home. I don't get a chance to look at anything while upside down and he tosses me unceremoniously into the bed, causing me to bounce before I settle.

He's on me before I have a chance to even move. Using my own knife to cut my clothes from my heated flesh. The knife pressed hard enough to cut lines, drawing beads of blood to bubble up to the surface. Once my clothes are removed, and I lie naked in front of him he slides his tongue along those cuts, licking up every drop of my blood. Knowing his thirst for blood is like mine, drives me even higher, my hips jerk up and down against nothing as I try to force some pressure onto my needy clit. I remain silent, I won't beg him for anything, I won't show any signs of weakness, no, he will give in to his lust before me.

CHAPTER SEVEN

Lucian

"I've been obsessed with you since I watched you kill our father," I whisper against her skin, my warm breath causes her to shiver. "You did what I longed to do. What I never had the courage to do until I saw you do it. I relished in knowing I wasn't alone. That you were just as fucked up as me." My voice lowers as I admit something I have never told another soul and never will again. "He took me too." My eyes flash away, the anger still burns under my skin. "Took my ass and forced me to enjoy it. He'd jerk my cock, making me cum every time." My teeth grind, the noise loud enough to hear over her panting breaths in the room.

The whole time I tell her my story her face stays blank. Controlled. My little sister longs for the control our father took from her. But I do too. "You are my obsession, Sister. And I won't hold back any longer. I've waited. I've done my time and now it's your turn. You will give me what I need or I will take it without your consent." My tone remains calm, though the thought of raping her only turns me on more.

"Do you want your big brothers' cock, Sissy?" I purr, the lewdness of it making my rock-hard cock even stiffer. I can feel my cum leaking from my tip, begging me to fill my sister up.

Trying to gain back control, she rips my jeans open and jerks my cock out of my briefs, finally getting her first peek at what's bound to be inside her. Using my cock she pulls me forward until I'm kneeling over her face, her mouth opens and she forces my thick, veiny dick as far back into her throat as it will go. Her moans and groans vibrate against me causing my hips to jerk forward.

"That's right, Sissy. Take your brother's massive cock. Choke on it." I brace my hands forward on the bed, leaning all the way forward so my pelvis is against her nose. Stuffing her throat full of me and effectively suffocating her. I barely pull back out, only doing small thrusts to keep her throat clenched around my bulbous head. I moan as she gags, her nails clawing my ass. The pain makes me thrust faster, loving it mixed with my pleasure. I can feel the small drips from those cuts as she gathers it on her fingers before swirling it around my asshole. My body clenches, drawing tight. I haven't had anyone in my ass since our father. Using my blood as lube she thrusts her fingers inside me, deep enough to rub my now enlarged prostate.

"Fuck!" I hiss, knowing I won't be able to hold on much longer. "You going to make me cum in your throat, sissy? Our shared blood in my ass." I see her eyes start to close slightly and I know she's close to passing out. Her fingers thrust harder as she swallows around my head, sucking my dick like she's trying to suck my goddamn soul from my cock. It feels so fucking good. "Yes... Fuck yes! That's it, Sissy. Does my cock taste like Daddy's?" I growl seconds before I blow my hot load down her throat, pulling out and spraying the rests onto her face. It gets all in her hair and nose and even her eyes.

She growls and I know my last comment upset her. I smirk, good. "That's why you wanted me so bad, huh? Cus' I remind you of Daddy. Even though he fucked us up so badly you can't

THE BLOODY MASSACRE 325

help but long for his dick." Her eyes flicker away as she pants to catch her breath. Drawing in big pulls of air after being deprived for so long.

"My turn." I groan as I work my way back down her body, taking the knife that was embedded in my stomach not but thirty minutes ago, and place it in my mouth. She watches, her eyes drawn to what I'm doing, not wanting to miss any sick moment of it. I lift my tongue, cutting the tendons that attach it to the bottom of my mouth, allowing me to extend it further. My own blood puddles in my mouth. With a tight grip on her throat I force her mouth open before spitting all the blood into her mouth. The second my blood hits her tongue, her eyes bulge and her body shutters and jerks and I know she just came. She moans so loudly that if I had neighbors, I'm sure they'd have heard. It makes me almost wish I did. "How do I taste?" I ask without actually wanting an answer.

I yank her legs apart, stretching them farther than is comfortable and I see her face scrunch in discomfort, but I don't care, she's feeding my obsession now. She won't get out of this unscathed. I smash my face roughly against her still pulsing pussy, tasting my blood mixed with her cum. Her sweetness mixed with the copper tang of my blood makes my cock hard again. I grind myself against the mattress to relieve some of the pressure. Her hands dig into my scalp as she yanks my hair, trying to force me to stay flush against her dripping cunt. Little does she know I like being suffocated and I'd happily die with my face buried in her sweet honey. Fuck, the forbidden taste of her pussy is more enticing than I could have imagined. It makes my cock so fuckin' hard.

"Yes, Lucian. Yes!" she moans as her hips thrust against my lips, causing my teeth to push against her clit. I bite down on her plump lips, hard enough to draw blood, wanting to mix us all together. She moans again, loving the pain. I force three fingers inside her at once, her pussy is wet enough it doesn't hurt as much as I would have liked. I bend my fingers, rubbing her g-spot roughly, as I suck her nub in a hard rhythm in my mouth. "Fuck. Daddy, make me cum!" She yells as her squirt sprays out of her with enough force to almost waterboard me. I don't think she meant daddy in the fun, kinky way and I almost blow my load. I open my mouth, wanting to catch as much of her spray as I can.

"Hmm... You regret killing our father?" I ask as she finally comes down from her orgasm. "Sounds like maybe you are only upset he stopped fucking you." I hunger to feed that deep seeded darkness that lurks inside her. The twisted, depraved, disgusting part of her. "Did you like coming on our fathers' cock? I could pretend to be him if you want?" I watch her eyes, her pupils still blown and her lids half-mast against her eyes. "My cock is bigger than his was, but I still remember the way he worked it in and out of my ass so I can probably mimic it." Without waiting for a response, I thrust my cum soaked cock into her swollen, used up twat.

I thrust inside her, recreating the same rhythm our father always used. I bring my hand up to cover her mouth. "Be quiet for me, baby. You don't want to wake up Mommy." I whisper in her ear, and she moans loudly against my hand. Loving the fact that I'm fucking her like our father used too. As much as I like fucking with her mind, I don't want her to forget who's really fucking her. "I may fuck you like Daddy, but don't forget that it's Bubba whose huge, thick cock is making this pussy spasm. Daddy wished he could fuck you like I can." I emphasize this by thrusting my hips as roughly as I can. Slamming so deep inside her, I know I'm hitting her cervix with every thrust. The sound of my rapid pounding echoes in the room. It's so fast and hard it sounds like someone's clapping, a standing ovation for my performance. I feel her juices leaking out from around my cock, the fit so snug, her tight ring is forcing it out. As she moans her pleasure, I see her eyes close tightly and her face hitch as I give more pain than pleasure. But I won't stop, it feels to fucking good.

THE BLOODY MASSACRE

I push her spread legs closer to her chest, causing her ass to lift. Without warning, pull out too far with my back thrust before wedging myself to the hilt in her barely used asshole. "Now, I'm just like Daddy aren't I." I groan as I watch her blood tint the cream on my cock from the tear I just made in her asshole. Tears stream down her face but she thrusts back into me, wanting me to force her. My hand connects with her face, her head whipping to the side with the force.

"Look at this tight little asshole. Taking your big brother so well. You like having your blood covering my cock? This cock is yours. It only gets hard for you! It's you I think about as I sink into the asses of my victims. It's your ass I wish I was fucking." I groan, the feel of her tight hole bringing me closer and closer to the edge. I've never felt anything so tight in my life. It's even better than I could have dreamed. And I have, for years. The thought of her body has been my only focus as I jerked myself or slit the throats of my victims with my cock buried deep in her ass.

Leaning forwards on her legs, I rut my hips against her fat ass, watching it jiggle as my pelvis connects with it. My eyes are drawn to the main event though, the vision of my dick sliding in and out of her tight ring. The blood and cum that's coating it and making it shine. I release her leg for a second to slap her clit, feeling her asshole tighten around my thick girth.

"You want big brother to cum deep inside this ass? Come on, Sissy. Scream for me!" I growl, my voice is harsh and deep. I lean forward sucking her dark pink nipple into my mouth. I suck as hard as I can, my hips not missing a beat. I bite down at the same time I feel her asshole clench and hold. Knowing she's coming forces me over the edge. I unload my full balls deep inside her ass, painting her walls white with my thick seed. I pull out and watch it drip as she continues to pulse. Using my hand to cup it, I gather all that's drained out before stuffing it into her pussy. "That's it. Take your brother's cum. Maybe if we're lucky you will have my baby. You think I could fill this pussy full enough to breed you? Have your son/nephew." I chuckle at the thought. I don't mind it actually. I never wanted kids, it would interfere with killing. She smirks.

"I have an IUD. Too bad." She chuckles as if she's won. But she's forgotten an important detail, I still hold the knife. Without warning I bury the knife to the hilt in her pussy, using it to open her up before forcing my fingers inside. Her screams bounce off the wall and this time they aren't from pleasure. Once I feel the cord, I yank it as hard as I can, ripping the plastic contraption right from her uterus. I hold it in my hand, admiring the blood that's coating it, knowing that there is nothing stopping it now.

She growls as she swings a sharp fist towards my face and for the first time I see fear in her eyes. She's worried. It's gone from a fun game and some hot sex to something more serious.

"What the fuck, Lucian!" she roars as her fist connects with my jaw. Without a seconds hesitation the knife slices down her chest, carving a nice line between her juicy tits.

"You are mine, Sissy. Now there will be nothing between us." My voice comes out sounding like a prayer.

"I will never be yours. You are mine." She says before her fingers are digging into the wound I had completely forgotten about, just above my hip. She's forcing her fingers to gape the hole, finger fucking it as if it were a pussy. The pain feels so good. When my cock hardens, and she sees she's not achieving her desired effect she growls in anger before fighting me for the knife.

I'm stronger than her typical victims and she doesn't hold the advantage she usually does. I can taste her fear, bitter in the air as I draw it closer to her flesh. Wanting... no... Needing to taste, needing to have a part of her inside me. We grapple with the knife as it cuts a jagged line across her full breast, cutting deep to the muscle. I continue to cut, removing the piece as if it's a puzzle. She bleeds and cries out, the true fear of possible death leaking from her eyes. Jerking the knife from her grasp, I dig my

THE BLOODY MASSACRE 329

fingers into the now cut patch of skin, before stuffing it into my mouth and chewing. She's bleeding from multiple places, and I can smell it perfuming the air. I watch the blood run from the hole in her breast into the divot I created down the center of her chest, it travels down her soft belly like a river. Not being one to waste, I lick it up, swallowing as much of her as I can.

"Lucian." Her voice is firm, but I can hear the fear behind it. She doesn't want to die, and if I continue to let her bleed that's exactly what will happen. Not even bothering to clean my cock I force my dick back into her cunt, enjoying the friction from her lack of wetness. I rock my hips, forcing my cock farther inside her with each thrust. I place the knife at her throat, needing to feel more of her fear, needing it to feed my darkness. Her eyes flash and although I still see desire and her pussy dampens for me. There's an unsteadiness of her vision, her brain burning with the undeniable truth of this encounter. She will not survive it.

I push my cock to the hilt at the same time I dig the knife deeper into the side of her neck. I can feel her pulse quickening against the blade. I use her body as my own personal playground, not giving a fuck if it hurts or not. She's held my desire for so long and now she's paying for it.

"Such a good little Sissy, taking bubba's cock so well. Your pussy's stretching as far as it can for my thick shaft. That's it, little one. Milk my cock like you wish it was Daddys." And she does, she comes hard on my cock, pinching me in a tight grip, but it's not enough to push me over. *No.* I need her blood. I slide it through her jugular, the blade so sharp it slices through her flesh like I'm spreading butter on toast. I groan at the feeling, so utterly satisfying. I continue to fuck her as she bleeds out in front of me, enjoying the sight of the life leaving her eyes. I always knew my obsession would be the death of her. I just had hoped I would have the wherewithal to resist until I had my fill of her tight little holes. Lucky for me, I did.

I fuck her corpse, watching as it jerks lifelessly with each of my harsh thrusts. I finally release the knife, letting it clang to the floor with finality as I put all my effort and focus on her. On this moment. I groan at the contradictory feeling of her flesh cooling, but her pussy's still warm. I want to feel more, but not yet. I rub her clit, manipulating her body as I see fit as I work out all my desires on her empty shell. Her eyes stay open, those golden eyes that match my own staring at nothing, seeing nothing. Her jaw is slightly slack as her full lips remain pursed. I lean forwards taking her lips with mine, sliding my tongue inside to taste her, taste the forbidden fruit that I had denied to myself for too long. I fuck her mouth with my tongue as I fuck her raw pussy. It feels to fucking good. I've never fucked anyone dead before, but in the irony of it, I decided my sister would be the perfect candidate to try it on.

And oh, was it worth it.

"Delicious," I purr into the empty room, filling her empty skin sack with my cum.

I stare down at her in awe. She's so beautiful, she's like my own personal porcelain doll. I want to keep her forever...

EPILOGUE

"Hey Sissy, I'm home!" I yell into the house as I open the door. I'm met with silence, but then again, I usually am.

I set my stuff down by the door and kick off my boots before making my way down to the basement.

"How was your day, Sissy?" I ask before quickly continuing, "My day sucked, I missed your tight pussy so much," I groan as I make my way over to the table where she lays, the cords stuck in her skin causing the machines to beep. I quickly strip down before stuffing her full of my cock. I lean forward to hum in her ear, "Hmmm... My perfect little Sissy."

I thrust hard as I use her body. I will never get enough of her, her pale skin and her plump lips. The gold of her eyes has dimmed but it doesn't matter, they still look like mine. Now they're just filled with storm clouds. Her pussy is warm thanks to the machines circulating the blood, keeping her body alive while her brain is dead. I run my hands over her swollen belly, she's about to burst and I know it won't be too long before our child is born. I groan, the thought makes my cock twitch, knowing I'll have a piece of her forever.

I use her body like I always do. Her only purpose now is to be filled with my cum. I groan as I squeeze her full milky tits roughly. I lean forward to slurp on the colostrum that I force from her breast. Groaning at the sweetness. Sometimes I miss her screams. Seeing her face scrunch up in pain as I force her to take all ten fat inches of me, but it's worth it. It's all worth it for my perfect little Sissy doll.

The End

About the Author

E.R. Hendricks is originally from Connecticut but now lives in Missouri with her husband and kids. She is a hot mess mom, to five kids and two fur babies. If she isn't reading books, she's writing them. Her hobbies include reading, writing, and COFFEE. She is new-ish to writing but truly loves it. She writes spicy romance and is even venturing into Horror. The tropes vary depending on her mood. She writes anything from fantasy/paranormal to contemporary, dark romance, and even horror. The only limit is her twisted imagination. With a soft spot for psychotic men and strong, badass MFCs, you won't find any meek, frail women in her books. She hopes you enjoy her books as much as she enjoys writing them.

Printed in the USA
CPSIA information can be obtained
at www.ICGtesting.com
CBHW030801011124
16733CB00020B/181